I was ....t
m..t ....od with my nose in a book. When I was
seven .....ote my first proper story about a magic puddle
that flipped up to reveal a secret world underground.

I'm now a non-practicing engineer who works in project
management. I write romance and young adult stories. I've
been a voice-over and radio continuity artist. I love country
music and used to have my own radio show. My boyfriend
says I have an unhealthy obsession with Kenny Chesney. I
live in London.

No One Wants to Be Miss Havisham

BRIGID COADY

Harper*Impulse* an imprint of
HarperCollins*Publishers* Ltd
1 London Bridge Street
London SE1 9GF

www.harpercollins.co.uk

A Paperback Original 2015

First published in Great Britain in ebook format by Harper*Impulse* 2015

A catalogue record for this book is
available from the British Library

ISBN: 9780008119423

Automatically produced by Atomik ePublisher from Easypress

Printed and bound in Great Britain

For my family with love and thanks.

Chapter 1

Jessica Marley was dead: to begin with. The notice of her death had been in all the major newspapers, her Facebook account was now a very sparsely populated memorial page and Edie Dickens had been to her funeral. Yes, Jessica Marley was as dead as a doornail.

This didn't stop Edie from hoping that it had all been a bad dream. She glared at the calendar on her computer. The words 'Mel's Hen Night' stared back at her. It was a mere two days before this ordeal and her greatest ally on the battlefield of nuptial nonsense was gone. Dead. Pushing up the daisies. Whilst Edie was stuck with going and worse, she was the maid of honour, which meant participating in the damn thing. Mel might be her oldest friend but they differed wildly in their views on weddings and suitable hen activities. Jessica hadn't.

Who would complain with her about the ridiculousness of venue, the trite jokes and obscene games, plus the awful tackiness of the regalia that all, not just the hen, would be forced to wear?

And at the wedding itself... Edie would have no one to take bets with on how long the marriage would last and whether the groom had had his hand in the bridesmaid's posy.

The thought that it was irrational to blame Jessica for dying did flit across the front of her brain, but it was quickly brushed away. Jessica was a veteran of the nuptial war and one of the rules was always "eye the food warily". She should've spotted the cocktail stick holding the mini burger together. If she'd spotted it she wouldn't have swallowed it, therefore causing the onset of peritonitis.

Death by canapé.

Another casualty of a wedding, just a little more final than the normal crushed dreams and plundered bank accounts.

Edie locked her computer screen, breathing more easily when the screen showed the regulation company logo, 'Bailey Lang Satis and Partners'. She grabbed her bag and jacket and left to get a late lunch. She glanced at the empty seat at the other desk in her office. Rachel, her trainee, was taking yet another long lunch. It was getting ridiculous.

Edie swept along the corridor, taking some pleasure that people stepped out of her way.

Never let anyone stop you from being the best you can be.

She couldn't remember who had told her that, but it stuck with her. Along with her mother's maxim of 'never let the bastards see you cry.'

"I can't believe he's actually working here!"

It was another solicitor, Caroline, who was speaking in a breath-less voice like a boy band groupie.

"He's so sexy. When he smiled at me as he held the door open this morning I swear I almost fainted."

Carmel, one of the partners, was giggling.

As she passed them all standing in a knot by the Ladies she frowned. The office was not a place for socialising. It was a place to work. When she reached partner, there would be changes. Ever since her mentor, Ms Satis had been put on gardening leave for alleged work place bullying, it had gone soft. Was it bullying to expect the best from everyone? Edie pressed the lift button hard.

"Looks like the Shark is in a snit again."

She heard the whisper as it carried across the marble floor and hard walls of the lift lobby. The doors opened and she got in.

Never let the bastards see you cry.

The smell of cinnamon and buttery pastry filled her senses as she stood at the counter of the local sandwich shop. Her mouth watered at the memory of it melting on her tongue. An image of her dad laughing as he wiped the crumbs from her cheeks.

She thrust the memory back behind the walls in her mind. It was better to forget that and only remember that her mum never allowed pastries. Too calorific.

Plus Ms Satis had always advocated that a widening waist showed that a lawyer wasn't taking care of the little details. Edie wasn't sure she would ever reach the greyhound leanness of her mentor but she was giving it a good try. The thought of Hilary Satis kept the memories safer. Emotions had no place in a divorce lawyer.

"Oh come on," she couldn't help muttering under her breath.

Edie wanted to leave the shop as fast as possible whilst her memories were still ruthlessly corralled. But the one person who stood in front of her in the queue wasn't moving. Why were people not prepared with the correct change when they came to pay for their sandwich? She tapped her foot and started tutting.

"I'm sure I have it right here." The woman in front was digging through her purse and beginning to count copper coins out onto the Plexiglas counter. A key chain with a cube of photos of grinning children swung from it.

"For the love of God," Edie didn't explode so much as fire the words with laser pointedness at the back of the woman's head. Edie took in the messy and poorly cut hair and wondered how the woman could've allowed herself out looking like that.

The woman turned in shock.

"Some of us work and you are costing me money. If you are incapable of counting out change then I suggest you ask your children to teach you." Edie pushed past the woman as she said it, leaving the woman open mouthed and with tears starting in her eyes.

I'm only doing it for her own good, Edie thought, pushing any

3

twinge of shame down behind her walls to join her cinnamon flavoured memories.

"Smoked salmon on granary, salad and no butter," she calmly ordered.

The owner of the shop, a burly Italian cockney glared at her but slapped the bread onto the board.

"No butter," she said it sharply as she saw him start to dip his knife in the tub. He threw the knife down, muttering in Italian.

People had to learn. They had to toughen up. Life wasn't a Disney film full of helpful woodland creatures and funny animated snowmen. If you didn't look after yourself no one else would.

She paid with the correct money, and took her sandwich in silence. She stared pointedly at the now crying woman standing with a handful of change and left the shop the doorbells chiming accusingly behind her.

Walking back onto her floor from the lift, she noticed that there were still people gossiping. She could feel her lips tightening. It was a dog eat dog world; that was what made her a great lawyer. No distractions, no diversions. What she hadn't learned by herself, her mother or Hilary Satis had drummed into her.

These people needed to get with the programme.

"Edie?" A weedy voice said.

Sighing, Edie turned away from the screen.

"Yes, Rachel?"

Edie asked herself, yet again, why she had been assigned the most colourless and ineffectual trainee solicitor the firm had ever taken on. Didn't they know that a divorce practice needed sharks? Go-getters? Ever since Hilary had been forced out it had gone soft. Mind you the trainee before Rachel hadn't been much good either and Hilary had been around then.

"I have to leave early tonight," Rachel said bouncing from foot to foot.

It was the most animated Edie had ever seen her.

4

"Early?"

She'd already taken a long lunch. Edie would have to check her billable hours carefully.

"Yes… it's for my wedding dress fitting!" Rachel fairly glowed.

And another one was seduced to the dark side. No wonder she wasn't good for anything. Weddings turned people's mind to porridge. And if they didn't have much of a mind before, it went even quicker.

Edie looked at Rachel, really seeing her for the first time. She shone from within, transforming her dirty dishwater coloured hair, her scrawny figure hidden in a polyester black suit and her cheap shoes into something touchingly pretty.

Weddings? Pah.

It wouldn't last.

"And you think that takes priority over Mrs Robinson-Smythe's settlement?" Edie asked.

"I can come in early tomorrow?" Rachel's bottom lip wobbled.

"You should be coming in early anyway if you want to get ahead. Oh don't cry. Just go. But this will be going on your permanent record." Edie said and turned away from her in disgust, ignoring her until she left the office.

Edie found that firing off an email to the HR department about the lackadaisical attitude of her trainee lifted her spirits, and she carried on working with a small smile. If you didn't watch the trainees they were apt to slack off, she knew this. She'd been taught by the best. Really, between Rachel's sloppiness and the other solicitors spending the time gossiping about men, it was a surprise that Bailey Lang Satis and Partners was still as successful as it was. Standards were slipping.

At eight pm, she shut down her computer, removed all papers from her desk, averted her eyes from Rachel's teetering piles of briefs and left. She strode confidently through the office, and noted she was the last to leave. Good. It gave her a sense of pride, and also relief that she didn't have to make small talk with anyone.

Exactly twenty minutes later she was outside the door to her building, a red and white mansion block just off Victoria Street. It was a quiet and elegant place and an easy bus ride from work at the edge of the City. The double doors were half glazed and led through to a tiled entrance way. Above the doors was a stained glass semicircular window showing flowers, misplaced Edwardian whimsy, Edie always thought.

The last rays of the sun on this June evening were shining directly onto the window. As Edie put her key in the lock, she glanced up.

Instead of the whimsical flowers she'd expected, a face stared down at her. The face of Jessica Marley.

It glowed in the light of the setting sun. It had Jessica's perpetual look of superiority; her chin length bob moved slightly as if touched by a faint wind. And perched on top was a cheap silver tiara. Brown eyes stared beadily down at Edie. There was nothing whimsical about them.

Edie blinked.

No, it really was just a stained glass window.

The blood from her face was now pooled somewhere round her knees. With her hand shaking, she turned the key in the lock and stumbled through the front door.

That didn't just happen. It couldn't have done.

"Low blood sugar. It's just low blood sugar," she whispered as she took the lift not trusting her legs for the usual brisk walk up the stairs. She'd seen Jessica because she'd been on her mind earlier; that was it. It had to be. It was the only logical explanation.

Once in her second floor flat, she rapidly turned the locks and put the chain on. Back flattened against it, she lifted a hand to her forehead. It was cold and damp, but not from fear; she didn't do fear.

She could hear Ms Satis' voice telling her to pull it together.

"Get a grip Edie. It was just a trick of the light." Maybe if she said it enough she could believe it. It was a technique she knew well.

Taking a deep breath she walked to the kitchen through her bland and colourless flat. There was not a personal touch anywhere, not a photo or a knickknack; it was more like a hotel room. She could move out at a moment's notice and not leave an imprint of herself behind. And what was in the flat was perfectly aligned; everything was in its place.

In her spotless and almost clinical kitchen, Edie prepared dinner with automaton precision: organic chicken, no skin and grilled to reduce the calories, organic vegetables steamed and not a touch of a starchy carbohydrate because it was after six pm. The work soothed her, all the boundaries and rules giving her structure, making her feel safe. Her phone rang, and she automatically checked the caller.

Her mother.

Her lips pursed. She didn't have time to speak to her mother, Edie lied to herself, when what she meant was that she didn't have the energy to deal with her. She sent it to voice mail.

Then, as was her routine, she sat at the small breakfast bar that divided the kitchen from the living room and carefully placed a forkful of food made up of perfect proportions and dimension in her mouth. She chewed exactly thirty times before she swallowed, and, because she'd had so much practice at ignoring anything that made her uncomfortable, she successfully dismissed the thoughts of weddings and stained glass windows as she reviewed Mrs Robinson-Smythe's settlement.

By exactly ten thirty pm Edie was in bed, a solitary figure lying in her cool crisp white linen sheets. It was as if she was laid out, arms by her sides or occasionally crossed across her chest. All neat and tidy, nothing messy.

OK, so tonight she might have checked under the bed and in each wardrobe before she lay down, but those were just sensible precautions for a single woman living in the centre of London. And if she'd never done it before tonight, it was never too late to start. At least that is what she told herself.

On that fuzzy edge of sleep, that time where you walk on the verge between the waking path or the field of dreams, she heard an electronic click, the sound of a text message being delivered. It jolted her awake.

Who could be texting her now?

And then as her brain woke up, she remembered she didn't have an alert for her text messages, her phone was set to vibrate mode. Then as if to underline her thought and highlight it in bold, she heard it again, and again. And then it seemed that every electrical appliance in the flat turned on and began to beep, the sound getting louder and louder.

What the…

Edie's heart was hammering so loudly that she almost didn't hear the sound of stiletto-heeled shoes tapping slowly and laboriously towards her and the clanking sound of a chain being dragged over wooden floors.

It came closer and closer.

"Bugger this!" she whispered. "It's just a dream."

And as she said it, something came through the bedroom door. Right through it, without opening it.

"Jessica?" Edie whispered.

She pressed her hand against her ribcage as if trying to keep her slamming heart from leaping out.

The same face that had stared at her from the stained glass was right there in front of her: the superior look, the chin length bob. But Edie had never seen Jessica in a bridesmaid's dress before. It was peach satin, cheap looking and so full of frills and lace, it was the embodiment of the dream of a demented four year old. And Jessica had a chain dragging behind her. It was fastened about her waist. It wound around her and fell behind her like a train. It sparkled with pink glitter; and woven between the links were pink feather boas, 'L' plates and bunny rabbit ears, penis-shaped straws, red devil horns and fairy wings.

Her body was transparent, so Edie could see the massive bow that adorned the back of the dress.

She'd always suspected Jessica was full of hot air.

"What the hell do you want? You're dead." Edie said.

"Oh come on Edie, of course I'm dead. Do you think if I were still alive I'd be here? Also, you know, see-through…" The shade gestured to her body.

"But J-Jessica…" Edie wasn't sure why she was trying to argue with a mad bridesmaid ghost in her bedroom; maybe she needed to humour it until she was certain what she was dealing with.

"You know, that is the first time I've heard my name since I died. Nothing worse than having been someone and then to be reduced to wandering around without anyone knowing you," the spirit said.

Edie suddenly remembered that although she and Jessica had known each other since secondary school and were united in their hatred of all things nuptial, she hadn't actually liked Jessica very much. Too full of herself.

"Can you sit down?" asked Edie, doubtfully.

The ghoul raised a withering transparent eyebrow.

No, Edie hadn't really cared for Jessica at all.

"Well… erm… make yourself at home."

Make yourself at home? What was she saying? She'd never had Jessica to stay in her flat when she was alive and now she was asking her spirit to make herself at home. In fact she couldn't remember ever hanging out with Jessica except at various weddings of mutual acquaintances. Not that Edie went out much anyway.

Edie watched as Jessica positioned herself on the end of her bed. There was no corresponding dip in the mattress; it was like the ghoul floated on the duvet.

She must be dreaming.

"You think you're dreaming," stated the ghost.

"Well I must be."

"Edie, for once in your life stop being a lawyer and doubting everything. Use the senses God gave you, why question everything?"

"Because senses have a habit of being hijacked, that's why. Little

9

things can affect them; I could be overworked and hallucinating."

Edie knew she was clutching at straws, but what was the alternative?

The beady gaze of the spectre was making her uneasy. Added to that was the way that whilst the ghost sat still, her hair, gown and wedding ephemera were agitated. It was as if someone had opened an oven and let the hot vapour out.

Odd, very odd.

"If I wanted I could have had a piece of cheese after dinner and I'd be imagining George Clooney instead. It's all bollocks." Edie said going on the attack as she always did when feeling uncomfortable. But also wondering why she hadn't imagined George Clooney.

At this, see-through Jessica gave her a scathing look and then raised a cry, so truly gut wrenching and melancholy, that the hairs on Edie's neck rose and she clutched her duvet closer to her, moving it to her mouth so she could bite on it and stifle her scream.

"OK, OK. I believe in you." Edie said.

"Thank God for that, those cries are hellish on one's throat." The apparition coughed politely.

"So it's lovely to see you and all Jessica, but why are you here?" Edie's voice trembled even as she tried to sound calm and professional.

"I can tell you where I would be if I had a choice. I would be living it up the other side of the pearly gates. As it is I'm stuck round here doing the spiritual version of social work." The ghoul sighed and slumped slightly.

Edie waited. The spectre then sat up straighter and fixed its stare on her.

"OK so here's the thing, Edie, supposedly everyone is required to love selflessly. I know; I rolled my eyes too. You are supposed to go out and 'spread the love.' Not just love of course, but also all that hope that it supposedly produces, and share it. With the whole world. All a bit vomit inducing, I thought. But that wasn't the end of it. Oh no, and this is the doozy… If you don't go out and 'spread the love,'" Jessica-that-was used her fingers to make quotation marks, "well, you spend death wandering the earth, witnessing all that love and stuff and not being able to share in it. Did you know there was a contract? People should let you know these things. I was told it was all set out in the small print. But who has time to read that?"

That which had been Jessica threw up its hands causing the chain to rattle and a blizzard of pink glitter to fall on the duvet.

"And the chain?" Edie asked.

"Another one of those pesky Ts & Cs which no one tells you about; allegedly the links represent every time I scorned love, focused on work and the minutiae of weddings. When I didn't see through the glitter and the tat to what was underneath it all, I made one of these damn links. Something about free will, I zoned out around then." The ghost sighed.."And if you think this is bad… well you should see yours. You get extra links every time you act shark-like in those divorces instead of going for mediation. I particularly like the fetching penis deely boppers and magic wands they've put on yours."

Edie was horrified. Not the boppers.

Chapter 2

Edie was shaking, her teeth chattering. Frantically she looked around her and peeked under the duvet.

No boppers. No chain.

She checked again just to make sure.

"Oh, you won't see it."

Jessica's superior voice was beginning to grate on Edie's already frazzled nerves.

"But believe me," she rattled her chain spewing more pink glitter over the duvet, "it is much, much longer."

Edie couldn't see the end of Jessica's chain; it stretched from the bed and through the closed door to the room.

And hers was longer?

"But we aren't evil people, Jessica. We sent all those wedding gifts and some bloody expensive ones too. We gave up our weekends and went to all the hen parties and all the weddings, even the ones we knew weren't going to last. We said all the right things. And we get this?" Edie pointed at the chain. "Tell me it isn't true," she implored.

"Empty gestures, Edie. When did we ever congratulate them from the heart? We shut ourselves off from their happiness and our own. We had withering hearts behind our withering put downs. You remember don't you? All those conversations and bets on who would be divorced first. We said how stupid they all were for believing in fairytales. And how we knew better. Well at least they did believe. Because I'm stuck carrying this chain on my own. Alone. For eternity."

The ghoul shook its chain and sniffed back tears.

Edie shivered at the misery that came off it in waves.

"But you have a chance, Edie. You can change." The spirit eagerly leaned towards her as she spoke.

"But how?" asked Edie.

"You will be haunted," Jessica the ghost said, "by three Spirits."

She was going to be haunted by more ghosts? This wasn't happening. She was going mad. Maybe she needed to take some time off. She hadn't had a holiday in years.

"Three Spirits?" she said.

Jessica nodded.

"And this is my chance?" she asked falteringly.

"Yes."

"My only chance?"

"Yes."

"No other way?"

"No, if you don't do this…" the ghost paused and then gestured down towards her outfit. Edie shuddered; the peach shiny dress and the pink glitter encrusted chain made her feel ill.

"Expect the first tomorrow, when the bell tolls one."

"Can't I take them all at once? I mean three nights of interrupted sleep are going to play hell with my work schedule," Edie hinted.

The spirit Jessica ignored her.

"Expect the second a week later at the same hour; and the third in a fortnight. Edie, please, for your own sake remember this." The ghoul stood as she said this and wrapped her chain around her arm.

A set of fairy wings fluttered against a pair of devil's horns.

"I've got two weeks of this?" Edie's voice rose an octave or two.

"Better two weeks now than an eternity later," the ghoul retorted.

When it was put like that…

"Will I see you again?" Edie asked.

Did she want to see Jessica again? She hadn't been overly keen on her when she was alive. But maybe she could have someone to talk things over with after the haunting? Edie was used to dealing with things alone, but this was huge.

"No, this was my one chance to right some of my wrongs. My one chance to save you from the same fate," The spirit walked towards the window, heels tapping and chain scraping.

"Remember Edie, it's all in the small print of the Ts and Cs. Let the love in." The spirit paused. "I can't believe the crap they've got me saying," Jessica muttered as the sash window flung itself up and open of its own accord and she stepped out.

Edie threw back the covers and rushed to the window.

Hovering just over the sill, Jessica stared back at her.

"Remember!" she wailed and turning joined the throng of similarly clad women and morning-suited men who suddenly appeared. Glitter, fairy wings, handcuffs and dodgy hats filled the air.

"Remember!"

The ghoul rushed away from Edie and up over the rooftop of the mansion block opposite. And then she and the rest of the wedding crazed ghosts were gone.

"Madness," Edie whispered. "Complete and utter madness. That chicken must have been off."

But still she slammed the window shut and double-checked the locks. She leapt back into bed and pulled the duvet up to her chin. She absently picked at her manicure.

"It was just a dream, just a dream," she repeated to herself, ignoring the glint of pink glitter that dusted the end of her bed.

She was still saying that under her breath as she marched through the reception area of the office the next morning. Edie ignored the receptionist cringing behind the large wood and chrome desk, she forgot to sling her usual scathing comment on the state of the poor woman's dress or that she'd let the flower arrangement droop.

"It was just a dream," she said softly while she waited for the lift.

Edie had already said it as she sat up in bed, as she showered, as she dressed, as she made breakfast and in a frothy white mumble as she brushed her teeth.

The lift arrived empty, for which she was thankful. She especially didn't want to deal with people this morning. She got in, jabbing the button for her floor.

As the doors were about to close a large be-suited arm, stopped them.

Damn it. She shifted to the side without looking up.

"It was just a dream," she whispered to herself. "I must cut down on meat."

"I did that, did me the world of good but there were times I'd kill for a steak or a bacon sandwich," a deep voice said in her left ear.

Chapter 3

Edie jumped.

"What?" she said and looked up at the man next to her.

He was looking down at her with a friendly smile. Looking down from a long way up. And it was a very charming smile. Edie's hackles went up. She didn't want to deal with people today. Especially charming ones.

"Cutting back on meat, you were just saying," he explained.

"Kindly keep your dietary tips and stories for someone who cares," she said. She didn't need charming. Ms Satis had warned her to look behind the charm because they were normally hiding something. She was usually right.

The tall dark man's smile faltered under her icy blast.

"Hey, you were the one sharing your dietary story first," he said his hands held up in peace in front of him. "I thought maybe this was a new Friday office policy people had instigated while I was away."

Edie stared at him confused. Why was he still talking? No one talked to her in the lift and never after one of her put-downs. And who the hell was he anyway?

The silence stretched for three more floors.

"This is us," he said brightly.

Edie could feel rage building in her. She didn't do brightly and she definitely didn't want brightly charming people on the same floor as her.

The doors slid open and he gestured for her to leave first. She stalked out of the lift and tightened her grip on her briefcase.

Turn left. Turn left. Turn left. She willed him as she turned right. But no one was listening because there he was coming up behind her.

"I'm Jack Twist." He was so close it felt as if he was speaking in her ear directly.

She stopped.

He wasn't going to give up, she thought, until he had some sort of conversation. Tenacity was a good trait for a lawyer but not when they were garrulous as well.

It went against her work principles to indulge in chitchat but she needed to set him straight.

She turned on her heel and found herself inches from a very broad chest. It was currently clothed in a crisp striped blue and white cotton shirt. The tie was discretely and geometrically patterned in blue silk that soothed her somewhat. Then her attention was caught by the lining of the charcoal grey suit.

Cerise.

She blinked.

It was still cerise pink. The colour hurt her sleep-deprived eyes.

"Well Mr Twist, thank you for letting me know that you sometimes crave a steak or a bacon sandwich." She tore herself away from the pink lining and moved her gaze to the determined and tanned chin at the top of the shirt, "I feel I can now begin this day with more of a spring in my step from this minutiae. But for future reference I don't wish to hear about that or, in fact, anything else about you ever again whether in the lift or anywhere else. Good day."

She swivelled on her heels and stalked off without waiting to see what Mr Twist had to say about it.

Who the hell did he think he was? OK so she had been talking to herself, which wasn't something she usually indulged in but after last night…

Edie shivered, it was a dream. Just a dream.

She opened the door to her office.

No Rachel.

And after she promised to come in early.

Edie sniffed. The email she'd sent to HR last night would be followed up by a phone call today. How could she work to her best ability or expect to succeed when the people around her were substandard?

Edie marched to her desk. She placed her briefcase in the centre of it, adjusting it slightly to align it with the edge of the desk. She flicked open the locks, leaned forward to switch on her computer and then sat down in her chair all in one fluid take.

Work. Where she could forget about hallucinating. Where she could forget about ghosts and soft things like loving unconditionally. Where she could concentrate on at least making some money for those poor unfortunates who made the colossal mistake of getting hitched and believing they could have a happily ever after.

As she clicked to open her email, her last thought before she lost herself in work was;

Had some woman persuaded Jack Twist that cerise was a desirable lining for a work suit?

"Having reviewed the joint assets and the pension owed to Mrs Samuels, it is our belief that a fair settlement for my client is…"

The door to the office crashed open, banging on the wall and then almost ricocheting closed again. Edie paused in the middle of dictating her letter on the Samuels settlement. She clicked off the recorder, as Rachel, almost brained by the rebounding door, staggered into the room.

Edie lifted one carefully groomed eyebrow and surveyed the wreck of a girl before her.

"Well hello, Ms Micawber, it is good of you to grace us with your presence," she said. "But if I could draw your attention to the clock over the door it is now nine fifteen am. If this is your idea of coming in early, I would hate to see you come in late. And may I also point out that you seem to have your skirt on backwards, your tights are laddered and there is a suspicious stain on your shirt." Edie summed up.

She didn't mention the call she'd made to HR fifteen minutes before.

"Oh God, I am so sorry I'm late!" gasped a red-faced Rachel. A drop of sweat traced a path down her cheek.

"Timmy was sick in the night, and by the time we got him resettled and ourselves back to bed I was so exhausted I missed the alarm," she stopped to gulp in more air.

"And then Rob gave me a lift to the station but we got a flat," Rachel peered down at her shirt and made some vague rubbing motion over her left breast, smearing the stain into a bigger circle.

"I think that might be oil or grease from when I was trying to stop Timmy from lifting the spare tyre by himself. He is such a sweetheart, I can't wait until the wedding and then I'll be his stepmum properly."

Edie could feel her eyes beginning to roll back in her head from boredom. It was too early to have to listen to Rachel's witterings about her allegedly perfect fiancé Rob and his kid Timmy. Actually there was never a good time to listen to her. Edie knew more than she needed to about poor Timmy's health issues and how his mother had rejected him at birth.

"Rachel," she said sharply. "Enough of the family spiel, we are behind enough already without a rehash of the touching family bonding experience I'm sure you all shared. Pull yourself together and when you have you can tell me where you are with the McCartney-Mills case."

Edie clicked her Dictaphone back on.

"Half the pension, five thousand pounds a month maintenance and the London flat," she carried on as if Rachel's entrance had not happened at all.

Edie pinched her nose as a dull throbbing headache, probably caused by her interrupted night's sleep, hit her.

And it was still only lunchtime.

She stretched out her arms, laced her fingers and pulled, loosening herself up.

At least today was Friday; she could have a small lie in tomorrow and then she would have the whole weekend. Two days where she could get some work finished uninterrupted by colleagues or clients, two days without Rachel's snivelling.

But what about ghosts? An inner Edie whispered.

There was no such thing as ghosts; last night had been a very vivid and detailed dream, she told herself.

She was obviously fixating on weddings because Mel's was coming up in a fortnight. Why had she ever agreed to be bridesmaid, sorry no, make that maid of honour in the first place? It was only due to the length of time that she had known Mel that had made her say yes. And when had maid of honour become such a big thing? She shuddered when she thought of it. Not only would she have to sit through a wedding, she was actually having to take part in one as a member of the wedding party. It was enough to make her break out in a rash.

Yes, it was the stress from the wedding that was getting to her. That was probably why she'd dreamt of Jessica. Really it was funny when she thought about it, how her subconscious was playing tricks on her. And everyone knew you shouldn't read into dreams.

Then a memory tickled the back of her mind and as it poked a bit harder at her, a black cloud of dread appeared on her horizon, it loomed and crept closer. It was something to do with the wedding… the clouds gathered into a storm and closed in. There was a sinking feeling in her stomach, her recently stretched shoulders tightened.

What was it?

And simultaneously at the exact point she could put a name to her dread, a calendar reminder on her computer bleeped and named it for her.

Mel's Hen Weekend – 1 day

The hen weekend.

Her vision of a blessed free weekend was winked out in the flip of a binary switch, the production of a calendar reminder. This time tomorrow she would be in the midst of the most hellish endurance sport known to womankind… the hen party. And as maid of honour there was no way she could miss it or even leave early. She was in for the duration, no time off for good behaviour.

And even she wouldn't back out and blame work. She might hate weddings but she really did love Mel. She owed her for making her teen years at least partly bearable. For giving her a refuge from the coldness at home.

But Edie knew that every one of the other hens were card-carrying members of the 'happily ever after' clan.

Her phone rang, thankfully distracting her from the need to think any further about the hen night. She lunged for it without checking the caller ID.

"Edie Dickens," she answered.

"Edie! It's a disaster!" a voice squealed out of the earpiece.

She should've checked. Edie frowned as she moved the earpiece further away from her ear.

"Hi Mel," she said, "What is it this time? The caterers have run out of pink icing? Barry has run off with the best man?"

And of course the other point of being maid of honour and best friend to the bride was that you were supposed to be available to calm down any nerves and last minute panics. It was a bit of a stretch because all the advice Edie had was to tell her to cancel the whole thing, run very fast in the opposite direction and use the money for something more sensible… like taking a course in underwater basket weaving.

"No! As if! Although now you say that I think I'll just give the caterers a quick ring after we've chatted… just in case. God wouldn't it be awful if they didn't have pink icing for the cupcake cake? It would blow the entire colour scheme!"

Edie looked upwards in disgust. This was why she didn't do weddings. And to think she wouldn't even have Jessica to take the piss out of it with her.

Jessica.

She hadn't really visited last night had she? She couldn't have done. All that funny stuff about contracts and loving unconditionally… it was a load of bunkum obviously drawn from some weird and wonderful part of her mind and mixed with dodgy meat.

"Anyway what I phoned about is my bloody parents," Mel had obviously finished worrying about the caterers.

"What's up with Maggie and Doug?"

Mel's parents were the only married couple that disproved Edie's theory. They had been together for thirty-nine years and even though Doug was a workaholic surgeon and was away working more than at home, they would be together for thirty-nine years more. They were safe and solid and completely unlike her own parents. When she was a teenager she used to wish they'd adopt her, that she could be part of their normal family. In fact she'd spent almost all her time round at their house. It was more of a home than the one she'd shared with her mum.

"They are acting like five-year-olds. They are squabbling in low, angry voices and whenever I ask them what's wrong they both clam up and say there is nothing to worry about. You don't think there is a problem with paying for it all, do you? Maybe they forgot to pay the deposit on the golf club? Oh God, I hope Dad isn't going to be completely inappropriate during the speeches."

Edie sighed. It was nothing startling then, no world-shattering event, Mel just needing to vent to the one person who had to listen. Her maid of honour.

"I'm sure your parents are fine," Edie spoke absently as she opened her emails at the same time. "Doug probably brought up

22

some surgical procedure at one of their charity dinners or something and put everyone off their scallops."

"Yeah. Of course. You are so right Edie. I don't know where my head is at."

I know, thought Edie, your brain is on Planet Wedding and it has sucked any sense out of you.

But she didn't say it. She also didn't say she thought Mel had lost a fair few IQ points ever since she got engaged. Hell, who was she kidding? Ever since she fell in love. Why couldn't Barry have run off with the best man? It would solve all manner of things. For once Edie kept her opinion to herself, Mel meant too much to her.

"OK, well I'll see you at mine at eleven am, and no ducking out of anything. You promised." Mel carried on.

"I'll be there." Edie promised as she said goodbye.

She even had to drive herself to her own execution. A three-hour car journey with the blushing bride before they even got to the hen weekend; if Edie's body wasn't so well disciplined her shoulders would have been round her ears, her back bent and she would be wringing her hands. Instead she picked at the chipped varnish on her thumbnail.

At six thirty, Edie repacked her briefcase with less work than she would have liked. She turned off her computer and left the pale and red eyed Rachel still at her desk.

"Oh, are you off?" Rachel sounded surprised.

Edie knew it was earlier than normal but if a hen night called then she would need to make sure she hit the gym that night instead of tomorrow.

"Good night, Rachel," she said repressively. There was no need for her to keep Rachel up to date with her social life.

Marching out of her office she headed for the lift, thinking as she walked that she would do a quick five miles on the treadmill and then some weights.

Pressing the button, the chipped varnish on her thumbnail

where she'd been picking at it caught her eye; she wondered whether the manicurist could fit her in tomorrow morning.

"We must stop meeting like this." The deep voice from this morning spoke from somewhere behind her.

Her back tensed.

It was bad enough that she was haunted in her dreams now it felt as if she was being haunted in real life.

She ignored him.

"Tough day at the coalface, huh? So tired and drained from saving people's marriages that you can't speak?" the bass voice rumbled on.

Really. Saving people's marriages? What kind of divorce lawyer did he think she was? It was in the title 'divorce.' Hilary Satis had taught her that when she'd been her mother's lawyer and then again when Edie had come to work for her.

"I think you'll find, Mr Twist, that saving marriages is for marriage counsellors. Not for lawyers."

The lift arrived and she marched in. Turning to press the ground floor button, she got a good look at her nemesis as he followed her in, grinning.

She had forgotten how tall he was; she only came up to his chin. His face was square and saved from beauty by a broken nose, a scar through his left eyebrow and another just below his lower lip. Although the scar brought attention to a bottom lip that begged to be kissed.

What?

She caught herself from thinking further about his lips.

She looked up and caught hazel eyes glinting, laughing at her.

"Well, I believe we will have to agree to differ then," he said following her in. "Ms Dickens, isn't it? Your reputation precedes you," he continued.

The way he emphasised 'reputation' caused Edie to go on alert.

She knew his type. They were always trying to convince people that if they just worked at it they could get back together or at least come to an equable settlement. As if. That wasn't what the job was about.

"I take it you believe mediation is the panacea for the masses then? All the touchy feely new age stuff," she said.

As Edie said 'mediation' a shiver went up her spine.

Mediation.

Wasn't that what Jessica had said she should be pushing her clients towards?

"New age? If you want to call it that, then yes, Ms Dickens I'm one of those touchy feely new age types. But maybe you'd care to tell me where I'm going wrong over a drink tonight. Dispense your theories. Maybe take pity on the prodigal son returning to the fold."

His hands were held out in supplication. They were as rough and battered as his face. One of them could've easily held both of hers.

Where were these thoughts coming from?

And what was this prodigal son stuff? Did he think she had nothing better to do than gossip about her colleagues? A drink? As if.

She opened her mouth to tell him and as she did a faint shimmer of pink glitter fluttered out of thin air and landed on his shoulder. The few specks winked in the fluorescent lighting.

Pink glitter.

Just like the glitter she had found all over the end of her bed that morning.

The same pink glitter that had wound a path from her bedroom window to disappear somewhere in the middle of her living room.

It hadn't been a dream.

Edie felt the blood drain out of her face. The cerise lining of Jack Twist's suit went grey. She put a hand out to steady herself.

It hit solid muscle; muscle clad in cotton and wool.

"Whoa there. I know I'm not much of a catch but you don't need to faint to get out of it. A simple no would have been fine," Jack Twist joked as he grasped her arms to hold her steady.

He smelt of coffee, shampoo, laundry detergent and something citrusy. Clean. Normal. Not the sort of man who would have ghosts haunting him. Well of course he wouldn't, he was the saintly sort who believed in mediation.

And yet there was the glitter.

It winked and blinked at her, a warning light.

Stop.

Wait.

Go.

Go, she had to go.

"Excuse me please," she said.

Wrenching her arm away she staggered to the lift doors and as soon as they were at the ground floor and opening she slipped through the gap.

"Edie! At least let me get you a cab," his voice called loudly causing everyone in the lobby to look and see what was happening but she ignored it. She ran out of the building and bumped and careened her way through the commuters on the street.

Chapter 4

Edie lay in her solitary but very well appointed bed. She had spent a quarter of an hour smoothing the sheets before she got in, trying to make herself calm.

Then she'd gone through all her yoga relaxation exercises and when that hadn't helped she'd used the self-hypnosis sleep app on her phone. But she was still awake. Every time she heard the sound of Big Ben chime the quarter hour, her body tensed and she found herself grasping the duvet.

She was being silly. The whole thing with Jessica had been down to dodgy meat; she knew that. She did. That glitter on Jack Twist's shoulder in the lift was just something left over from whatever birthday celebration was happening this week, there was always one. Not that she was ever invited to them. He'd obviously brushed up against a banner or a card. It had taken her running almost halfway to the bus stop before she had thought logically about that one.

So there was no ghost coming.

Why she was allowing some bad dream to dictate her life? She'd never let anyone else dictate it before. And she wasn't about to start tonight.

No, she was being silly. Now she'd thought it through logically, she would sleep. And setting her formidable mind and iron willpower to it, she drifted off to sleep.

When Edie woke up, it was so dark that, staring round she could scarcely distinguish the window from the walls of her bedroom. She was still squinting trying to see, when the chimes of Big Ben struck the four quarters, she listened for the hour. She reckoned it must be about three o'clock.

The heavy bell went past three and struck twelve; then stopped. Twelve. But it had been past twelve when eventually she'd closed her eyes and gone to sleep. The clock was wrong. A damn pigeon must have got into the works. Twelve. This was going to be all over the news and she'd have to listen to everyone witter on about it for weeks until something equally as trivial occupied them.

There was no way time moved backwards.

She reached to her bedside table and checked her mobile phone. Twelve. Frowning, she looked at her radio-controlled clock. It lit up and confirmed the time.

Twelve.

"This isn't happening," she said, "there is no way I've slept the day away… no way. Someone would have called."

But maybe she had.

No, her, Edwina Charlotte Dickens sleeping in and missing a day? Never. It would never, could never happen. And on the few occasions she was sick she'd always phoned in and then worked from her bed. But this wasn't work she was missing, but a hen night.

She could see herself subconsciously sleeping through it. But there was no way that Mel would allow her to miss it. And she wouldn't let Mel down. Edie had promised to do this for her. And she didn't break promises.

Edie scrambled out of her bed, and groped towards the window. Which was frosted. In June.

She rubbed the frost off with the sleeve of her pyjamas; nothing unusual. It was just very foggy and extremely cold. Global warming? Freak weather? Time standing still? But the street was silent; no hysterical people running round like headless chickens so probably not a major global catastrophe.

Then she must have got the time she went to sleep wrong. Mustn't she? She hated this feeling of being out of control, of doubting her own mind. Her mind was the one thing that had never let her down

Her stomach clenching in trepidation, Edie climbed back into bed again, her mind spinning. Thoughts racing; too many strange things were happening.

"There must be some logical explanation," she said to herself.

Jessica's ghost bothered her the most. Although she had spent most of the day ignoring the memory, it still festered there in the back of her mind.

And another Spirit was due… if Jessica was to be believed. Had it really come to this? She was taking the word of a see-through former person?

Big Ben chimed again.

Edie checked her phone, it shone and showed 00:15. Forty-five minutes to go and logic said Edie would be left alone. It was the twenty-first century… people didn't get haunted the way they used to. It just wasn't done.

She lay on her side in bed, knees curled protectively towards her chest.

"Ding dong!"

"Half past," she muttered as she reached out and checked her phone yet again.

"Ding dong!"

"A quarter to," Edie whispered into her pillow, her hands clutching it tightly.

"Ding dong!"

"One o'clock," she said out loud, her body relaxing, "and not a strange visitor in sight!"

Edie didn't bother looking at her phone; the quarter chimes of Big Ben were good enough for her. And once the hour bell had sounded, she would be getting some sleep.

How stupid had she been? Believing some dream she had last night.

"Terms and conditions. I mean, really."

Edie bashed her pillow into shape and pulled the duvet up to her chin as the hour bell sounded a deep, dull, hollow, melancholy one.

As the sound ended, light erupted in the room, as if a thousand camera flashes were going off at once.

With a small scream, Edie catapulted upright in bed. Her eyes were blinded by the flash of light. Rubbing them she tried to rid herself of the black spots. Opening them again, she was confronted with a visitor.

She rubbed her eyes again.

Opening them still showed the same visitor.

What was a six-year-old flower girl doing in her bedroom?

The child was dressed in a pink dress; the bodice heavy with embroidered flowers and seed pearls, the skirt fell in folds like a fairy princess. On her blonde and curly hair sat a circlet of sweet peas and roses with bits of baby's breath, gypsophila, peeking out here and there.

Clutched in her hands was a flower basket but instead of flowers the basket held the light that had blinded Edie earlier. It lit the whole room, a blue white light shooting up from the basket to hit the ceiling like a thousand spotlights. Nothing could hide from that light, it illuminated all shadows.

Solemn blue eyes stared at Edie. Eyes too old for a six year old and like the light, they scorched bright. They tore through Edie's outer layers and the mask she showed the world to see what was hidden beneath. Edie's soul shrank and tried to hide but found its darkest corners exposed.

"Erm…" Edie's voice faltered and faded under the child's stare. Why did it have to be a child? Edie never knew what to say to them.

"So little girl, are you the Ghost that Ms Marley told me about?" Edie tried to smile encouragingly at the youngster, but it felt more like a grimace.

The child raised an eyebrow, shook her head and sighed.

"I might look like a six-year-old but you don't have to talk to me like I'm stupid," the child Wraith replied.

Just my luck, thought Edie, I'm being haunted by a precocious poltergeist.

"But yes, I am the Ghost that Jessica Marley told you about."

The Ghost had a soft voice and low but it echoed as if it were at a distance.

"And who and what are you exactly?" Edie asked her body tense for the next shock heading her way.

"I am the Ghost of Weddings Past."

"Like history past?" inquired Edie. It was bad enough going to weddings but to have to go through some sort of history lesson as well.

"No. Your past and the pasts of those close to you."

Oh.

"Well, while you do that could you turn down the light?" Edie said.

"Turn it down?" the child swung the basket as she put both hands on her small hips. "Turn it down? This light doesn't have a dimmer switch you know. It isn't to be commanded and leashed like you do everything else."

Edie's eyes watered as the light shone in them and her skin stung where it hit her as if caught out in the sun too long.

"I'm sorry, Edie you'll just have to get used to it." And with that the Spirit folded her arms, knocking the basket even more. The beam careened around the room.

"OK, so the light is staying," Edie conceded reluctantly. A good lawyer knew when to give ground in an argument and when to strike to win.

"But what exactly is the reason you're here?"

Information was key, and Edie needed it. There was one thing she hated and that was to be flying blind.

"Your welfare, of course," the flower girl rolled her eyes again.

"You did listen to what Jessica had to say didn't you?"

"Well yes," Edie replied but she thought how much better her welfare would be for having a full night's sleep.

"Sleep? You'd rather sleep than be reclaimed? Saved?"

Edie jumped. Not only was she invaded by ectoplasmic presences, they had ESP.

Chapter 5

The little girl unfolded her arms and held out a hand. Edie looked at it as if it would bite her. She remembered all the other little flower girls she had held the hands of. She remembered the sticky residue, the snotty slickness.

"Come on! Get up! We have to get going," the hand was shaken closer towards her. Edie wanted to say she wasn't dressed, that it was cold outside and didn't the little girl have parents who would be worried about her? Instead, Edie reluctantly took the hand. It was soft and warm, dry and without stickiness and it was very strong.

With a raised eyebrow the Ghost said,

"Stop letting outside appearances blind you to reality."

And then it pulled Edie from the bed and took her towards the window.

Edie didn't have time to grab her robe, her bare feet squeaked on the floor and she shivered in her t-shirt and cotton pyjama bottoms.

"I'm not going out of the window," she said.

The Ghost reached out and up and laid its small hand on Edie's t-shirt, right over her heart.

"Have faith." The eyes were kind even though they still burned bright, "just put up with having my hand here and you'll be supported in all this and more."

And with those words they passed through the wall.

"What the…"

There was no plummeting to the ground, as Edie had tensed herself to expect. In fact they were already on the ground but they were definitely not in London any more. Instead of her street of mansion blocks, they were outside on the verge of a lane beside a country churchyard.

Instead of darkness and that weird fog, it was a bright summer's day. The sort of June weather that happened when June behaved properly and it was the way Edie remembered her childhood when she thought about it, which wasn't often. Butterflies flitted from cowslip to buttercup.

"Oh my God…" breathed Edie.

Her hands shook as she reached to touch a flower. She slowly turned on the spot, drinking in the scene. "This can't be, this is the place where I grew up. This is Little Hanningfield."

Her hand went to feel the rough stone wall that separated the grass verge they were on from the tiny cemetery and the small squat stone church.

The Spirit looked up at her, a strange smile hovering round her little girl lips, but it was a grown-up, wise smile.

Edie rubbed her chest; she could still feel the imprint of the little hand on her. She could feel each finger and along with it she could smell her childhood. Freshly cut grass, the smell of warm tarmac and horses. And with the smells came rushing in all her childish thoughts, hopes and dreams. The dam she had barricaded them behind had been breached by the touch of a tiny hand and she was flooded.

"You OK?" the Ghost asked. "Your lip is trembling and… are you crying?"

"No, no… just a touch of hay fever," muttered Edie with a husky catch to her voice. "So where are we going?" she changed the subject.

"Where do you think?" the Spirit asked.

34

"Home," breathed Edie.

"Do you remember the way?" The flower girl asked, staring hard at Edie.

"Remember it! Of course I remember it!" she scoffed.

"Odd, it isn't like you visit here often," the Ghost replied.

Edie rushed off the grass verge and headed down the small country lane, away from the church and towards the village green.

"Look that's old Mrs Scaman's cottage, it looks exactly the same. I used to come here because she made the most amazing lemon drizzle cake. And see, all the cats are out sunning themselves. There's Gerry and Dylan and Merlin."

She paused.

"But they died when I was a teenager."

She looked from the cats towards the Ghost who was standing in front of her.

"This is the Past, Edie. Shadows of what has been. They don't know we're here," she replied.

Tell that to Merlin, thought Edie, as the smoky grey cat twined itself between her legs, purring.

"Bloody cats," said the Ghost. "They never can stick to the rules."

Five minutes later they stood by a worn wooden gate, a garland of flowers and ribbons covered it. Red balloons bobbed from the gate post.

"But this was Philly's wedding," Edie gasped, remembering. "But that was…" she did some frantic calculation in her head and came up with a number which shocked her.

"I told you, I'm the Ghost of Weddings Past," said the Spirit. "And this was your first wedding. Come watch."

Edie allowed the small strong hand to pull her to one side of the gate.

Suddenly, out of the front door of the house flew a little red whirlwind about the same age as the Ghost standing beside her. Fine dark hair in a bob was held ruthlessly back with a flower headband that allowed a mischievous freckled face with two front teeth missing to show.

"Look Mummy! Look! Daddy, come and see!" the girl cried as she started twirling in circles, looking down at the way her dress flew round her. "I'm a princess!"

"I felt like a princess that day," whispered Edie. Her eyes blurred as she stared down at herself. "I used to dream that I could have that day again. That I would have a wedding day and feel like a princess again."

Behind the young Edie came a woman who was about Edie's age now.

"Mum!" both Edies cried.

"She is so young," wondered the older Edie.

"She's younger than you are now," pointed out the Ghost.

She was, thought Edie. And she had a family and a home then. It had all gone wrong; everything did, but her mother had known it however briefly. What did Edie have?

A job, a voice in her head said. It sounded like Ms Satis. Edie had a life where she didn't have to answer to anyone but herself. And that was just fine, wasn't it?

"Oh this is where my Aunt Philly comes out!" Edie remembered. "She looked like a queen. I wanted to be just like her. We had so much fun planning the flowers and putting together the orders of service. Did you know that flowers have a language? That if you use different blooms they mean something?" Edie was smiling; tension that had been in her jaw for years was easing.

And then from out of the house came a glowing young woman, the dated gown doing nothing to dispel her beauty. Little Edie and her mother instantly surrounded her. When was the last time Edie had been with just her mother and aunt? Last Christmas? The Christmas before?

Oh no, not then. That was the year she had gone away on her own because she was too stressed from work to be able to deal with her mother and the empty space which they all tried to ignore.

And well, who had time at weekends to visit? At least she would see her at Mel's wedding. Edie's mood dipped.

"I wish," she whispered, blotting her leaking eyes with the back of her hand, "but it's too late."

"What is it?" asked the Spirit staring up at her seriously.

"No, it's just that my mother phoned me the other night and because I was too busy and tired and didn't want the stress I didn't answer and never called her back. I wish I had. She's all I have left."

And then from behind her aunt came a man. Her father. She looked at his face, her memory of it had been blurred by so many years without seeing him. That was what he looked like.

He was young and handsome.

She had his eyes.

He wrapped an arm round her mother's shoulders. She leaned into him and they shared a look. Edie's tears flowed again.

"Is that your father?" the Ghost asked but Edie knew it was rhetorical. She nodded as she drank him in. She watched as her younger self skipped round the couple, laughing while her aunt looked on. She'd been totally secure in that world, a world she believed centred round her. How wrong she'd been.

The older Edie ached. When was the last time she'd seen her dad? It had been a long time ago. Not too many years after this wedding.

The Ghost smiled thoughtfully, and waved its basket saying, "Let's see another wedding!"

The foliage grew and retreated, blossoms came and went, and little Edie went from six to thirteen in the matter of a minute. Her dress was now peach silk, and her body hovered on the threshold of adulthood. She was at that stage where she was neither fish nor fowl.

She picked at flaking paint of the gate, her face set in a sullen scowl.

"Hey Edie!" A bundle of blonde energy also in peach came running down the lane.

Teenage Edie's scowl lightened and she smiled.

"Mel! Can you believe it, my mother won't let me wear any make-up!" she grumped to her best friend. "She and Dad had the most massive row about it. God, sometimes I hate her. She never wants me to have any fun."

The older Edie felt the tears gathering. That had been the last big row she remembered them having, and then he'd left. Although she hadn't known that then.

And they'd rowed because of her.

"It's alright," the petite elfin face of Mel looked down, frowning as she rummaged through the funny bag that she clutched to her chest. It was a facsimile of a reticule and was done in the same shiny peach fabric.

"Here!"

Triumphantly she waved a set of cosmetics at teen Edie.

"Oh, I remember," said the older Edie, her face alight with memories.

She watched her younger self inexpertly apply lipstick and mascara while her best friend held the small compact mirror in front of her.

"There! Tom will have to notice you now," said Mel.

Little Edie's face flushed hotly and clashed violently with the peach dress.

The watching Edie's heart skipped a beat as she heard the name. The same way she knew her heart had skipped a beat all those years ago.

"Ah, so you remember Tom then?" the Spirit quizzed.

"How could I forget Tom," Edie said. But she had. She'd buried all those memories deep, locked them away. Even when Mel had told her that he was the best man at the wedding she'd ignored it. Nodded and then carried on as if she didn't care.

Edie and the Ghost moved to follow the teenagers as they piled, giggling, into the flower decked horse and carriage that had pulled up in front of the gate.

"Do you know where they're going now?" asked the flower girl Spirit.

"To the church," she replied. "It was our teacher, Miss Stray, getting married. She was marrying Mel's cousin, Charlie. Tom was, well, is his brother.

"He was fifteen that summer. And Charlie's best man and all I wanted was for him to notice me."

The scene dissolved into soft focus and refocused with them back outside the church. Edie jumped.

"Saves time," the Ghost apologised.

From the inside the church came the sound of the wedding march.

"Ready?" asked the Spirit.

Was she? Fizzing deep inside her was the teenager who wanted to see Tom again. She wanted to feel all the innocent pleasure of being in love for the first time all over again. That wrenching panic that they might never see you, might not love you back. But no matter what happened, you couldn't stop the hope and yearning from filling you all the way to your fingertips.

"Yes," she breathed.

Was this the last time her life had been uncomplicated? Mum and Dad had still been together and her world had been whole.

They walked up the path and went into the church; they went from the bright June sunlight to the cool darkness of the Norman church. They passed the font and began to follow the bridal party down the aisle.

"There's Joanne Kitchner!" Edie squeaked. "My goodness last time I saw her she was screaming at her kids in the supermarket. Wow, she looks so young.

"Jessica!" she called as she passed a teenage girl. The young Jessica wore the same superior look as the ghost from the night before. The only difference was age and spots. "I'd forgotten she was at this wedding."

Edie tried to grab her attention by shouting.

"She can't hear you; this is just a reflection of your past. She isn't here," the Ghost said.

Edie sighed. It would've been useful to have an ally against the tiny tyrant. She moved on down the aisle.

"And there is Justin Douglas. My goodness, how all the girls used to swoon over him. Mel used to doodle *Mrs Mel Douglas* all over her books." Edie cocked her head on the side to look at the gangly adolescent whose hair was gelled to within an inch of its life and still wondered what Mel had seen.

"And you?" the Ghost asked as she skipped down the aisle in a parody of the flower girl she resembled.

"It was always Tom for me," Edie sighed.

She remembered the love hearts she'd doodled with 'Tom + Edie 4 Ever' written in them.

They reached the bridal party; the teenage Edie was gripping her posy so hard her knuckles were white. Her face was flame red as her eyes kept darting to look to her right.

"There!" her older counterpart pointed.

It was Tom.

The Tom of all her adolescent dreams, the Tom who had turned into her dream man until she put those dreams away from her.

Standing solemnly next to the groom, watching the vicar and not glancing to the left at teen Edie or anywhere else, was a tall, slight man boy. His curly blond hair was ruthlessly held down by hair product so that only a slight wave was discernible. Edie's fingers itched with the memory of those curls unfettered between her fingers, the soft springiness. The way he smelt.

Her heart turned over as her eyes traced his profile. A smooth forehead unblemished by the frown lines she had carved there. Mouth full and slightly smiling. When had she last seen him smile? There hadn't been much smiling in that last year.

"How on earth are you doing all this?" she fought against the tearing feeling inside her. "Is this some complicated and sophisticated hologram? And who the hell told you about Tom?"

Yes this was better. Stop the maudlin memories. Edie rubbed her chest near her heart, she needed this to stop.

The Spirit raised an eyebrow, a very adult look on a six-year-old face.

"Edie," she said with a hint of exasperation.

"Well I suppose anyone could have told you about me and Tom! I mean all these people were at the wedding…" Edie's voice petered out. "I don't know how you made it all so life like, it must have cost a fortune but I've seen what they can do in films these days."

"You want more proof?" the little flower girl asked.

Proof? Hell yeah she wanted proof.

"Yes," she said it and jutted her chin out.

The pain in her chest retreated as she wrapped herself in her familiar blanket of stubbornness.

The Ghost sighed dramatically.

The scene vanished in a blink of an eye.

It felt as if part of Edie was wrenched out and left behind.

A scene emerged around them; they were inside a marquee which had fairy lights strung on the ceiling mimicking a star-studded night. The flashing lights of the mobile DJ twirled to the beat of the music blaring from the speakers.

"Oh no," Edie groaned.

"Well you wanted proof," the Ghost said sanctimoniously.

"No really, I believe you," she was desperate. "Can we just stop it now? Go back to my room? I've learnt whatever lesson you want me to learn."

She couldn't relive this again.

"So who is that over there?" piped the Ghost.

Surely it wasn't against the law to hit a Ghost who looked like a six-year-old girl?

"Me," she muttered.

"And what are you doing?"

No, she couldn't hit her; knowing her luck this was really some precocious stage school brat whose parents would sue her for lost earnings.

"I'm…" the words stuck in her throat.

"Yes?"

"I'm dancing," she said.

"Dancing? Really?" the Ghost was definitely trying not to laugh.

Edie's face burned for her younger self. She wriggled in embarrassment for what was to come.

"I think we need to get just a little closer," the Spirit said and for a six-year-old she had a freakishly strong grip and pull.

Edie got closer to the writhing flushed figure in peach silk. Oh God, had she really thought that she was dancing in a sexy way? Her puppy fat was spilling over the top of the dress and she was squinting up under her eyelashes. And to think she had spent hours perfecting her sexy gaze in the mirror thinking it would have a devastating effect on men. I suppose it did, she thought, devastating in a 'run screaming from this girl' sort of way.

She watched as the dance continued, her breathing increasing in time with young Edie's. The anticipation that she knew she'd felt as she danced closer to her quarry; the unsuspecting Tom, who was leaning against one of the marquee poles. He was surveying the dancers whilst surreptitiously drinking a stolen glass of champagne.

"Hi…" young Edie croaked out as she wriggled in front of him. It really did look like she was trying to shed a too tight skin.

He hadn't heard her.

"Hi!" she shouted.

It reached every corner of the marquee. Trust the damn DJ to cut the song for one of those shout back moments. Heads whipped round to look at her.

"Er… hi," he replied uncomfortably. He took another swig of champagne. His eyes were desperately looking round for escape; or was it to check he hadn't been seen with alcohol?

"Can I have some?" the teenage girl asked and the watching woman's stomach knotted in synch.

"Well, you're a bit young to be drinking," he said, worried.

"I'm old enough! I've drunk champagne loads of times!" Twice at least and then only a sip from her Dad's glass at New Year but this was Tom. She was going to lie, wasn't she?

He looked at her, unconvinced.

"Walk away. Walk away," whispered older Edie.

Oh God, it was like watching a car crash about to happen and having no way of stopping it.

"Come on, outside," he said as he looked round and snagged the whole champagne bottle and sauntered out.

The teenage Edie glowed.

It made the older Edie shiver; she had never seen that look on her face before.

It was the look that Mel had when she looked at Barry. What her parents had once had. Even drippy Rachel had looked like that. Lit from inside with the wonder that was love. But what she saw on her teenage face was even purer.

This was first love.

It was an effing disaster.

She lunged at herself. Her hands went straight through her own arms.

"We've got to stop her! I mean me!" she said.

"This is your past. You can't change the past," the Spirit said as she twirled gently to the music on the dance floor, making her skirt rustle.

"But she is going to be devastated. Mortified. For years she is not going to be able to look at champagne, never mind drink it. Or rather I won't." Edie was desperate and confused.

She had to stop herself from making this mistake. Again.

"You can't change the past," repeated the Ghost.

"Well I'm going to try!" she said.

She hurried across the dance floor, the dancers somehow avoiding her as if a force field surrounded her.

Her stomach felt as if it were round her ankles. Her skin flushed and then paled as she remembered; it crawled in repulsion at her stupidity. She'd relived it time and time again, woken up sweating on many nights. She couldn't go through it again.

She burst out of the marquee into the deep dark night. The stars scattered across the sky, twinkling down, winking at her. Was the whole world laughing at her?

"Ow!" she heard a muffled shout.

It was beginning… her teenage self had just tripped over the guy rope to the marquee. If she turned around she would see herself. Her dress would've flown up and she'd be sprawled across the ground.

She turned.

Yes, there she was.

And she really had shown her knickers to the world.

"I'm fine. I'm fine," young Edie said, voice high and squeaky.

"Give me your hand," Tom said putting down the stolen bottle.

He held out a hand and hauled her up.

Old Edie had to stop this.

"Edie!" she shouted, "Edie, go back inside!"

No one answered.

She jogged over to the teenage couple and tried to grab young Edie's arm. It passed straight through as if she were a ghost.

"You're only a visitor here," the small muffled voice came from the vicinity of her elbow.

"Really?" She was getting annoyed. "Well if that is the case where did you get the sausage roll?"

The Spirit gave a fake smile as she carried on eating the stolen sausage roll, then turned back to the couple in front of them.

"Oh dear"

Edie looked up.

Young Edie was attempting to pout sexily whilst leaning against a tree. It was less a pout and more a scowl.

And it was just about to get much worse.

"So can I have a drink then?" Edie junior croaked.

She really hadn't purred in the sexy way she had thought.

"Have you got a cold or something? Because I'm not having your germs!" Tom asked.

"No," she coughed. "No, I'm fine. No germs, honest."

No germs. Nothing contagious. Because it isn't like you can catch stupidity, the older Edie thought.

Tom passed over the bottle of champagne and young Edie took a large swig from it.

The watching woman's nose itched in sympathy as the bubbles hit the teenager and started her sneezing.

"You have got a cold! Sheesh, Edie! I've got my exams coming up I can't be ill!"

"No! It was the bubbles. I'm really OK." She spluttered.

For a few minutes they stood sharing the bottle, passing it back and forth. The memory of that night came back to Edie and she remembered her mind had been racing like a hamster in a wheel trying to think of something witty to say. And how the champagne was acidic on her stressed stomach, making it roil queasily.

"Hey Tom!"

And suddenly there was Justin, and Edie was now the third wheel.

The relief on Tom's face was just as hard to see a second time.

"Champagne! Good one! Hand it over, Dick!" Justin swaggered up.

Both Edie's top lips curled at the offensive contraction of her surname. But the younger one silently gave up the bottle.

"Ciggie?" Justin expertly tapped out a cigarette from a pack he conjured up from his pocket.

Tom took one like a proper smoker and then the pack was in front of Edie.

"Don't do it," she whispered. Please let this young Edie make a different choice. "Don't do it." Her hand was at her mouth.

The teen reached out and inexpertly took a cigarette. It looked awkward in her straight fingers, the tube of tobacco too near the palm.

A flame erupted from the Justin's lighter and the two boys leant forward and lit their cigarettes.

Teen Edie leant forward, the cigarette trembling in her hand.

The sudden smell of burnt hair and hairspray fought with the jasmine.

"Silly mare, you'll go up in flames!" Tom pulled her back and peered through the gloom at her fringe.

"You've taken off at least an inch. Here, take mine."

Tom passed over his cigarette and took Edie's unlit one; which he soon had lit.

The larger Edie groaned.

"That bad, huh?" the little Ghost whispered mesmerised by the scene, the half-eaten sausage roll was hovering by her mouth.

Bad? The worst was just a few drags away.

The glowing end of the cigarette wavered as she brought it up to her mouth. The teenage Edie sucked on it quickly and coughed out the smoke immediately.

"Have you never done this before?" Justin asked.

"Of course I have," she spluttered.

"Yeah right! Well you're supposed to inhale," he said and proceeded to demonstrate.

Edie lifted the cigarette again. This time she inhaled.

The memory of the acrid smoke filling her mouth and then her lungs came burning back to her as she watched. Older Edie knew the moment when her teen body rebelled against all the abuse. Her older body tried to relive the memories as she watched herself experience them.

The terror from the lack of oxygen and her dizzy head added to the roiling stomach from tension and champagne. The eyes became wide with the dawning horror that the old saying 'better out than in' was about to play out. The sheer panic as her body convulsed, sides aching.

And then came the eruption.

All over Tom's shoes.

Mortification flooded both of Edie's bodies.

"Ahh man! That is gross!" cried Justin.

Bent over, all the young Edie could do was throw up again and again, tears dripping from her nose until they were the only liquid left for her to expel.

She had wanted the earth to swallow her up then and there. Even all these years later she would happily wish for it again. She watched as Justin backed away in disgust. Hadn't Tom gone as well?

But he hadn't. She didn't remember him staying. She watched open mouthed as she saw Tom hesitantly raise his hand and slowly rub her young back in sympathy.

He'd rubbed her back?

Dumbfounded, the older Edie watched. How come she had never known that he'd stood there rubbing her back? She would've known surely.

"Go away!" rasped the teen.

And he went.

Edie looked at herself. The bedraggled vomit sprayed hair, the green white face with black streaks from too much mascara, which had now been cried off.

"Take me home," she turned to the ghost. "I've learnt whatever you wanted me to. I'll agree to anything just let me go home."

The flower girl looked up at her pityingly.

Pity. Edie cringed. She wasn't pitiful, goddammit.

"There are a few more things you have to see," the Spirit said solemnly.

"No!"

"No?" the Spirit raised an eyebrow.

"No. N.O. I've had enough of this circus, I want to go home to my own bed."

"Oh you'll be lying in your own bed soon enough, wrapped in a chain," the Spirit retorted.

A small sprinkle of pink glitter fell from its fingers.

Edie shuddered.

Not the pink glitter.

She caved.

"OK, your way then," she sighed.

Chapter 6

Another fade out. And then fade in.

Another wedding reception, she recognised the Little Hanningfield village hall again. Green and white bunting and streamers covered the walls and the ceilings. Lights flashed as the disco played on the small stage at one end, the stage that had held the annual nativity play but now played host to a middle aged man who was dad dancing behind the decks.

Tables at the other end were groaning with a buffet of pork pies, sausage rolls, cheese and pineapple hedgehogs and sandwiches, punctuated by bowls of crisps.

The hall was full of people either hanging round the food or in the middle of the floor, dancing. They were dressed in the style people had worn when she was at university.

The she caught sight of herself, happily dancing with Mel. Her hair was much longer, her face smiling. Glowing with hope and ideals.

"This was Justin Douglas' wedding," she said, remembering, "It was my final year at uni. Mel and I were invited for the evening do. She said it was the wake of our childhood dreams. She had still been hoping Justin would marry her."

She smiled as she watched herself twirling Mel around wildly by the hand, neither of them caring about the boys who were circling them on the dance floor.

"We were so happy that summer. We'd got jobs at the local pub." Her foot tapped along to the beat of the song. "We thought we could rule the world."

She missed the certainty that everything would somehow come out right. She didn't know why, she already knew by then that life wasn't fair.

And then she saw him. He was just coming through the door. Tom. He was taller than he'd been at his brother's wedding and his shoulders had filled out from the rowing she knew he'd taken up at Oxford. His hair was longer and not suppressed by hair gel. The curls and ringlets were spiralling onto his forehead.

The older Edie smiled. She looked at her younger self who was twirling, oblivious to the look of admiration that was written on his face as he watched her. She'd never known he'd looked at her like that. As if struck by a thunderbolt and as though he suddenly saw her for the first time.

"He looks smitten. A smitten kitten," the flower girl said smugly. Edie could feel herself blush like a teenager.

"Don't be silly." She wanted to nudge the little girl with her elbow and then tell her more about how this beautiful boy loved her. Or had loved her.

"He told me that this night was when he fell for me." She watched as her student self stopped twirling, looked up and saw Tom watching her. His face was neutral by then, he'd hidden the look that her older self had seen earlier behind a mask. Maybe if she'd seen his face that night things would've been different?

"You really think just seeing the smitten kitten look would've stopped everything that followed?" the ghost raised an eyebrow and looked at her dubiously.

"It might've done." Edie lied to herself.

The ghost tutted and shook her head as if Edie was a hopeless case.

Edie watched as Tom came walking towards her past self and

Mel.

She hadn't thought about it in years. The way her heart had stuttered when she realised that Tom had finally noticed her. The way he'd brushed past Mel, just like he was doing now. The way Mel started to laugh, startled by his single mindedness. The way he'd grasped Edie's hand. The way her entire world, at that moment, became focused on only him. She couldn't catch her breath. She thought she'd faint.

Older Edie felt a faint echo of that feeling rush over her.

"You really need to work on that sexy look," the little Ghost had her face scrunched up in disgust as she watched the scene.

Edie had to agree; love really must be blind because her student self resembled a goldfish. But she glowed. How she glowed.

And then the music slowed.

"This was our first dance," Edie felt dreamy, she watched as Tom grabbed her hand and drew him to her. "And this was our song."

She remembered her heart racing in double, even triple time to the music. She'd worried that her palms would be sweaty and he'd run away in disgust.

But the words of the song wound round her, heartbreak, regret and lost love. She shivered. Their story had been foretold in that song if only she'd listened to the words.

"Bit depressingly true to life don't you think?" the Ghost piped up.

Edie wondered if damnation was preferable to listening to snarky asides from a pint sized pot of ectoplasm.

"Don't even think it." The wise old eyes of the flower girl stared up at her fiercely. Edie quickly held her hand up and shook her head, backing down.

She looked back at the dance floor. Tom's hands were holding her younger self closely; she had her head tucked into his shoulder. She'd always fitted perfectly in that space, as if it had been specially made for her.

What if? She thought as she watched him bend his head.

If only, she sighed as she saw their first kiss.

Tears welled up, her heart felt as if it would break all over again. They'd lit up that dance floor with their love; it had been perfect.

She remembered the feeling of his lips on hers, burning away all the yearning she'd had for years into a perfect moment. The way her body had wanted to merge with his.

"Oi you two, get a room." The drunken groom came barrelling into them and tore them apart. "Hey, what you snogging Dick for?" Justin screeched with laughter but Tom had grabbed her and held her close.

"I get it." The older Edie could feel the tears burning on her cheeks. "I should never have broken up with Tom. You need to understand it was…"

"No, Edie," the Ghost stamped her foot. "You need to understand. This isn't about being with this boy or that man. This is about you and your choices."

"I get it, I need to make better choices. Can I go back now?" She wanted to go home and curl up in her bed and cry for her old self. Tears for the girl on the dance floor. Where had she gone?

"Not yet. You need to see one more thing."

"But I…" Edie wracked her brain for another wedding. There were so many going back over the years. From the bright primary colours of her teens, gradually fading to pastel and then grey in her memories. The fun was sucked out of them until it was all just ashes in her mouth.

The spirit grabbed her hand and with a lurching twist and turn they moved location.

A restaurant, a familiar restaurant with people dressed in the fashion of the last decade or so. She wondered absently how anyone had ever thought it had looked good.

"This was Tom's and mine favourite restaurant," she said confused. "This is where we celebrated our first jobs," she spun round looking at the place. "But I don't understand? There hasn't been a wedding here. Or at least I've never been to a wedding here."

When was the last time she'd been here? Not since they'd broken up. At first it had been too difficult. She snorted, as she realised she had been about to say 'it had been too full of ghosts.' And then she had put all thoughts of Tom and her life with him in a box in her mind, shut it tight and carried on.

Never let the bastards see you cry.

The Ghost beckoned her to the far corner without speaking. And there in the shadows at the back, at the most intimate table was Tom. A grown-up Tom, the age he'd been when they were last together.

Blond hair ruthlessly held down and cut short to eradicate the curls he hated but she'd loved. His face was not the boy who had rubbed her back or the face of the student who'd kissed her at a wedding but the face of the man she had lived with, loved.

"But... I don't understand" she whispered. "I'm not going to have to watch him cheat on me or anything, am I?" She recoiled at the thought.

"Never have I had a client so completely blind," the Ghost said. "Of course he didn't cheat on you. You were the one doing the cheating." She looked disgusted, as though Edie was failing a test.

"I never even looked at another man." Edie said. She wanted to throw something at the Spirit for saying it. "I know what cheating does to people." She shuddered as she thought back to her mother and the fact that she never smiled the same way since Dad left.

"There is more to cheating than being with another man. You cheated on him with your job, your time, your attention until there was nothing left of you for him."

"It wasn't like that," she said.

"Wasn't it?" the Ghost countered. She gestured back to Tom.

Edie looked. She didn't remember this night. Not in this corner. Not with Tom wearing that dark suit that had been tailored to show his leanness, the lining a sedate navy. The light blue shirt made his eyes glow, or was that something else? And that was the tie she had bought for him the last Christmas. Well she hadn't

53

actually bought it. One of the secretaries had. But he'd loved it and that was what mattered, wasn't it?

There was a bottle of champagne chilling, unopened beside him. She saw the yellow label. They had always said they would only drink that brand for truly special occasions, she remembered. There was a little bunch of her favourite tulips in reds and oranges on the side plate of the place setting opposite him. But this had never happened. Was this some sort of fantasy? Her mind was conjuring up a scene where everything turned out right; it was taunting her with what could've been.

She watched as Tom craned his neck every time the door to the restaurant opened and someone new came in. She saw the way his eyes lit up as the door jangled and how they died a little when it wasn't the person he expected.

For forty-five minutes she watched. And with each minute his shoulders slumped a little more. She sat at a table nearby, rubbing her chest, which ached more with each drop, with each bit of light that faded in his eyes.

"Would sir care to order?" a waiter would ask every five minutes.

"No, I'll wait," he assured him.

And as time went on the waiter's attitude changed to one of pity.

Who the hell had the audacity to stand him up? Just look at him! She thought.

His phone rang and even the shock of seeing how phones had changed didn't disturb her as much as the thought he'd been left alone.

"I hope he gives the silly cow what for," she said, "I mean look at all the trouble he went to."

"Shug, where are you?" his face bright and eager.

Shug.

That was his name for her, short for 'sugar' because he said she was as sweet as it. It tugged at her heart and exploded in her brain.

She was the one he was waiting for.

"Not going to make it at all?" his face fell. No, it crumpled.

His whole body seemed to curl in on itself. Like the air had been let out of him.

"No, no I understand. Your work is important and if Hilary needs you to stay, you have to. Yes, I know how much she's done for you. I'll see you at home. I lo..." he winced at the sound of a dropped phone, which even Edie could hear from where she sat.

"I love you." He whispered to the dialling tone.

Edie's vision blurred.

"Would sir like to order?" the pitiful gaze of the waiter was again on him.

"Yeah, I'll have a double gin and tonic and take back the champagne. We won't be needing it."

As Tom stared dejectedly at the table his hand crept to his right hand pocket. Dipping in, he brought a small object up to the table.

A small, black velvet ring box.

No. Edie's stomach flexed like it had taken a prize fighting punch.

He flipped the lid and there nestled on white satin was the most perfect ring she had ever seen. Small and discreet, not expensive or showy but it wouldn't have mattered because it would've have come from Tom and that was enough.

"No," she mouthed.

"What was so important that you forgot it was your anniversary of your first kiss? What was so urgent that you couldn't make time for him? What blinded you to your life that you didn't know that Tom was going to propose?" The Ghost was implacable. Each question fell on Edie like physical blows.

"But we were busy, the Agnew divorce was complex and it was all hands to the pump. It was that work that got me the promotion. Hilary, Ms Satis, she told me I had to focus. That work would never let me down, that it wouldn't cheat on you. And he knew I wanted to do well. Always be the best you can be, he knew that. But he never said. If he'd said..." she faded out.

"If he'd said that would you have come?" the Ghost asked.

Would she? Would she have wanted to be married so young? She wasn't sure. Maybe a few years before she would have but then... then she was clawing her way up the ladder and getting married would have gotten in the way.

"We could have had a long engagement?" she said hopefully.

"Edie, you cheated on him. And you cheated on yourself. And you still are."

And with a twirl of flowers and pink glitter the Ghost, Tom, the perfect ring and Luigi's restaurant vanished.

Edie was alone at last in her cold and empty bed.

Chapter 7

Sunlight streaked in the window and struck Edie in the eye. It had drawn its bow and unleashed it right on target.

She groaned. She felt like she'd drunk a crate of wine and then gone five rounds with Mike Tyson. What had happened?

The scent of jasmine, sweet pea and roses was still in the air.

The Ghost.

Edie sat bolt upright in bed.

A Ghost had visited her, just as Jessica had promised. This was actually happening. She started to shake. People like her didn't get haunted. In much the same way people like her didn't turn into vampires or go to séances. It just wasn't done.

There was no logical reason she could come up with to explain it, though. Even if someone had managed to invent some sort of very high-end interactive experience it couldn't explain what happened. There were things that were shown to her last night that no one else could have known.

She was going mad.

She stopped shaking.

Yes, she was going mad. That was much easier to deal with than hauntings. Obviously she was overworked and needed a good rest or something. Or some pills. Maybe an extended stay at a health farm. Odd that being mad made her feel better. As if she'd regained some control.

She swung her feet out of the bed.

They were grass stained and muddy.

She began to shake again. She looked closer; a pink heart-shaped piece of confetti was stuck to the little toe of her right foot.

Mad. Crazy. Certifiable. Chased by the little men in white coats loop de loo. If only that was the explanation.

"Oh my God!" she screamed catching sight of the alarm clock. It couldn't be ten o'clock?

She had to be at Mel's in an hour and it was a good twenty minutes between here and there, even on a Saturday.

Confetti forgotten, the Ghost relegated to the back of her mind. Edie scrambled from her bed and ran into the bathroom.

An hour, later she pulled up outside Mel's in Clapham South. She'd made it. She winced as she looked in the rear view mirror as she reversed into an available parking space. She had made it but her grooming hadn't. Her dark hair, which had been damp and unstyled when she got in the car, was now windswept and curling into ringlets here and there. Her nose was shiny as she hadn't had time to put on any make-up and she struggled to remember what she had stuffed, willy nilly, into the overnight bag for the weekend. She was sure she had forgotten something.

"Edie!" Mel screeched as she came to the door of the flat.

The terrace of houses, now mostly divided into two flats, was the same as pretty much everywhere in this part of South London. Built sometime in the late nineteenth century as family homes for commuters they now were family homes again, just cut up to a much smaller scale. Mel and Barry had the ground floor of a corner house, giving them a garden that came into its own in the summer.

"Edie! Come in! Come in!" Mel called, oblivious to her neighbours and their Saturday morning comfort.

Edie grimaced. Typically, Mel had demanded she was here on

time and yet again she was running late herself.

Locking the Mini, Edie walked to the flat and wondered why she'd rushed. She could've at least taken the time to dry her hair.

"I'll just be a few more minutes," Mel promised as she ushered her in.

Edie followed her through the living room that the front door opened straight on to. The room was cluttered with fashion magazines and boy's toys. Games consoles and mountain bikes.

Edie carried on down the narrow corridor and into the kitchen dining room at the back of the house. The summer sun streamed through the glass ceiling of the extension.

Mel disappeared into the bedroom while Edie settled herself on a stool at the breakfast counter and tried not to notice the sink full of dirty dishes. Edie itched to wash them and to stack the listing pile of magazines into a perfectly arranged tower. Instead she chewed on her thumbnail. The edge was ragged and she grimaced as she noticed the polish was almost completely gone.

"OK, Edie you have to promise that whatever happens I am NOT to snog anyone or do anything that I might regret tomorrow morning," Mel called from the bedroom.

Regrets? Surely getting married would give Mel enough regrets. One more wouldn't break the bank.

"I'll make sure!" Edie replied, because she knew that as a maid of honour she had certain responsibilities.

"Oh and I hope Mum will be OK. Aunty Celia has had to pull out so I'm not sure how she'll feel being the only one of her generation at the weekend."

"I'll look after her," Edie replied.

Thank God, she thought, another grown-up. Now there would be someone as uncomfortable with all the pink glitter and stupid games as she was. Maybe this way she wouldn't miss Jessica's acerbic asides so much.

Thirty minutes later Edie had persuaded, cajoled and threatened Mel into the car. As it was they would be cutting it fine to make it to Bath, or rather the house outside Bath that had been rented for the weekend, in time for lunch.

Edie roared out of Clapham and hoped that they would at least be in time for the manicurist and massage therapist some enterprising sort had booked to visit them that afternoon.

"OK, we have to be at the restaurant for seven thirty," Jo, one of the other bridesmaids called over the high pitched and slightly hysterical voices of the hen party spread around the kitchen and living room of the Cotswold house.

"And as it said on the invite... LBDs, that is Little Black Dresses everyone! And I'll be supplying the accessories."

I'll just bet you will, thought Edie.

She'd caught a glimpse of what looked like feather boas in a rainbow of colours in a bag that Jo had slipped upstairs. She had also overheard people talking about fairy wings and tiaras. Why didn't they just tattoo 'hen party' on their foreheads and have done with it?

Edie went upstairs, her body more relaxed than it had been since the whole haunting thing had started. She might not enjoy the rest of the weekend but she had definitely enjoyed the wonderful massage. The therapist had set up his table and oils in the study cum library downstairs. The fact that the therapist was male and quite personable hadn't passed any of the party by. And the manicure; she inspected her nails. Perfect. Now no one would know she was stressed.

The hen party included the other two bridesmaids, Jo, Mel's best friend from uni and Sophie, Barry's sister. Edie couldn't work out why Mel thought she had to include her but maybe it was a love thing?

She shook her head; there was no point in worrying about it. They were stuck with Sophie. The rest consisted of Mel's mum, Maggie, and a collection of uni and work friends.

In the master bedroom that she was sharing with Mel, Edie took her overnight bag and began to unpack. Her toiletries, nightdress and clothes for tomorrow were all there, but no little black dress.

"No," she whispered.

She was sure she had packed it.

Edie thought back and suddenly she could see it in its dress bag still hanging on the back of her bedroom door. Put there so she wouldn't forget it.

Yes, she was going mad.

"What's up?" asked Mel as she came into the bedroom.

"I seem to have forgotten my dress," Edie said quietly.

Mel's mouth dropped open.

"You forgot something?" she came and sat on the bed, looking up at Edie concerned. "Are you OK, Edie? Is it work?" Edie noted that she didn't ask if it were a man.

"No, I'm fine," she said.

If you count seeing dead people as fine, she thought.

"Well, if you're sure. You do seem a bit distracted..." Mel waited and looked at Edie expectantly. Edie wasn't elaborating because if she did they would be on their way to the hospital rather than a nightclub.

Mel shrugged her shoulders and continued. "Good thing I bought a spare. Do you need shoes as well? Because someone else might have some," Mel went to her bag and started pulling out a mess of black material.

"Actually I bought three dresses because I couldn't decide and someone was rushing me!"

Edie blushed.

Untangling the three dresses Edie and Mel stared at them as they lay on the bed.

"Ah..." said Mel.

Ah indeed. The dresses were all on the 'lacking in material' side of fashion. And then of course there was the fact Edie was taller and curvier than her petite elfin friend.

"This one is stretchy," Mel picked up a jersey dress which looked

61

demure in front, which was unusual for anything of Mel's. "Give it a go."

Edie looked at it dubiously

"It looks like a tubey grip," she said.

"It stretches. It'll be fine" Mel said.

Five minutes, later having puffed and panted and wriggled into it, Edie stood red-faced looking at herself in the mirror.

"Obviously you'll have to go commando," commented Mel, "and you can't wear a bra because of the back."

"The back?"

Edie swivelled round and saw that what the dress had in coverage at the front was more than made up for with a lack of material at the back. The dress scooped down and fell in folds just above her bottom.

"But you'll be fine, you've got the body for it," Mel said as she straightened the seams.

"Body maybe, but not the mind," Edie said.

Or lack of it she thought.

"I'll wear what I came in," Edie stated.

"What, you can't!" wailed Mel. "The whole little black dress thing is a theme… Jo and I had it all planned. If you don't wear it, it'll throw everything out. We won't all match."

Why on earth was she the maid of honour? There was no way she could back out. She was supposed to be calming Mel down not winding her up. She was going to have to do this.

"I'll do it but I'm not wearing heels!"

"They aren't too high are they?" Mel asked later as Edie tottered out to the waiting taxis in the only pair of shoes that had fitted her in the whole house. She'd tried to force her feet into a pair of Jo's ballet shoes but it turned out the only person with the same size feet was Sophie.

"I look like a hooker!" she hissed back.

"No you don't. Admittedly you don't look like you. But you

scrub up very well." Mel grinned and then swinging her pink feather boa, adjusting her large garish tiara and wiggling her fairy wings she went to join the other hens in the cars.

Edie's nose tickled from the bright red feather boa that she had been presented with as she'd come downstairs and she hoped that the tiny silver tiara that she had managed to find wasn't too obvious in her hair; the hair that ever since this morning's fiasco refused to sit flat.

I look like I'm on the pull she thought grumpily as her Achilles tendons twinged from the vertiginous heels that she wore. They consisted of a few strips of leather attached to the Everest of heels. She now knew why Sophie had happily passed them over. She'd need a few drinks to just numb her toes that were already complaining about the funny angle.

"I've heard that the professional rugby players all go to the club we're off to tonight," crowed Sophie, flicking her mane of red hair over her shoulder. Edie shuddered; so they were going to be fighting off Neanderthals all night. She tried to get into the taxi without the nonexistent skirt part of her dress riding up round her waist.

"Phwoar! I love rugby players…" giggled Mel.

Edie closed her eyes. OK, so she and Maggie would be the only ones not interested in the Neanderthals. And so it begins, she thought.

Three hours later, full of food and lubricated on enough alcohol to sink a small ship, the hen party stumbled into the club. The music was so loud and full of bass that Edie could feel it in her chest. The club was dark with flashing lights; and the decor featured too much chrome and black velvet. There was only one dance floor with a bar down one long wall. Mel was already on the dance floor, feather boa aloft shedding feathers as she shimmied unsteadily.

Edie winced as her shoes made themselves known over the alcohol yet again. She needed more drink and she needed it now. Maybe she'd black out and be carried home. She started to pick her way to the bar.

"Regroup!" hollered Jo. "We've got a table in the VIP section!"

Edie sighed and looked longingly at the bar, so near and yet so far.

She winced her way to the VIP section. It was in the corner of the club furthest from the bar and across the dance floor. Behind the roped off section crowded with full tables was one long empty table and champagne bottles in buckets of ice. The surrounding tables were full of men the size of mountains, with cauliflower ears and scars. But all were grinning at the approaching party. There weren't just foxes in the hen house, there were wolves.

How many of these will I see sneaking out of the house tomorrow morning? she thought. There would be a fair few and most will have been with the married or attached hens. Something about hen parties made the paired up types worse.

"Someone drag Mel off the dance floor." Jo crowed. "It's time for 'Truth or Dare!'"

Maybe if I drink enough I can numb my feet and my brain, Edie thought. She grabbed a seat at the far end of the table, furthest from the ringleaders and from the hungriest looking wolves. But nearest one of the champagne buckets. If she kept control of the bottle she would be fine.

She wanted to slip her shoes off and massage her feet but she wasn't sure she'd ever be able to get them on again.

Maggie, Mel's mum, sat down next to her. She was leaning a bit after being persuaded in the restaurant that Mojitos were non-alcoholic.

"OK! Time for the first Truth or Dare…" Jo dug into the pink and marabou trimmed Stetson that she had been wearing earlier and had decided to use as the receptacle of shame.

"Mel! Truth or Dare?"

Edie poured herself a glass of champagne and cynically sat back to watch the show.

"Dare!" screamed Mel.

It felt as if the wolves moved a little closer, poised for the kill; they were obviously familiar with hen night dares.

"OK if you take a Dare now you have to have a Truth later… your Dare is to collect at least one pair of men's underwear."

Edie sipped the champagne and looked up at the ceiling and then back to table, shaking her head, as the rest of the group howled in approval.

Mel staggered off to the nearest table of wolves and in a moment was sitting on one guy's knee whilst the others told her they couldn't help as they had all gone commando. Not that Edie could hear them, but she could see their demonstrations when Mel required proof.

Five minutes later she came back victoriously waving a pair of black cotton jersey shorts that she had removed herself in some dark corner of the VIP area.

"Oh my God! He was this big!"

Mel used her hands to indicate size.

Edie chugged down her glass of champagne.

"OK, who's next?"

It carried on down the table. The dares got more daring, the truths more outrageous until they got to Maggie.

"I'll take a dare," she declared drunkenly.

"Maggie, you don't have to if you don't want to," Edie shouted in her ear.

"I want to and I will," her chin was thrust forward and there was a look of combat in her eyes.

Edie backed off.

"OK Mrs R," called Jo "Your mission, if you choose to accept it, is to snog the man of your choice!"

"Excellent!" Maggie said.

Edie caught her arm,

"Don't do it!"

"Oh but I'm going to. What's sauce for the gander is sauce for the goose."

And with that cryptic utterance she made her way to a table of slightly older men, in their late thirties and early forties. She bent down beside an outdoorsy looking guy. Rough round the edges with an open smiley face and a rangy body.

"You go Mrs R!"

"He's fit!"

"Phwoar! Look at his arse."

The hens were hollering over the music.

He stood up grinning, took Maggie Remington in his arms and proceeded to give a masterclass in sexy kissing. Taking her face in his hands he leaned down and gently kissed her; drew back and went in again. Edie could see Maggie's knees give way and suddenly she threw her arms round his neck and that was it.

Full frontal snoggage.

"Go mum!" cried Mel! "I never knew she had it in her."

This was all going to end in tears; Edie could feel it in the pit of her stomach. Women who were happily married didn't go round snogging random men. They also didn't go round squeezing the arses of said random men.

After what seemed like an age, they came up for air. Maggie was flushed and smiling like the cat that got the cream, her younger partner in crime looked shell shocked, as if he had gone to pet a kitten and found that he was playing with a full on cougar. He dug in his pockets and with a shaky hand gave Maggie his card.

"And she got his number!" someone shouted.

Maggie was smiling as she wove a wobbly line back to their table, gently fanning herself with the business card.

She settled down next to Edie who stared at her in awe and terror.

"Erm… Maggie?" she said, "Was that really wise?"

"Oh yes, Edie darling. You see I've left Doug and I hear that to get over a man it's best to get under another," she said it with a purr and fluttered her fingers at her recent conquest.

Left Doug?

Edie's heart stuttered.

"But why... what... how?" she said.

Maggie's face took on a steely look although Edie could see the hurt round her mouth.

"If he will have affairs with nurses and generally act like a teenager on heat then I don't see why I have to put up with it any longer. I've sat back and let him rule everything for years, now it's my turn."

Edie thought she had no illusions left about marriage, but as Maggie ripped the veil from her eyes she realised she hadn't been as cynical as she'd thought. How was she supposed to change like the Spirit said when not even Maggie and Doug could make it?

Chapter 8

"Alright! Now it's the turn of the maid of honour!"

The gang whooped and hollered.

Edie sat mouth still ajar. How could they all be so happy? Didn't they realise the world had just tipped on its axis? She looked over at Mel's smiling and flushed face.

"Mel doesn't know does she?" she shouted in Maggie's ear.

"No she doesn't, we're waiting till she gets back from the honeymoon. We don't want to ruin her wedding."

So if Mel didn't know, it wasn't for Edie to tell her, was it? Not to ruin Mel's day and destroy the foundation of her life? No, it wasn't for her to tell.

"Oi Dickens! Stop trying to avoid this thing! Truth or Dare?" Mel hollered.

Truth? What was the truth?

She wasn't sure any more. Hearing about Maggie and Doug was almost as hard as when her own father had walked out because he couldn't live a lie, because he didn't love them any more. Because he didn't want her. She felt detached, light-headed. Suddenly the music wasn't too loud any more; it faded to a buzz in the back of her mind. The truth?

She wasn't up for any more truth tonight.

"Dare!" she called back, crossing her fingers that it would be low on the embarrassment scale.

She was out of luck. Which was pretty much standard for her these days.

And due to that lack of luck, she was walking towards the bar with Jo, Mel and Sophie. They had picked out her target and were all there to witness the dare.

"Maybe I will take Truth instead," she shouted.

"Nope! You said Dare, so you've got a Dare!" Jo said, taking her job as games master seriously.

Edie wouldn't have been surprised if she started to announce every Dare with the phrase, 'May the odds be ever in your favour.'

Sophie seemed to be in it for voyeuristic reasons, she was enjoying Edie's discomfort a tad too much. She had a death grip on Edie's arm. Crescent indentations would probably be left on Edie's biceps from those acrylic nails. Edie was trying to remember what she'd done to earn it. They'd only met a few times.

"Can't have the maid of honour backing out." Her grip tightened harder.

Ah, that was probably the issue; Sophie wanted to be the maid of honour. Edie wondered if there was a way of resigning. She would gladly let Sophie have the job.

"Look we picked a nice one, it's not like we chose a complete loser," Mel slurred.

Edie looked again at the target.

He was tall, dark and filled a pair of jeans very well. Broad shoulders stretched a rather too bright red jumper and she wasn't sure it went with the shirt underneath which looked cerise but that could've been the light. Or she was beginning to see cerise everywhere.

OK, from the back he wasn't bad but she still had to do the dare. "Come on!"

Edie tried to dig her heels in and you would've thought with heels as high as these they would make great anchors. Instead they threw her off balance, making her take tiny steps so she didn't wrench her ankles. She was dragged behind the other women in an undignified scramble, and then when they reached the unsuspecting man Sophie heaved her forward, propelling her like a stone from a catapult. Stumbling on the impossible shoes, she managed to somehow stop herself from careening into him.

For once, she thought, something was going right. She was an inch from his back.

He smelt familiar; her stomach fizzed.

It was obviously the champagne.

He was very tall, if she moved slightly she could kiss his shoulder and that was only because of the blood depriving heels she had on. Which meant... she was going to have to say her appointed dare phrase loud enough for him to hear. Her whole plan to lean in, pretend to whisper the words in his ear and then run away was now busted.

"How about giving me a Long Slow Comfortable Screw Against the Wall?" Edie rushed out, heat rising in her cheeks as she named the infamous cocktail.

What were they, seventeen? These were the sort of games they'd played at school and uni. Thank God no one from work could see her.

As she backed away from him, ready to make a run for it or at least a high-heeled hobble, he turned and one arm snaked out, grabbing her round the waist.

His hand burned against the bare skin on her back, it felt like a brand. Her centre of gravity shifted and now off balance she fell onto a chest that was like rock.

A determined and somewhat familiar chin came into view.

"Don't leave sweetheart, I haven't said no yet. Although I usually like to have a bit of conversation before I do that for a girl," the voice was low in her ear, she felt the words rumble through his chest.

How could a stomach fizz and flip at the same time?

No wonder he'd smelt familiar. And it explained the red jumper and cerise shirt. There was only man who had invaded her space

70

closely enough for her to smell this week. Who was she kidding? There was only one man who had invaded her space in much longer than a week. And it was the same man who believed that cerise was a valid colour choice.

Jack Bloody Twist.

He was stalking her.

"Oh my God, it's Jack Twist!" Squeals from Mel, Jo and Sophie pierced her ears worse than the music.

They knew him?

"Ladies!" he rumbled.

Edie ducked her head down, letting her wild hair fall over her face. Hopefully he wouldn't recognise her.

"So which of you ladies is disappointing the male race by coming off the market? Please tell me it isn't Long and Slow here."

His thumb gently stroked the curve of her back and set goose bumps racing round her body and spiking her body heat.

"That would be me!" shouted Mel.

"No. What a travesty. Whoever he is he's a very lucky bloke," Jack said.

"You know him. I'm marrying Barry Jones." Mel slurred and was looking at Jack in a distinctly dodgy way for a bride to be. "I'm Mel."

"Mel? But of course." Jack leaned down and kissed her cheek but still his hand was glued to Edie's back. "Thank you for the wedding invite. Haven't seen Jonesy so happy and I promise to make sure he behaves at the stag night."

"Don't you remember me? I'm Sophie Jones, Barry's sister. You used to be so sweet to me when I was little. I had such a crush on you." Sophie fluttered her eyelashes and tried to look coy whilst also squealing like a teenager faced with her boy band pin up as she butted into the conversation. "I'm one of the bridesmaids."

It sounded as if she was advertising her services, as though bridesmaid was a synonym for easy. She would have shoved Edie out of the way to get closer if she could have. Edie hoped Jack would have more taste than to go for a hen, even if he had known her as a kid. Not that she cared what he did. It wasn't any of her business. And if he was at the wedding... she figured it would be big enough for her to avoid him. Edie squirmed a little trying to ease her way out of Jack's embrace. He was too close, making it difficult for her to think.

The arm tightened round her.

"I loved your match winning try the other day," Sophie giggled and tried to wiggle round between Edie and Jack.

"Why it's little Soppy Jones."

Edie sniggered. Soppy? Ha! Sophie's face fell.

"Sorry, Sophie isn't it? Great to see you and thank you, but the try was a team effort."

There was a small beat when they all looked at each other.

"I think your party wants you back." Jack pointed back across the dance floor where Maggie and the other hens were waving wildly. "I'll see you all at the wedding?"

Edie tried to follow them but between his arm and her heels, she was stuck.

"Now I believe, Long and Slow, you and I have some business to take care of." His voice was gravelly and it made her shiver as he whispered in her ear.

He used a finger to tilt up Edie's face.

Or at least he tried to.

She tucked her chin closer to her chest. Who cared about double chins and wrinkles? There was no way he was seeing her like this. And of all the people she could've said it to? It was as if she were cursed. She wondered whether this was her hell? She was paying for failing Tom by being embarrassed in front of Jack.

"No, we're good, we're fine," she squirmed against him, trying to get the iron arm to loosen its hold.

"If you carry on like that it will be short and quick," he said in her ear.

She froze.

His hand slipped lower, his little finger stroking her skin beneath her dress. If he moved the finger a millimetre more, he would find out that she was wearing absolutely nothing underneath.

The fizz and flipping increased; joined by heat that spread from her stomach down through her legs. The hair on her arms rose.

"Edie Dickens, don't be such a prude!" Mel yelled.

A prude? Not with what her body was begging her to do. She wanted to wrap herself around him. Melt into him. It was torture.

The arm around her stiffened.

"Dickens?"

Damn it, she had been so taken in by that small movement of his finger that she hadn't realised the implications of what Mel had said. But now her cover was blown. Fizz and flip collided and heat drained away leaving cold.

She'd never live this down.

Summoning up every pig-headed part of her, and with the mantra 'don't let the bastards see you cry,' echoing through her, she put the thought of the office gossip behind her, lifted her chin from her chest and raised her head.

She looked up slowly into stunned hazel eyes.

"Wow! You definitely loosen up when you're out of the office," he said.

"You know each other?" Sophie didn't seem happy about this and Edie hadn't noticed that she still hadn't left. Jack Twist was upsetting her mind just as much as the ghosts.

"No."

"Yes," said Jack in direct contradiction to Edie.

"We met in the lift yesterday," Jack continued, "and it looks like we're fated, the way we keep bumping into each other like this doesn't it, Slow?"

He smiled down at Edie.

She didn't trust him. There was a glint in his eye as if he knew she wasn't as immune to him as she made out.

And his smile got bigger as his little finger resumed its

exploration of her back. Fizz, flip and heat came rushing back. What was she still doing plastered up against him? What was happening to her?

She was going completely and utterly mad.

Wrenching herself away, she stood up as straight as she could in the crippling shoes.

The heat left her but her skin tingled as if he still stroked her.

"OK Sophie, I did my Dare. Let's go," Edie ignored Jack next to her. Or tried to. Her body wanted to lean back against him. It was just hormones, she thought; she didn't need to lean on anyone.

"So no Long Slow Comfortable Screw Against the Wall then?" he teased.

Pausing to look over her shoulder she narrowed her eyes and glared at him. He laughed at her. Her body fizzed for him.

"Come on!" she snapped and staggered away. She wouldn't look back. She wouldn't.

"So tell me all about your try. Specially as we're old friends." Sophie still wasn't following her.

Edie felt her head drag itself around; like a compass to magnetic north. Sophie was taking advantage of Edie's leaving and had plastered herself against Jack's side. Her talons now clasped around Jack's bicep.

She was probably testing it for firmness like she was buying fruit, Edie thought.

Jack caught her eye, raised an eyebrow knowingly.

Edie spun her head back again.

They were welcome to each other she thought as her stomach sank.

"Maggie. The cabs are here."

Edie tried to pry Maggie away from the lanky guy she was glued to.

She whispered thanks to the heavens that it was the end of the night and Mel was too drunk to notice her mum's behaviour.

"Lemme alone," Maggie mumbled between kisses.

No one should have to get this close to two drunk people snogging, Edie thought.

She shuddered.

If the whole Jack Twist episode hadn't burnt away all the alcohol and so sobering her up; then watching the antics of the hen party would have finished the job. The single girls had all danced the night away on the dance floor whilst every married or engaged one had plastered themselves against some random bloke.

Not one of them was with their respective partners.

She should leave them all to it.

This whole wedding malarkey was just a storefront and façade applied by people who didn't have the imagination to see any other way of doing things.

No wonder the divorce business was so brisk.

She went to leave Maggie playing tonsil hockey with her chosen beau. Maggie was a grown-up. It wasn't for Edie to make her leave. If this is what Maggie wanted then she washed her hands of it.

As she turned away, a sparkle of pink glitter winked at her from Maggie's hair.

Logically she knew it was off one of the tiaras or fairy wings. Logically.

The tingle of dread left over from the Ghost's visit ran down her spine. There was nothing logical about being haunted by ghosts. And there was nothing logical at the dread that filled her as she stared mesmerised at a small spangle caught in greying curls.

She would do something. She had to do something. Maggie might have given up on her marriage but Edie hadn't. Not yet. She remembered that Maggie had been there for her when her own mum had been too involved in her own anger and grief over the divorce. How Doug had been there when her own father hadn't. He'd ferried her and Mel in his car, acting as their taxis service to parties and covering for them with Maggie and her mum when they came back tipsy. And her own dad hadn't even sent birthday cards.

She looked round the club. Seeing all the cracks in marriages and relationships that were developing in front of her, she thought of all the collateral damage. Somewhere there could be a little girl like her. She'd do something. She had to.

Not that they'd be grateful but she would help them maintain the façade of their marriages.

Turning back she stiffened her spine, ignored the slurping and spit, and tapped Maggie on the shoulder.

"Maggie!"

"She's alright love, I'll take care of her," the rangy guy peeled his lips from Maggie briefly.

"That's what I'm afraid of," she said.

She grasped Maggie's shoulders and began to haul her off.

"Need a hand?" a familiar voice rumbled in her ear.

She stiffened.

"We're fine thank you."

"It doesn't look fine," he sounded amused.

"Why don't you get back to Sophie?" she bit out nodding her head towards the pouting redhead by the bar trying to attract his attention by waving a bottle of beer she had obviously bought for him.

"Because I'm not keen on groupies no matter how long I've known them and I'd rather help you," he replied.

"I don't need your help, thank you."

"Are you sure, Dickens? Or are you going to try and get your whole party moving and unsnogged all by yourself?" he gestured round the room.

It resembled the end of a school disco. Couples were scattered across the dance floor and perched on chairs, bodies were sealed together from lips to feet. She didn't want to know what was happening in some of the darker corners.

It would be like herding cats.

Once she'd got one couple undone, they would have re-stuck by the time she had turned around to work on another. It was as if they were covered in hormonal Velcro.

"I don't…" she faded.

She did. She needed help and he was the only volunteer.

Now if she could stop her own body from sealing itself to him like it wanted to, everything would be fine.

She stepped back and waved Jack forward.

"The most sensible thing you've done all night, Slow," he whispered in her ear.

Jack tapped the rangy guy's shoulder.

"Whaaaa…"

"Sorry mate but this lady needs to get home. Family emergency."

"Family? Is Mel OK?"

Maggie's lips unsealed themselves. Her maternal instincts overcame her oxytocin levels

"I think she's looking a little peaky…" Edie lied.

Mel was actually outside the building, serenading the leaving club goers with Abba songs. Edie had escorted her there personally before coming back inside.

"I must go!" Maggie untangled herself after one last wet snog and wobbled out of the club.

Rangy guy stood, looking puzzled, his arms still in place as if Maggie was going to come back any minute.

"One down, five more to go. Shall we?" Jack gestured Edie in front of him and they went off to tackle the next couple.

With a few well-placed words in each bloke's ear coupled with their shock at being spoken to by Jack Twist, each couple was successfully unstuck and the female halves were led out of the club with their belongings. They then staggered and slide drunkenly into the waiting taxis.

Jack gave the last girl a push into one of the cars and turned to face Edie.

She glared silently at him. Damn him for being so efficient. She should be thanking him, but being mad at him was safer. Maybe she had papered over some cracks in people's lives but it made her realise the chasms in her own. And standing next to Jack reminded her of what she didn't have, what she could've had.

Edie moved towards the last taxi, she should join the rest of hens and move far away from him. Reclaim some part of her shredded mind.

"You're welcome," Jack said.

She stopped.

She wanted to get in the cab, slam the door on him and pretend the last few hours hadn't happened. Cut herself off from everything. But that was before last night.

The look on Tom's face when she had shut him out swam in front of her; the ache in her chest came back. Should she try something different? Stop slamming the door on people? She looked at Jack, Tom's face fading into the past as she was faced with the present.

"Thank you," she said stiffly.

"Is that all? No Long Slow Comfortable Screw? With or without the Wall?" he joked.

She should have slammed the door.

Men. They only thought about one thing; last night had made her soft. Made her think the unthinkable. She had always been clear-headed; she prided herself on it. She saw the truth of the world. And she was going to make a stand now. All the turmoil of the past few days churned up in her. She turned away from the cab. Well she would give him something...

"I'll take a Long Slow Comfortable kiss?" Jack said, his hands up placating her. His shoulders raised and his head on one side.

She came closer; this is what she got for being nice. A guy thinking she was a pushover and only good enough for sex.

"A quick peck?" he asked.

"If you don't cut it out all you'll get is a short sharp clip round the ear!"

"I love it when you talk dirty," he said.

This was pointless. He was deliberately winding her up. She

took a deep breath; she'd just turn around, ignore him and leave.

Behind her a car door slammed and with a screech of tyres, the last cab pulled away.

"Hold on! Wait for me!" She twisted round and tried to run after it down the road.

Once again the heels hit back, she clipped them on the curb and would have fallen if a large hand hadn't grabbed her arm.

"Fuck. Fuck. Fuck. Fuck."

Edie's eyes burned. Tears. No tears for years and in the space of twenty-four hours she had cried twice.

Well she wouldn't cry. No, she wouldn't. And she definitely wouldn't cry in front of him.

Ever since bloody Jessica had arrived in her room nothing had gone to plan. And she liked her plans. Instead, she was floundering around and knee deep in wedding stuff. Wasn't all this haunting supposed to get her away from tacky nights out?

"ARGHHHHH!" she threw back her head and screamed to the sky.

"You OK?" Jack asked from behind her.

Would he stop being nice and funny? How rude did she have to be before he would leave her alone? Before everyone would leave her alone.

"I am perfectly fine. Thank you. But I would be even better if I was currently in a cab on the way to the house," she said.

How was she supposed to get home now? The street was deserted; not a taxi in sight.

"Well you can't blame the girls, it did look like you were heading towards me for some hot and heavy action…" he said.

There were times, and now was one of them, that Edie wished she had taken criminal law. Then she would know a really good barrister who could defend her for justifiable homicide. How could one person make her feel so angry and so turned on all at the same time?

She growled in the back of her throat and clenched her fists,

79

trying not to go for Jack. But whether to kill him or kiss him, she didn't know.

"From behind, of course. Not from the front. No, from the front they would never have left me alone with you. They would have feared for my health," he said.

"Don't you ever shut up?"

She couldn't think when he joked like that. Or when he looked at her like that, as if he saw through the mask to the real Edie.

Edie stamped her foot in frustration and fear, forgot about the damn torture shoes again and toppled into his arms.

He smiled crookedly down at her and in the dark she thought she saw his pupils widen.

"I'm pretty quiet when I do this."

And he bent his head and kissed her.

What the…

Edie's mind went momentarily blank.

And then her body was full of sensations that her head tried to keep up with.

His lips were soft but strong, hot but cool.

The contradictions of the kiss echoed Edie's confusion. She was quivering with anger and desire. She desperately wanted to sink into his arms, sink into this kiss, lose herself in it but she also wanted to run away. Far away. Somewhere safe. But then she felt safe here. There were goose bumps on her arms but her skin was on fire.

Edie hadn't been kissed like this since… Tom? But had Tom's kisses ever been like this? Yesterday she thought she hadn't remembered Tom's kisses, then last night they had come flooding back. But now… now they were receding overwhelmed by the kisses of this man. Tom faded like an old Polaroid, two dimensional and bleeding colour. Jack's kisses were three dimensional, high definition and here.

Jack moved his mouth against hers. He stroked her lips with his tongue.

Tom who?

She wanted to open up and show herself to Jack, she hadn't felt like this... ever? She loosened her hold on the reins of her heart; she wanted to let go, to fall deeper.

And then her hair was ruffled by a breeze that seemed to come from nowhere. It blew Jack's scent away and brought with it the faint smell of jasmine and sweet pea. It was the scent of weddings and first love, of innocence and hope. It was the fragrance of new beginnings. It was the perfume of Weddings Past.

She froze.

It was one thing to be haunted by ghosts when you slept, but it smelt like they were interfering in the real world as well.

She tightened her hold on the reins that she had almost let run through her fingers. There was no falling here. Was she being manipulated? Was this real?

She wrenched her lips from his and pushed away from him, all the time her hormones screaming to let this carry on. Her hands shaking, she pushed them through her hair to stop from reaching for him again.

"I think I prefer you talking," she said.

She couldn't help her tongue licking her lips, tasting him, testing the swollen feel of them.

Jack wasn't smiling any more; he stood with his hands on hips, glaring at her.

"Dear God, woman don't you ever have a good word to say about anyone?"

The shaft hit true. She didn't, but then why should she? It wasn't as if anyone had anything good to say about her any more.

A small voice asked her, *and whose fault is that?* She hoped the voice was in her head, she hoped it was her rarely present conscience. If it was some spiritual manifestation then she was indeed ready for the men in white coats to take her away.

Now she was no longer plastered against him, she shivered. It wasn't only from the cool evening air.

"I need a cab," she said, dodging his question.

"I'll drive you," he replied.

"There's no need, I'll get a cab," she said.

"There is every need! One: you can't walk in those ridiculous heels."

He ticked off the reasons on his fingers.

"Two: your bag went with the rest of the hens in the taxi," he paused and stared hard at her unsmiling. "Three: you are way too sexy to be wandering round Bath on your own in that dress."

He thought she was sexy?

She hadn't been called sexy since Tom. He said it when they lived together, when they were curled up in bed, she in her old pyjamas, or when she'd dressed up for a night out and she definitely hadn't been sexy near the end. The disappearance of her bag was less important... she was sexy. Jack Twist said so.

Although at this precise point in time he was looking at her like he wanted to shake her rather than kiss her.

"Will you have some sense and let someone help you?"

It was her only option. It could be worse, she thought.

"OK, but no mauling me," she said.

"Honestly the whole mauling thing is looking more and more like an aberration," he said. He gestured to a line of cars parked on the side of the road across from the club.

Walking towards a low-slung sports car, she snorted to herself. Typical boy's toy. She stopped near the passenger door and was surprised when Jack carried on past it to a dusty Golf.

"I'm too tall to fit in one of those sports cars very easily," he grinned at her as if he knew what she'd been thinking. "Had one and almost gave myself a hernia every time I got in and out."

Another point in Twist's favour; not that she was keeping score.

Damn.

Jack held open the passenger door. Edie slide into the car making sure her legs were together and her skirt kept decent. Jack still looked appreciatively down at the large expanse of leg

82

she showed as she swung them inside. The leather seat was cool against her bare back.

Jack closed the door and walked round the front of the car. She watched the way he strode to his door and in the beam of the streetlight, he looked like the stranger he was. Not the man she had just been kissing. She absently touched her fingers to her lips.

He took up too much space, she thought as he got in the car. His shoulders were wider than the seat. His legs, long and muscular, were close enough to touch.

"So where to?" he said as he turned the engine on.

Edie told him the name of the house they had rented and the road.

"Very nice," he commented as the car pulled away and started wending its way out of the city.

"I take it you come from round here?" she asked.

Not that she was interested, or usually did small talk. It was just that silence with Jack seemed more dangerous. Talking broke the tension.

"This is where I started my rugby career," he said.

"Rugby?"

"Yeah, that's what I've been doing instead of working at the law firm. I turned professional and now I've retired from the firm," he speeded over the bridge out of the city.

A professional rugby player?

Edie looked at him out of the corner of her eye. That explained the size and the scars. It also explained Sophie being a groupie.

Twist? Edie turned his name over in her mind. An elusive memory came to her. Two years ago, the papers had been plastered with his face snarling in triumph as he crossed the goal line in the finals of the Rugby World Cup. She remembered being annoyed by the whole kerfuffle as it had kept any serious news off the front page for days.

She opened her mouth to say something, and closed it. Small talk had deserted her.

They lapsed into silence. The lights of the city flickered through the windows, highlighting his hands as they changed gear, the white traces of scars. And then they were in the dark country and she was blind except for the hedgerows that flicked past in the headlights. The only sound was their breathing and the whirr of the wheels on the tarmac.

But she could feel him next to her. Could feel every breath he took. And burning her back as it leant against the leather, was the place where his little finger had stroked her as he'd held her. She licked her lips. She could still taste him.

The spot over her heart jabbed her.

What was stopping her from kissing him again? On her terms; not his or any ghost who was not above pushing them together. The fizz and flip was back. Maybe it was because she was taken by surprise the first time and she'd invented the scent to get back some control? But if she were in control when they kissed again, what was stopping her?

She didn't remember the drive being this long. Would he just hurry up!

And then they were there. The headlights picked out the gate-posts and then the hedges that curved round the small circular drive in front of the neo-Georgian house.

Lights blazed from each of the downstairs windows and the upstairs ones too.

"Looks like the party is still going on. Want me to come and check for any stray men who might have snuck their way in?" he asked as the car came to a stop in the soft gravel of the drive.

"No." she said quickly.

They sat in silence again, the engine idling.

Edie's hand was on the door handle. She should say something. Say thank you and good night. Shut the door on him and walk away. Never looking back.

Or she could lean in for another kiss. On her terms this time. Prove to herself that she could reach out; prove that she could stay in control. And maybe show some interfering ghosts that she was taking a step in the right direction.

She could do this.

Taking a deep breath, she licked her lips and turned towards Jack. She put her hand out to grab him and went in for the kill.

Chapter 9

"Well goodnight then," Jack said as he shook the hand that she had put out. The hand she was going to use to grab him and pull him down for a kiss.

Her face heated. The jab above her heart became an ache. Fizz and flipping flopped.

That first kiss had just been a pity kiss then.

And people wondered why she didn't do love and stuff. She didn't because for her it meant involving men and, she decided, they were all freaks. Ms Satis was right; men weren't worth it.

"Goodnight." She said and she pushed open the door of the car and stumbled rather than marched round on the gravel to the front door.

"Oh and Edie…" Jack had wound down the window.

She stopped with one hand on the front door.

"Next time we kiss it'll be because you want to and not because you need to prove it to someone."

The gravel crunched under the tyres as he drove off.

She'd prove something to him all right. She would prove to him just how much she didn't want to kiss him again.

She pushed open the door and was hit by the noise of Abba coming from the living room and was soon swamped by the drunken hens.

"So did you kiss him?" Mel asked.

Edie ignored her and went to bed.

"I feel like death!" Mel groaned as she stuck her head under the pillow trying to hide from the sun.

Edie lay beside her staring at the ceiling. She didn't know whether she preferred waking up to Ghosts or to a hangover and the feeling that something disastrous was just around the corner.

"Did I imagine it or did my mother snog some bloke last night?" Mel's voice was muffled under the pillow but Edie could still hear the worry in her voice.

And there was the disaster, turning the corner and waving its hands in Edie's face. Her mouth was dry but now she wasn't sure whether it was from fear or the hangover.

Maggie and Doug were getting a divorce. And Mel didn't know, couldn't know. Edie might not believe in weddings but Mel did, and her parents announcing they were splitting up just before the wedding was not going to happen.

"As if. Maggie would never do anything like that," Edie tried to put the sight of Maggie snogging the rangy bloke to the back of her mind. "I think you had one too many glasses of bubbly," she lied.

Now she had to make sure no one else spilt the beans.

She sat bolt up in the bed; this called for serious emergency work. She had to speak to every one of the hens before Mel got up so they could get their stories straight. And she didn't trust that cow, Sophie, not to try and use it as a way to make Edie look bad.

Not on her watch.

"Why don't you stay in bed?" she told Mel. "I'll go and get breakfast started, make sure everyone's OK." Keep it light Dickens, she thought, don't overdo it. She hoped her smile looked a little genuine but it felt more like a rictus grin and she was glad Mel was still covering her face with her pillow.

"If you don't mind that sounds great," Mel snuggled further under her pillow "and if you could find some aspirin then I will

87

give you my first born."

Edie shuddered; kids. She pulled on her clothes from yesterday, giving the jersey dress from last night a kick and a quick stamp with her foot, and then promptly regretted it as pain shot upwards. Her feet were swollen and sore from those heels.

First things first, she needed to make sure Maggie's secret little mistake was going to stay little and secret even if she had to keep Mel in seclusion for the rest of the weekend.

She limped out of the bedroom, went out into the hallway and knocked on the first door.

"Hi, it's Edie, can I come in?" she slide through a crack in the door and Operation Cover Up was on.

Forty-five minutes later, she sagged against the wall in the kitchen. The story was straight. Admittedly Sophie had been a little difficult by trying to blame Edie for Maggie's bad behaviour. A few harsh words about how it hadn't been her idea to do Truth or Dare and an unexpected ally in Jo had Sophie toeing the party line. Edie really didn't know what the hell she'd ever done to Sophie, and she was beginning to think Barry had to have been a saint to put up with her as a sister.

But Sophie notwithstanding, Edie had made sure that Mel had her aspirin and she had also started breakfast. Now she just needed to find Maggie. She hadn't been in her room.

Edie chewed on her thumbnail, ruining her new manicure.

She was worrying needlessly. Maggie was probably up for an early morning walk, just like she did at home. Mind you, after the amount she had put away last night, Edie was surprised she had the energy to make it out of bed. But still, it felt as if something wasn't quite right.

Edie poured herself a mug of coffee and went to the back door of the house, taking a five minute break before the bacon needed turning again.

The sky was the deep clear blue of an early summer morning; some bird was making a racket in the trees. In the house she could hear people moving around, dressing, showering. She preferred the wildlife of the trees than the wildlife inside. She had only a few precious minutes before the hen house descended.

Edie looked at the little gazebo that was at the end of the garden. Maybe, she thought, they could have coffee out there later before they went back. She admired the sides of it, which were shielded by wisteria and she watched as a butterfly alighted on it and waved its wings gently. The sun lit it and turned into a jewel.

And then it was gone. Disturbed by a sudden bang in the gazebo, the sides shaking. Who was out there? And what were they doing?

Looking down at the dewy flagstones, she wrinkled her nose. They were wet and slimy and she didn't have any shoes on. The gazebo shook again. Pouring the left over coffee out of the mug, she wielded it like a weapon and stepped outside. She picked her way carefully down the path; her feet complaining from the damp and the abuse from last night.

"Who's there?" she called.

She held the mug over her head, she hadn't heard of any violent crimes going on in the Bath or Cotswold area but with her recent track record of things going wrong...

"Hello?"

She got closer and peered inside.

Operation Cover Up was about to be Operation Blown Up.

"Margaret Remington," she said. "Put him down right now!"

Maggie's hands stopped groping a firm behind that Edie was sure she had seen before. A behind clad in jeans but with a back that was bare and bore a few scratch marks.

With mussed up hair, Maggie peered over the scratched shoulder.

"Hi Edie!" she said looking sheepish.

"Don't 'Hi Edie' me!"

All the injustices from the past week, all the frustrations and 'why me's?' from being haunted by ghosts from her past rose up. All the unfairness of last night, kissing Jack, and then not kissing

Jack bubbled. Having to play mother hen to a group of women who should know better grated. And on top of that, the fact that just this morning she had spent forty-five friggin' minutes trying to cover up for this middle-aged hussy. All of this welled up inside her. Mel's hen party would not be ruined. Not when she was in charge. It swelled from deep inside and then erupted.

"You will go into the house." Edie was shaking with rage but her voice was quiet and precise. Each word bitten off and clipped.

"And you," she pointed a trembling figure at the familiar outdoorsy guy that had been attached to Maggie's face the night before. "You will get your arse out of here and you will do it without being seen."

He grabbed his shirt, and put it on. He was confused for a moment when it became obvious that no buttons had survived Maggie's onslaught, so he wrapped it round him.

"Out!" she said.

He used his thumb and little finger and held them to his face and mouthed

"Call me."

Edie spun on her abused feet in time to see Maggie blowing him a kiss and giggling.

Heaven deliver her from hormones.

"There is nothing to laugh about, lady," Edie said.

Maggie drew herself up and failed to look in anyway like the serious maternal figure she was aiming for. Wearing a housecoat over nothing wasn't going to cower Edie at all.

"Well Edie, is that any way to speak to me?" Maggie spluttered.

Edie raised her eyebrows.

"Ever since you decided to share your little secret with me I've every right to speak to you how I feel. Do you know that Mel woke up this morning worried that she had seen you snogging some bloke last night? So to keep yours and Doug's precious secret, I lied and said she'd had too much champagne and then spent the last forty-five minutes making sure none of the other hens blabbed." She took a breath and flexed her hands to release the tension and anger.

"And then what do I find? That somehow you managed to make an assignation with that man and proceed to make out like a teenager not more than a stone's throw from your daughter. Are you sure you don't want to tell Mel before the wedding? Because you don't see to be very cautious about it!"

Had she really wanted to get Maggie and Doug back together? She had made that promise last night before she remembered all the crap that hormones did to you. They obviously didn't calm down with age either.

"Sorry, Edie," Maggie whispered.

"You'd better be," she said.

"Now get back in there, deny everything and then on Monday I want you and Doug in my office first thing. I think it's time someone had a little chat with you both," and with that, Edie realised she was taking a step towards being the hippy new age lawyer type that she had accused Jack of being.

She was going to try and get them back together. It was one step away from calling in the mediator. Or of course it could be a call away from UN peacekeepers instead. Her skin crawled at the thought. All the lessons she'd been taught by Hilary Satis about going in for the kill and not letting emotions get in the way, were going out the window. Edie hoped she never found out. She wasn't sure she could justify it to her Botox and filler filled face. Even if Hilary couldn't express disappointment any more, she could make you feel it.

But this wasn't about her. This was about getting her brownie points with whatever being was sending her spiritual advisers, so maybe they would forgo the rest of the visits.

Chapter 10

Hen dos didn't leave one rested for the next week especially when the weekend had started with a review of your past mistakes via some unearthly Jerry Springer. It also didn't help when the hen weekend had included a run-in with the only man she had been attracted to since Tom. And she'd kissed him.

Oh, and he happened to work with her.

And not forgetting the crowning glory of the weekend, which was the news that the bride's parents were divorcing. Topped that off with the bride not knowing and the mother of the bride partaking in some extracurricular activities when she should have been ordering her hat and sorting out the flowers.

If Maggie acted like that at the hen night, Edie squirmed to think what could happen on the wedding day itself. Maybe she'd try to smuggle that man in, disguised as a waiter. Edie shuddered. Or maybe she'd move onto the ushers...

Edie sat at her desk early on Monday morning her hair ruthlessly tamed once again, her hands hovering over files. She let her gaze skip over her shorter than usual nails, the thumb nail on her left hand had been bitten to the quick and the polish was picked at. Saturday's manicure was completely wasted.

Edie wasn't stressed, no not at all.

She shuddered when she remembered the drive back yesterday.

There was Maggie muttering darkly in the back when she wasn't coldly ignoring Edie. Mel, oblivious in the front, wittering on about the wedding preparations. Edie was surprised she hadn't dropped them off at the first service station and left them there to hitch-hike home. And it had only been some quick thinking that had stopped Sophie getting in the car; she'd been angling for a lift back. Luckily Jo had seemed to interpret Edie's horror and subsequent death glare correctly and managed to usher her into a different car. Maybe Jo should be the maid of honour?

As a result she was in early to deal with work. Of course she was. Not to avoid meeting Jack in the lift. No, not that.

She also needed to reorganise her day now that she was about to embark on her very first reconciliation or mediation or whatever it was going to be. She'd get Doug and Maggie back together by Friday if it killed her. She didn't want to know what the next Ghost had in store for her but the carnage and disruption that was becoming her life couldn't continue.

This was a simple reconciliation.

And doing it in work hours might be a little unethical but Maggie and Doug were insisting they paid for her time. How difficult could it be? Jack Twist was supposed to be an expert in it and she didn't rate his intellectual prowess. An ex-professional rugby player? Come on, he was one step up from a Neanderthal.

Edie was still thinking about him when she ushered the sheepish looking Maggie and Doug into the conference room that afternoon. It would be a piece of cake.

"So Maggie and Doug, thanks for coming in." Edie lined up the pad on the table and looked up at her new clients. She'd written down a step-by-step plan of how this would happen. If they hit all the steps then they would be sorted by Friday.

Back together. Loved up. She pressed the point of her pen harder into a full stop.

"Thanks for seeing us, Edie." Maggie said.

"Yeah, thanks." Doug seemed a little less enthusiastic. But Edie could change that.

"So, where would you like to start?" Edie asked trying to inject some brightness into her voice.

There was silence from the other side of the table. Edie noted that Maggie and Doug were avoiding eye contact with each other and her. Doug was staring with a fixed fascination at the oil painting over Edie's shoulder.

She didn't blame him. It was a painting of Hilary Satis and no one could say she wasn't striking. The painting showed her in all her power dressing glory, shoulder pads reaching for each sides of the frame. The artist had gone for a bit too much realism on her face though; Hilary believed that she should freeze herself at the age of thirty. That was when she had divorced her husband. Botox, fillers and, Edie suspected, a few facelifts had left her with a glossy, unnatural visage.

Edie knew the eyes followed you round the room. She hoped they wouldn't be judging her too hard as she went against everything that Hilary had taught her.

She quickly glanced over her shoulder, yes those eyes were judging her. But then she couldn't help but look at the painting of the pendant that Ms Satis always wore. It was rumoured to be her wedding ring and engagement ring that she had hammered flat with a tyre iron the day she found out he had cheated on her.

Edie shivered.

No, she didn't blame Doug for being mesmerised.

Maggie was looking at the table and drawing circles on it with her right index finger.

"OK so how about I start you both off?" Edie said.

Maggie and Doug nodded whilst still looking at the table and the picture.

"Maggie, could you maybe explain what it is that you would like to say to Doug?" Edie figured if they could air all their issues they could get on with things. Lance the boil, as it were. It wasn't

94

as if these two middle-aged people could have anything shocking in their backgrounds. It was probably something so petty that they'd realise it and laugh, then kiss and make up.

Edie smiled to herself. Piece of cake. She'd be able to face that painting of Ms Satis again.

"Well, I don't know. I'm not sure." Maggie stuttered.

Doug let out a snort of derision.

"Doug, was there something you'd like to say?" Edie asked.

"Yes, Doug. What is it you'd like to say? Because of course everything is about you and your opinion." Maggie snapped.

"Oh great, playing the victim again, Maggie? You're never the one at fault, are you?" Doug said as he turned to Maggie.

"Ha! Well I'm not the one who has been screwing his secretary and one of the nurses am I?" Maggie retorted.

Edie could feel her smile slipping.

What had she done? Maybe she shouldn't have sat them next to each other? It obviously aggravated them both.

"Well if you didn't keep brushing me off with excuses like you're too tired. Too tired from what? Spending my money? And if you do deign to let me do anything you just lie there."

"Just lie there? I can't move because you've gained three stone so you've got me pinned to the bed. And by the way, every time I said 'Oooh baby, you're so big, just like that, oooh yes, you fill me up' I was lying! You're average in size. And technique!"

Edie flinched and wondered whether she shouldn't have issued protective gear and invited the UN.

Doug's come back was equally as cringe worthy.

"Well everything might be bigger and better if you hadn't turned into such a stuck up prude. Be a little adventurous. I haven't had any complaints recently!"

Edie wanted to slide under the table. No one should have to hear this sort of thing.

"If I could just ask you…" Edie tried to interrupt, to ask them to make more positive comments about each other, anything to get them off this subject.

"Complaints? Of course you don't get any complaints because they were after your wallet, you great oaf. I found your credit card statements. Most young women will 'put out,'" Maggie used her fingers as quotation marks, "if you buy them Chanel handbags and take them to fancy restaurants."

Doug was beginning to turn purple as he spluttered and tried to think of a comeback.

He couldn't have a heart attack before Saturday. Mel would kill her.

"And I'll have you know that I haven't had any complaints recently, either." Maggie said and Edie watched as Doug puffed up like a blowfish.

She was going to be the reason Mel's dad died before the wedding.

"OK! If we could get back to the plan." Edie almost screamed to get them to face her.

They both blinked as if they'd forgotten she was in the room. Edie could feel Hilary's eyes boring into her back. She could almost hear her voice.

"Mediation! What use is mediation? Go for the throat and the balls and take 'em for everything. There's no such thing as love forever; that is just a panacea for the weak, Edie. It is for the people that don't know what the real world is like."

She looked at Doug's purple face and Maggie's white one.

For a panacea, it certainly seem to hurt a lot to be much of a cure.

Later that afternoon, Edie was staring down at her desk, stunned. Her mind was tangled and bruised. How she'd managed to make it back to the office from the conference room she still didn't know. One minute she'd been saying horrified goodbyes to Maggie and Doug, she thought she might have organised another meeting as well but couldn't be sure, and then she was back at her desk. She had no memory of the walk, her brain had been too full of other things. Horrible images. Her hands trembled as she lined up the notepad in front of her to a more pleasing position.

How did anyone think that reconciliation was a good thing? Curing cancer was a good thing and probably easier than this. Or world peace. She could do that.

"Edie?" a small voice from the corner piped up.

"What?" Edie didn't have the patience to deal with little Miss Homemaker of the year.

"I was just going to say I think it's a wonderful thing that you're doing for your friend's parents," Rachel said.

"Wonderful?" Edie's voice held a touch of hysteria. "I have just spent the past hour trying to keep two normally sensible middle-aged people from throwing furniture at each other! And the stories…" she shuddered. "There are some things you really don't need to know about your friend's parents."

"Really bad?" Rachel asked.

Edie cringed as she remembered.

Her stomach churned. She had thought the wedding was going to be tough before. How the hell would she be able to keep it, and them, together now? And how could she ever look at them again?

"Oh yes, Rachel. Really very bad," Edie said.

And they still hadn't reached any sort of consensus about how they were going to attend the same wedding and how they could keep the split from Mel. The hour had ended with both howling threats at each other and Edie cringing in the corner. If they couldn't be civil for an hour together sober, who knew what sort of trouble they would both kick up at the reception with the addition of alcohol.

And Edie had to do this with them all over again tomorrow. They were all on a fast track programme to either reconciliation or hell. But she would do this, because she never let anyone stop her from being the best…and she'd do anything to put off Friday's ghostly visit.

Edie wondered if anyone would notice if she slumped against the wall of the corridor. It would be uncharacteristic for her to be anything but poised and perfect, but even she had a breaking point.

She stood beside the closed conference room door and leant her body very slightly against the wall and hoped no one would walk past. She shut her eyes and tried to relax, letting the wall take her weight.

"Everything alright?"

Ah yes, the person she had managed to avoid for almost an entire week would find her right now.

"Everything is just peachy," she lied as she quickly pushed herself upright and opened her eyes to see Jack staring down at her, frowning.

And to underline her lie was the sound of a book being thrown at the wall of the conference room. Edie flinched and hoped they hadn't knocked Hilary Satis off the wall.

There then followed a roar of rage and some muffled shouting.

"Yes, I have everything under control," she said.

In my dreams.

"Edie, it sounds like people are killing each other in there," said Jack.

"One can but hope," she whispered.

It was Friday and even with a meeting every day this week, the bloody Remingtons were in an even worse state. Edie could only be thankful in terms of her blushes that their insults had moved on from sex. On Tuesday they had focused on Doug being a workaholic and Maggie being a 'parasitic lay about'. Wednesday had focused on Doug's numerous affairs, which were blamed on Maggie's lack of interest in his life. Thursday's highlights were Maggie's over protectiveness as a mother and her inability to let Mel, grow up which was countered with Doug's absences as a father and complete lack of interest in his child's life. Which brought them neatly to today. Friday. Which was a wonderful mélange of the four previous days, peppered with even more spicy revelations about their respective love life.

She'd had to get out. She'd slipped out the door while they were shouting at each other, she'd refused to meet Ms Satis's accusing gaze.

"Are you really going to leave them in there unsupervised?" Jack asked.

Edie looked up at him through gritty, tired eyes. She hadn't slept for more than a few hours each night. She woke up in the middle of nightmares about glitter and Doug wearing fairy wings while he shouted at Maggie who was wearing a wedding dress. Or nightmares where she was banging on a glass wall as she watched Jack walk away from her, the cerise lining of his pinstriped suit glowing like a beacon.

He wasn't wearing his suit jacket, which she was thankful for because if he had been she might have lost it right then and there. As it was he was in his shirtsleeves, the blue and white checked shirt rolled up and his forearms, firm with muscle and sprinkled with hair, called to her. What she wouldn't give to fall into someone's arms, his arms, and just cry from sheer frustration and tiredness.

He looked solid, dependable and gorgeous.

He wouldn't have clients remove the need for divorce by conveniently killing each other.

"Hey, I've tried to reason with them, I've tried to get them to listen but all they do is shout back at me or ignore me," she said.

"When you say reason with them, would that be your usual reasoning? I.e. it's your way or the highway?" he asked.

"I'll have you know that my way was the most logical, sensible way. It was the way that was fair and would get them to realise they should get back together in the shortest possible time," she answered.

Damn it, why did she say that?

"'Get back together?' Edie, mediation is all about compromise and sometimes the best way to part. If you don't know that, how the hell can they?"

Jack thrust his hands through his hair.

"OK. I'm going in and sorting this out before someone calls security."

His hand went to the doorknob.

"And don't you dare come in until I tell you. You seem to have done enough damage already."

And with that he went in and shut the door.

The roars subsided until there was silence.

Then Jack's voice rumbled but too indistinctly for Edie to understand. She moved to the door and, quickly taking a look up and down the corridor to check no one was around, pressed her ear to it.

Still nothing.

A rumble from Jack, a lighter rumble which was Doug and then a twitter from Maggie. More Jack rumbles, Doug then Maggie. How on earth had he done that? Every time she had tried to get them calmed down they boiled over.

The door was pulled open quickly, surprising Edie. She jumped back, her cheeks hot.

"Well Mr and Mrs Remington…" Jack said as he frowned down at Edie.

"Please call me Maggie," Maggie positively simpered up at Jack.

"And it's Doug," Doug put his hand out.

"Doug, Maggie," Jack shook their hands.

"Now I'll see you on Monday and we'll take it from there, OK?"

"OK," they chorused, beaming at Jack and then turning that beam on Edie.

"Oh Edie thank you for recommending Jack here!" Maggie chirped, "A great choice, he seems so familiar."

Well of course he does you silly old bat, Edie thought, he was the one who dragged you away from your conquest on Saturday night. But the words stayed in her mind battering against her forehead while she turned the sides of her mouth up in a facsimile of a smile.

"Edie. You never told me you worked with Jack Twist. Capital rugby player, it was a sad day when he retired." Doug boomed. "And he's a friend of Barry's so he'll be at the wedding. Can't wait to tell the boys at the club."

Oh yes a sad day indeed, she thought. Instead of tackling other men on muddy fields he was here ambushing her at every turn.

"Edie, if I could have a moment?" Jack asked, gesturing her into the meeting room.

Edie watched as the Remingtons, in sudden accord, bustled their way to the lift. After wishing for most of the afternoon to be elsewhere, suddenly her only wish was to join them.

"Edie?" Jack said.

She turned her back on the Remingtons and went back into the conference room. She walked to the table and gripped the back of the chair hard.

Jack closed the door and came to her left and stood at the head of the table.

"What are you playing at Edie?" he said.

"I don't know what you mean." she said playing for time.

"You know exactly what I mean. In no way, shape or form are you qualified or experienced enough to be dealing with people like that."

"You have no idea what I am experienced enough in," she said. Jack raised one eyebrow and Edie blushed. "And you definitely don't have the right to speak to me like that. I am a senior associate in this firm."

"I don't care what seniority you have when you are doing work you are clearly not qualified to do."

"I don't have to listen to this," she could feel the anger rise and it warred with frustration because she knew he was right. She wasn't qualified to do any sort of mediation. She was only good at confrontation. She was good at breaking things and then sweeping up the pieces to make it tidy.

"Yes, you do. Mucking around like that could get this firm

101

embroiled in a nasty lawsuit and then you can kiss partnership goodbye."

He moved so he loomed over her. His face darkened, his brows drew together and the lips she kissed at the weekend thinned to a straight line.

He was furious.

And he looked gorgeous.

At the moment and for the first time in years, becoming partner didn't mean anything. Only two things meant anything.

Jack.

And getting rid of the ghostly guides determined to point out her faults.

"I… well…" Edie stumbled.

Jack's face relaxed, his lips curved up wryly.

"Look, I'm sure you had the best intentions. Your best friend's parents and all, I know you just want the wedding to go smoothly," he said.

The wedding? What wedding? She thought. She stared blankly at Jack for a few seconds, with the word 'wedding' crawling round her brain trying to make contact with another word or idea. She shook her head when it made contact with the idea of herself and Jack… and in shaking her head the word finally made contact with Mel. Mel's wedding. That was what he was referring to.

"Mel's wedding? Smooth? After the hen weekend from hell? And you did just hear her parents in here yelling blue murder didn't you? Smoothly! What a joke. You think I want this to go smoothly? I'd rather it didn't happen at all. What kind of person voluntarily shackles themselves to another? You've seen what happens? It's all hearts and flowers until BOOM! Someone's hormones take over and they're screwing their secretary or the nurse or the next-door neighbour. No, I think weddings are an abomination. The only good thing about them is the divorces they eventually lead to that pay my salary."

Edie's chest heaved from the shouting as her stomach sank.

Everything she had ever thought about weddings and marriage was now out in the open, laid bare for Jack to see. All the good intentions she had made this week were gone. She was definitely getting haunted tonight.

Jack blinked down at her.

He opened his mouth to say something, and then closed it. He frowned and opened his mouth again. He looked down at her, puzzled.

"If that's what you really believe, I feel very sorry for you," he said.

"Sorry? I don't need your pity," she said as she walked towards him, the index finger of her right hand pointing at him, jabbing the air to make her point. She came right up flush with him and tipped her head to keep eye contact as she poked her finger into his chest.

"And I don't need your help!"

"It must be a cold and empty bed you lie in every night," he sounded sad.

Emotion welled up in her, choking her, constricting her breathing, stopping her from talking.

She shook her head vehemently, denying it and then attempted to make a sound to deny it.

"No," she croaked.

Backing away from him, she needed to get out, eventually finding the door handle by touch. She looked up to see Hilary staring at her; Edie had never noticed the smug twist to her lips before.

"No," she whispered to them both as she opened the door and fled.

Maybe if she didn't go home this evening, the Ghost wouldn't find her. She could stay out all night. Or maybe not sleep and then carry on the way she always had. She sat at her desk, her mind whirring as she looked for ways to stop that night's visit from happening.

OK, she had failed in her first task this week, which was to get the Remingtons back together... and yes it burned. Never let anyone stop you from being the best you can be, she thought and flinched when she realised she hadn't. But the ghosts didn't have to know that. Maybe she could claim credit if Jack got them sorted out? She had introduced them, so that could count in her favour.

Edie pulled a piece of paper on her desk towards her. She would make up a credit and a debit column and mark down what good things she had done this week that should be part of her spiritual balance.

Credit:

Got Maggie and Doug in for mediation. Tick.

Debit:

Made them argue more. Cross.

Credit:

Introduced them to Jack. Tick.

Debit:

Managed to spill exactly what she thought of marriage to Jack. Cross.

Credit:

She chewed on the end of the pen and then tapped it on the desk. What else had she done this week?

Oh, she had saved all those women at the hen party from making huge mistakes. Definite tick.

Debit:

The whole hen party was pretty pissed off with her for playing goody two-shoes and then copping off with Jack. Cross.

It looked like she had come out about even... a definite haunting tonight then. She sighed.

Unless she could do what she had first thought... stay out. To not be caught.

Go on the lam.

Picking up her mobile, she dialled Mel.

"Mel, hi! Fancy a night out on the town?" She forced brightness into her voice. Surely Mel would want to see her and talk wedding stuff. And if that was what it took then Edie would pay the price.

"Erm… well… I'm sorry we've got wedding stuff to do, that's right, *wedding* stuff," there was an awkward silence.

Edie then heard furious a whispering between Mel and Barry on the end of the phone. She could hear some words "*Not enough space and they don't like - mumble mumble - and we've got - mumble mumble - coming.*"

Then Mel came back on the phone.

"Sorry Edie we've got all this wedding stuff to do. What about tomorrow night after the dress fittings? We can all go out again. A mini hen night. I know Jo and Sophie would be up for it." Mel sounded happy and relieved with the solution.

A sharp pain hit Edie in her chest. Wedding stuff, sure. There was something going on and she obviously wasn't invited to it. Well that was OK because she didn't fancy being somewhere she wasn't wanted…

But it hurt, it hurt much more than she expected. She called up every piece she had in her arsenal of coolness and rang off without making definitely plans for Saturday night. She wasn't sure she could handle a repeat of last weekend even if it didn't include Jack Twist. Especially if it didn't include Jack Twist, the little voice whispered. She pushed it away.

Who else could she call?

There was no one.

Not one other person in the world that she could call up to go out for a drink. Not one other person that she had social contact with.

Edie sat at her desk, stunned. How had she let that happen? Where was the social butterfly she had been at uni? Where were all the people she used to hang out with when she first got to London?

Probably all paired off and settled down in domestic drudgery, she lied to herself. But she knew she had lost touch with them all before that.

When she first came to London she'd had it all, a great job, a fantastic boyfriend and great friends. Every weekend there had been parties and then there were always those 'quick drinks' after work that had turned into getting home in the early hours. Then they'd all get up the next morning and go into work.

Then it had all got out of whack. Being good at your job and having ambition wasn't wrong; it was just that it took priority, as it should. She couldn't go out on the lash every night of the week and still perform at the level that was expected. So she'd started to really only have a quick drink, and then she'd stopped turning up at all.

And maybe she didn't have go to every party.

Then when Tom had gone… she had shut down so she didn't have to feel the gaping hole beside her and see the pitying looks. Then it was as if all her friends had gone too. Oh, they might have tried to get her out but she knew, what use was going out and being with people? They let you down. Hilary Satis had been right. The one thing that didn't let you down was work. She hadn't pushed them away, they had just left, like everybody did.

She shied away from the truth, all the times she cancelled nights out and her last minute let downs. She tried to forget that they had phoned her and phoned her until they gave up when she never returned their calls. Until she wasn't even a name on their Christmas card lists.

Edie shook these thoughts out of her head… all this introspection wasn't getting her nearer escaping her flat for the night. Hiding from the Ghost.

"Rachel," Edie said, breaking the silence that had fallen over the office since her conversation with Mel.

She looked across at her trainee. Why didn't she do something about that long stringy hair? She was always trying to hide behind it; she was doing it now as if she didn't want to make eye contact with the world.

"Rachel, I was wondering whether you were up for a girl's night tonight?" Edie tried to inject a chumminess and girls' together camaraderie into her voice; she cringed inside when it came out Head Girl-ish.

Rachel stared up through her curtain of hair, mouth wide open. The silence stretched.

Edie could feel a blush begin on her chest and slowly move up her neck. Is this what she had been reduced to? Begging for company from someone she neither cared for nor respected?

"Well?" she said.

"I... well... we... and..." Rachel said.

"Spit it out," Edie said.

"Well Rob and I are... and Timmy... DVD... night in... all planned," she managed to stutter out.

Edie filled in the blanks. The Domestic Goddess was being domestic; what a surprise.

"Another time, maybe?" Rachel said.

Edie snorted and slapped another file onto the desk.

So that was it. Even Rachel had something to do on a Friday night.

Who was she left with?

Jack Twist's face flitted across her mind.

No.

But he did ask you for a drink last week, the traitorous voice in her head wheedled.

Yeah and then on Saturday he'd kissed her and this afternoon he had hauled her over the coals about her work. She would rather face the Ghost.

Which was worse she thought, facing herself or facing Jack Twist? Either was scary, Jack saw too much and didn't hesitate to voice his opinion. I'll have an easier job fooling the Ghost, she thought.

Chapter 11

Edie jolted awake and sat up quickly. Through her foggy brain she tried to put her thoughts together. As she sat there, Big Ben tolled one. There was no mistaking it.

Just one stroke.

It seemed to reverberate in her ears.

She was awake and in the nick of time. By some horrible trick of fate she hadn't slept through the next visitation. Bloody Jessica Marley was definitely going to pay if she ever saw her again.

Edie wasn't going to be taken by surprise again… Oh no. She was taking control of this whole enterprise, no Ghost was sneaking up on her. They would see that no one messed with Edie Dickens.

It didn't matter what turned up, be it an extra from Thriller or something from Ghostbusters, she'd be ready. Although she did hope it wasn't Mr Stay Puft, he'd always given her the heebie jeebies as a child and put her off marshmallows, snowmen and anything in a sailor outfit.

Her mind was running in circles as she braced herself for anything that might come at her. But she wasn't braced for nothing.

The hour had definitely struck, she thought, but there was no Ghost. Nothing.

She shivered.

She watched the clock on the bedside table count the minutes past. Five, ten, fifteen, and still she was sans Ghost.

But although she was sans Ghost, as she told herself with slight hysteria, she wasn't without was a very sophisticated lighting effect. It was something she had been trying to ignore for the past fifteen minutes.

Where she sat in the middle of her bed had become centre stage for a bright and warm gold light that streamed from the living room. The longer she sat there the more she thought she might be in the midst of some spontaneous combustion experience but she just hadn't quite caught up to the combustion bit.

She wasn't quite as in control as she thought. Ghosts she was prepared for… Academy Award winning lighting effects she wasn't. But after fifteen minutes of shivering on her bed she gathered her courage. She was going to check out the living room. Maybe it was just a stray light from the building opposite, or a helicopter with a searchlight.

"A very silent helicopter," she said to herself as she swung her legs over the side of the bed. Was she really going to voluntarily search out the next Spirit?

She pushed open the bedroom door.

Yes, it looked like she was.

"Edie! You came!" shouted a strange voice in greeting.

It was definitely her living room, you could tell from the geometry of it but as to the décor… this was no longer the twin of a sophisticated hotel room. In fact the décor would never have been in the same genus never mind the same decorating magazine.

The walls and ceiling were covered with flowers and trees. There were roses, sweet peas, jasmine, and boughs from willows. It was a fairy bower. The air was redolent with the scent of summer and yet not cloyingly so. Small sparks of light flitted through the branches, fireflies alighting here and there on upturned blossom and blooms. Flowers that never shared a season were pressed cheek to cheek.

And the floor… Edie blinked.

Heaped on the floor rising up to form a throne were piles of salmon, chickens, great legs of ham, all manner of meat, suckling pigs and lobsters, vol au vents and hors d'oeuvres heaped on top of each other. Great pyramids of profiteroles, white icing encrusted cakes with bon-bons scattered over everything, cupcakes teetering precariously and rows of magnums of champagne on ice then next to the throne a precarious champagne glass fountain.

Pop.

The explosion of the champagne cork made Edie jump.

There, reclining in state on the throne, was the jolliest, roundest giant of a bridesmaid. In one hand she brandished a jeroboam of champagne that she was pouring, sending the frothy bubbles cascading down the champagne glass fountain. And in the other she held a glowing bouquet of golden roses, the light spilled from them, gilding everything.

She smiled down at Edie. Her cheeks, red and rosy, lifted so high from her grin that it squeezed her eyes to little slits of sparkling light.

"Well it took you long enough. I thought I was going to have to finish this whole bottle on my own!" the Ghost said with a belly laugh that sent her rocking on her throne.

Edie was flabbergasted. She thought she had been ready for anything. She wasn't ready for this.

"Have a glass."

The Spirit threw her arms open expansively, Edie ducked and cringed expecting the glass fountain to tumble crashing to the floor. She also couldn't quite meet the spark in the Ghost's eyes.

"No? Your loss. I suppose we should get on with the formalities… I'm the Ghost of Weddings Present," she said. "It would be easier if you had a quick look at me and then we can get on with the rest."

Edie realised that the Ghost had the whole Head Girl, jolly hockey sticks vibe going on and she knew better than to try and argue with that sort when they used that tone of voice.

She looked up at the Spirit. She, Edie decided calling her a she

110

was probably the best idea; there was a lush femininity about her as well as a sturdy practicality.

She was dressed in a simple silk forest green bridesmaid dress. It had an empire line and a cream sash. Her ample bosom swelled from the bodice and threatened to escape. The satiny whiteness of her skin glowed with health.

The dress fell in folds to her feet; which were bare of anything except for the dark red nail polish on her toenails and a cheeky toe ring with a bell on it, which adorned the second toe of her right foot.

On her bouncing chestnut curls that were cut in a bob, she wore a beautiful wreath of flowers. Every one of the flowers and plants from the fairy bower were represented. And here and there between the flitting sparks of light from the fireflies, there was the lazy fluttering of the wings of iridescent butterflies nestled within the wreath.

Brides everywhere would have killed for that wreath.

"Bet you've never seen anything like me before have you?" the Ghost exclaimed, her eyes smiling. They were kind, but very keen.

"I don't believe I have," Edie croaked out.

"Hmmm. Well that's a pity because my sisters and brothers are always out and about this time of year. Ah well," she huffed and then bracing her hands on her knees got up off the feast of a throne.

Edie's back stiffened. This was it. She lifted her chin as if she were on her way to the noose. She could do this and she was learning her lesson, wasn't she?

"OK, I'm ready. Last week I'll admit I was a bit stubborn but this week, anything you think I need to know just tell me. Anything you think I should be doing, let me know. I'm up for this," Edie rushed out her words. "I could make notes?" she ended hopefully.

"Hold on to my sash," the Spirit instructed ignoring her.

Edie reached a trembling hand for the silk and clung on tightly.

Roses, jasmine, sweet pea, sunflowers, lobsters, profiteroles, cupcakes, champagne fountains, they all disappeared in the blink of an eye. They were no longer in Edie's living room.

Instead they were standing with their backs against a wall. It was a familiar wall, in a familiar flat.

"This is Mel's flat," she said.

There was laughter and talking coming from the kitchen dining room.

The Ghost led her towards the door. Edie hung back. Did she really want to see this?

Peering round the corner, she took in the scene. There were empty bottles and used plates on the table, and four people were sitting relaxed in their chairs, drinking wine.

Mel, Barry, a little blonde woman and a man with his back to her, though his blond curls looked familiar. He turned to smile intimately at the small woman next to him and lifted his hand to hold the back of her neck.

Tom.

Edie's insides moved what felt like one foot to the left and her knees one foot to the right. She grabbed the doorjamb. She could feel the ghost of Tom's hand on the nape of her neck.

"Any gossip and stories I need to know before the big day?" the woman was asking.

"What sort of gossip and stories?" Mel laughed.

"Oh you know, which bridesmaid has got off with which of the ushers. That sort of soap opera thing."

The laughter faded as Mel and Barry held their breath and looked at Tom worriedly.

"Oh don't worry about that! Kitty knows that Edie is going to be there," said Tom laughing.

Mel and Barry breathed out.

"Oh good. There isn't going to be a problem with that, is there?" Mel asked,

So Mel was worried that she would upset Tom and Kitty? What about her, Edie? Didn't anyone care what she thought?

"Oh no!" Tom squeezed the back of Kitty's neck again. "Kitty

112

knows all about the Ice Queen. Don't you, sweetie?"

They all giggled at Tom's description.

"Oh Tom it isn't nice to talk about your ex like that! I'd hate to think what you'd call me if we broke up," she leaned into him with her hand on his knee.

"I am going to be sick." Edie said. "Ice Queen? How dare he? How dare they?"

"They can't hear you," the Ghost looked at her pityingly.

"We're not going to break up are we, Kitten?" Tom positively purred down at her.

Edie wanted to vomit as they rubbed noses. They were grown-ups and they were acting like besotted teenagers with the IQ of gnats. At least he didn't call her Shug, a traitorous voice told her.

"But I do want to know what Edie's like. Will you tell me, Mel?" Kitty asked.

Edie butted in. "Oh that's great. You come in here having taken the love of my life and now you want my best friend to spill the beans on me... you tell her, Mel! You tell her!"

Mel squirmed in her seat. There was a moment of silence.

"Come on Mel, say something," Edie said, willing her best friend to open her mouth and say what a great person she was.

"You have to have known Edie a long time to see her the right way," Mel began. She had her face bowed and was picking at a mark on the tablecloth.

"You can do better than that," Edie said.

"Oh don't start with the whole no one understands her guff!" Barry interrupted. "She is a cold, hard and calculating bitch!"

Edie's mouth dropped open.

Barry thought... he... but...

"Oh Barry, I'll admit she isn't the warmest person in the world but she is to me." Mel said slapping Barry lightly on the wrist.

"A light slap? I'd punch him in the face if someone said that about you." Edie was furious.

"You see I've known her most of my life and when we were

113

teenagers she was the warmest funniest person I knew, and she adored Tom."

Tom squirmed in his seat.

"Yes, you squirm, you smarmy git!"

"But then it all changed," Mel said.

Silence fell.

"What changed?" Kitty asked breathlessly.

"Her father left," Tom said.

"And that was when Edie started to build the wall around her." Mel continued. "She adored her dad. But when he left, he left. He never came back. Her mum told Edie he didn't want to see her. I'm not sure I believe that, but the damage was done. And then that lawyer, Hilary Satis, got her hooks in Edie and after that..." Mel made a motion with her fingers across her throat as if that was it.

Edie saw it and then stared at her nails, picked at her cuticles and willed her burning eyes to stay dry.

"Parents get divorced every day. That doesn't turn their children into the machine she is," Barry said.

"That's a bit harsh," Tom said.

"OK maybe I judged you badly, maybe you aren't such a smarmy git!" Edie said her heart lightening.

"She's more iceberg than machine." Tom laughed.

Edie tried to smack him on the back of his head, only for her hand to go right through it.

"You've been told," the Ghost said taking a swig of champagne, "You can't touch them."

But their words could touch her. She wasn't an iceberg, or a machine.

"Don't be nasty," Mel chided him. "I remember her twenty-first birthday; she was waiting and waiting for something from her Dad. A visit, a present, even just a card but then nothing came. I think that was the last time I saw her cry."

Edie could feel the tears on her cheeks. She felt raw and exposed.

"He never came," she whispered.

"Oh and she was very upset when you broke up with her." Mel looked over at Tom and raised a glass.

"And then…" Edie encouraged Mel but she didn't say anything else.

That was all Mel could say? Why wasn't she leaping over the table wielding her steak knife? Why was she marrying a man who hated her best friend so much?

"Upset? She had me out of the flat before I could finish my sentence. And then she sent me a detailed breakdown on a spreadsheet of who owned what, and how much we each owed the other. Down to the last penny," Tom shook his head. "Cold hard facts were all she dealt with," he said. "When I got that spreadsheet all the doubts I had about leaving, all the doubts about whether I had done the right thing, the urge I had to go back and ask to start again faded away."

"He had doubts?" Edie whispered.

Why hadn't she known? If he had wanted to come back, she would have had let him. Wouldn't she?

When he had gone, she had shut down, gone into automatic, sorted out everything that needed doing. She didn't want to be left with nothing, the same as her mother. She didn't want to be left with another hole in her life she couldn't fill. She wanted to be strong, she wanted to be Hilary Satis, she'd thought.

"Don't let the bastards see you cry," she whispered.

"But still you've got to admit she's done very well for herself," Mel said.

"Yeah but being on track for partnership in a law firm and a reputation as a shark doesn't keep you warm at night," Tom countered.

"I feel sorry for her," Kitty piped up.

Pity? She didn't want pity. Especially from some undersized pixie.

"Yeah, I know," sighed Mel.

"Pity?" Edie's voice squeaked.

115

Mel pitied her?

"Ouch. That's gotta hurt," said the Spirit. "And she's your best friend, huh?"

"She called tonight to see if I wanted to go out. She sounded desperate. I get the feeling I'm the only friend she has. I felt awful but I couldn't have invited her here with you two, could I?"

"I wish you hadn't invited her to our wedding. And made her your maid of honour," Barry complained. "It'll be like the spectre of your relationship at the party. But at least that girl Jessica isn't around any more. The two of them were always together at weddings, sneering at everything. They were only missing a third and it would have been the witches from Macbeth!"

"Invite that bitch, Satis and you'd have had your witches." Tom said and they all burst out laughing.

"I don't need to hear any more," Edie said.

"I have to say that Barry really doesn't like you, does he?" The Ghost gestured towards the giggling foursome round the table with the bottle in her hand.

Edie couldn't reply. She'd never really thought about Barry before. He was an annoying hindrance that she put up with because he came with Mel.

"I've never been awful to him," she eventually said.

Not awful. Dismissive and contemptuous when she bothered to think about him… yes.

"Ah. Not awful but not nice either, then?"

No, not nice, not nice at all.

"I think we're done here, as it is." The Ghost shook the bottle and held it to her eye. "And we're out of bubbles. First a refill and then on to the next stop. Hold on!"

Edie snatched for the sash and found herself squashed in the corner of a limo full of drunken women. Glitter, feathers and bubbles were everywhere.

"Ah, this is the life!" The Spirit said as she grabbed a bottle of champagne from the large bucket in the middle of the car and launched into an ear-deafening rendition of *We Are Family* along with the rest of the women in the car.

Edie watched the girls around her, their faces flushed from alcohol, eyes shining with happiness, their arms spread wide as they waved out the open windows to strangers they passed. No one would call these girls the Ice Queen, or a shark or a machine.

Something in her yearned to join them.

"You could do it," the Ghost said.

"No. Look at them making fools of themselves," Edie said.

"Yup, complete tits and they are having the time of their lives." The Ghost smiled widely. "Well if you aren't going to, can you just hold this?"

She handed Edie the bottle.

The Ghost manoeuvred herself onto her knees then stuck her head out of the open roof and waved her arms around, still singing loudly. She looked as if she were the centre of a bouquet of shining, happy women.

What on earth was she doing?

Edie cringed in the corner, waiting for someone to start noticing them. But they didn't. Much like it had been with the first Ghost, people didn't notice them; they would move out of the way so as not to touch them.

And waving out of the sunroof of a limo did look like a great idea. If these girls couldn't see her, then no one could. No one would know.

She put the bottle down and tentatively she crouched beside the Ghost and then stood up to put her shoulders through the opening.

The wind rushed through her hair and caught at her breath. Their limo was white and seemed, to Edie, to stretch forever. It was touring round Trafalgar Square.

She felt the anger and pain from Mel, Barry, Tom and Kitty's words blow away in the breeze. And underneath all that emotion was a pink piece of her that hadn't seen the light for so long. It swelled and she found herself opening her mouth and singing along.

Up Charing Cross Road, then left onto Shaftesbury Avenue, waving to the theatre crowds until the limo lurched to a halt outside a club.

"This is where we leave them," the Spirit said, grabbing the first bottle and then a second bottle of champagne.

Edie stared at her suspiciously.

"It's for the journey," the Spirit said.

Edie wasn't sure ghosts blushed and this one already had rosy cheeks, but she definitely looked pinker.

"Ready for the next visit?" the Ghoul asked.

Was she? She felt vulnerable and raw. She was exposed, but she knew the Ghost's question was rhetorical; she was in this till the end. She'd better get it done with.

"Yes, if I must," she said and took hold of the sash once more.

The limo dissolved and they were in a cramped living room in a modern house. It was a Lego style identikit house that builders like to throw up in great streets full as starter homes.

The floor was strewn with children's toys; a light sabre, toy cars and books. Edie and the Ghost stood with their backs against the staircase, which came straight down into the room. There was no hallway, just a front door straight onto the living room that then led into a kitchen diner.

Light steps came down the stairs, Edie turned to see Rachel Micawber, her trainee run down them with a tired smile on her face. Tired but with a look of contentment.

"Hey you!" she called.

Edie lifted her hand in a greeting before she remembered the rule. She wasn't here.

"Hey sweetie," a light male voice came from the kitchen. "Has his lordship gone to sleep?"

"He's watching the light show and listening to Harry Potter. I said he had twenty minutes before we went up," Rachel replied.

"You're too soft on him," the man came out of the kitchen.

So this was the famous Rob Cratchit, was it? Edie thought,

wrinkling her nose.

He was slight with mousey brown hair, which was receding fast. His face was long and toothy, his eyes behind frameless glasses. But when he smiled at Rachel, he was almost handsome. Rachel kissed him on the lips as he held her loosely in his arms.

"Wine?" he asked.

"By the bucket-load," she said.

"Bad day?" he asked as he released her and they moved together into the kitchen.

"Weird. The whole of this week has just been plain odd," she said.

"You can say that again," echoed Edie and looked at the Ghost. "Have you been haunting her as well? I wouldn't want to be greedy."

The Spirit raised an eyebrow.

Edie gritted her teeth and really wished they wouldn't do that, it made her feel about five.

"Not everyone is a desperate case like you. Some people know the meaning of love and sacrifice." Then the Spirit put a finger to her lips for silence.

"And the strangest of all happened tonight." Rachel giggled and that brought Edie back to the conversation. "You'll never guess who asked me out for a drink?"

"It had better not be that gorgeous rugby player you've been swooning over." Rob replied.

"Chance would be a fine thing," she retorted.

"Hey!" Rob flicked her with the cloth he was holding.

"OK, you know there is no one for me but you," she smiled up at him.

"Oh, please." Edie squirmed embarrassed to be eavesdropping.

"Anyway, it wasn't Jack Twist. It was Edie." Rachel continued.

"Edie? The shark? The borg?" he asked incredulously.

"Yup, Miss Snotty Pants herself."

Why?" he asked. "Not that someone wouldn't want to go out

with you, but why now?"

"It was really weird. You know I said that she had suddenly started doing that mediation stuff? Every day this week, she's had her friend's parents coming in for meetings and every day she comes back from them stressed out. And then today, off she goes as usual but then I heard from Angela in Commercial that she'd heard from Bronwyn in Litigation that Jack was going to be taking over this mediation because she was making a complete pig's ear of it all."

"A pig's ear?" Edie said her face burning with anger, shame and general unfairness. "A pig's ear is a bit strong. How about the way you dealt with the Cohen case, huh? You couldn't even get your client custody of their pet rat."

Edie crossed her arms and said to the Spirit.

"I mean, I know I shouldn't be doing mediation but I thought if I could just get Maggie and Doug talking it would get sorted out. Well I got them talking. Screaming as well. But there is no need for her to be saying things like that." Edie frowned. "Oh no! If Angela knows, then the whole office knows. Or if not, they definitely will by Monday."

She knew how the grapevine worked. There wasn't a part of Edie that didn't glow with humiliation.

"And then," continued Rachel, "she comes back from what must have been the disastrous meeting this afternoon and does bugger all work. Never seen anything like it. I almost asked her if she was ill."

"Oh maybe she and the rugby bloke have a thing going on?" Rob chimed in.

Jack and her? A thing?

Edie snorted.

"Ha!" Rachel started laughing. "Oh yeah that's likely. Jack could have any woman in the place. There is no way he and Edie…" Rachel laughed again, wheezing for breath.

"I'll have you know he kissed me last weekend." Edie waved

her finger in the face of the oblivious Rachel. "So take that and shove it up your…"

"If we could concentrate on the matter in hand and not focus on one-upmanship," the Spirit said taking a sip from the bottle of champagne, "although I wouldn't mind hearing about that kiss later."

"Anyway, Edie did no work and then phoned up her friend Mel, her only friend I reckon, to see if she wants to go out for a drink. I don't think I've ever heard of Edie going out on a Friday. She obviously got blown out, because then she turns round and asks me."

She sipped her wine and carried on.

"I swear, Rob, I almost fell off my chair in shock. Could you imagine spending a night out with her?" Rachel shuddered. "I think I'd rather have poked myself in the eyes with these chopsticks."

She brandished the set left over from their Chinese meal.

"Chopsticks in the eyes rather than a night out with you?" The Spirit looked at Edie with a mix of horror, pity and humour. "Boy, you must be a real treat to be around if these are the sort of reactions you are getting."

Edie's body was in knots. Her shoulders were meeting her ears; her stomach was wrapped round itself and then somehow round her knees. She was never leaving her flat again.

"This is what they think of me?" she said.

"Looks like it," the Spirit said.

"No need to sound so happy about it." Edie said.

"Da! Ray!"

A high-pitched voice slurred and called from upstairs.

"Yes, little man?" Rachel called back, full of love.

An incomprehensible babble came down the stairs.

Rachel and Rob listened intently.

"OK sweetie, we're just coming," she called.

Rob and Rachel passed Edie and the Ghost and carried on upstairs, holding hands.

"What the hell was that about?" Edie frowned.

She was sure Rachel had said that Rob's kid was at least five. Not that she paid much attention to The Domestic Goddess. That babble didn't sound like a five-year-old, it had sounded like a baby.

The Ghost turned to follow.

"Are you coming?" she asked.

As if Edie wanted to go and look at a child.

"Not especially…"

The Ghost thinned her lips and looked at Edie as if she were disappointed in her then grasped Edie's hand.

In an instance, they were in a darkened room. Projected images and lights danced across the ceiling and walls in a rainbow of colours. In one corner stretched a long vertical tube of liquid and bubbles that changed colour every few seconds. Rob and Rachel knelt by the side of the bed. The bed had sides to it, not quite a crib but not quite a hospital bed.

More babble came from the child that lay in it.

Edie peered closer and then she saw him.

This child might be five or so chronologically, but in other parts of his development he couldn't be more than a baby. He could obviously move of his own accord but his head flopped from side to side.

"Hey Timmy, you ready to be tucked in?" Rachel asked. She reached up with a cloth and wiped his mouth.

Edie was shocked.

"But how can she?" Edie whispered.

Timmy wasn't even Rachel's own child and yet here she was acting like he was hers.

"As I said, some people don't need to be haunted to understand the meaning of love and sacrifice." The Ghost stared at the scene, positively beaming. "Of course they will all be in for a whole lot of heartache later but they will always have their memories to warm them."

"What do you mean heartache?"

Edie looked at the child in the bed.

He was staring right at her; a small smile seemed to pull one side of his mouth up. His eyes were alight with laughter, humour and intelligence.

He could see her.

And he was laughing at her.

"Little Timmy over there was deprived of oxygen when he was born and it affects his movements. He also has cystic fibrosis. But inside he is a very bright and mischievous boy. However when Rachel loses her job in a few months and then when Rob loses his it will become a lot harder. No more extra private physio to help his breathing and mobility. And then…" the Spirit trailed off.

"But why would Rachel lose her job?" Edie said.

"Isn't that what you have been aiming for? All the emails to HR you've been sending, asking to put her on report? Surely you knew where it would end. Didn't you, Edie?"

The hairline cracks that had been appearing deep in Edie's soul, the fine lines in the wall that surrounded her suddenly gave way. She stood there, unmoving, while inside her, the pieces of the wall she lived behind lay shattered on the ground. Large fissures that were like crazy paving all across her heart. And coming through the gaps was the hurt she had been keeping back.

"Please, no," she whispered.

The hurt burnt like acid. Her cheeks were wet with tears.

"We still have a few more stops," the Spirit said kindly as if sensing Edie's inner turmoil. She grasped Edie's hand again in her warm grip and the eyes of a small boy that saw too much were no longer upon her.

Chapter 12

Light and laughter assaulted her eyes and ears. Edie scrubbed at her cheeks to get rid of the tears. She rubbed hard and wished she could remove the pain in her chest as easily.

"Now this is my sort of place." The Spirit threw back her head and laughed. Her body, if that's what it was, shook with it.

Edie peered round her to see where they were.

It was rugby player central.

They were in the kind of terrace house you find in posh areas like Fulham or Chelsea or Twickenham. Thin and long, it was packed with large men and little women. Rugby WAGs. Music blared out over the hubbub of voices. Edie felt like she was transported back to university days. Any minute she was expecting someone to break into the drinking chant of *Down you Zulu warrior. Down you Zulu Chief!* and then someone would start downing a keg of beer whilst the crowd chanted 'Chief! Chief! Chief!"

"Alright Waggy?" A man bellowed from behind her and right into her ear. "Down you Zulu Warrior!"

"Why?" she asked herself as the crowd went mental.

The majority of the front room along with the Ghost were chanting and roaring encouragement at the aforementioned thirty or so year old Waggy as he downed a small keg of beer.

"Men." She said. They never grew up, she thought.

She squirmed her way easily from the centre of the crowd. Yet again she was anonymous, but still possessing a crowd-parting ability which would come in handy at rush hour in the real world. She found herself at the far end of the house, by a pair of French windows that led out to the garden.

"So what's it like being back in Civvy Street?" a male voice was talking to another man standing in the shadow of the doors.

"It has its plus points and it has its pitfalls," the man in the shadows answered.

Jack.

That probably explained the rugby types then. But it didn't explain what he had to do with this introspection on her life. She had only known him a week. What insights could he provide that she didn't already know?

"Pitfalls? Oh come on. Are all the women throwing themselves at you and you can't cope? If that is a pitfall then I'll take it," his friend said.

"Why do you think it has anything to do with women? There are other things in life, you know" Jack replied.

Edie peered around the door to look at him. He was leaning against the wall of the house and held a bottle of beer.

She realised this was the first time she could have a good look at him without him knowing. Without him catching her drinking him in and raising an eyebrow or looking back with those eyes that saw too much.

He was tall, taller than most of the men in the house, probably six foot five she thought. She already knew about his wide shoulders, the stubborn chin that squared onto the world. But she wanted to see his eyes, to see the way they were when they weren't looking at her with pity, exasperation or just plain annoyance. She tried to squint further but the shadows from the door and darkness of the night outside defeated her.

"It's always got to do with women," his friend answered. "We all know you're a bloody good lawyer. What was it, top of the class at law school?"

Edie gasped. Top of his class? Her image of Jack getting his job through the old boy network shifted.

"You've got all that money from sponsorship deals, so it isn't that. So if it isn't work or money and you don't have the rugby to worry about any more then it has got to be women. Those legal birds throwing themselves at you, barristers in wigs wanting to see your briefs?"

"You're deluded and need to get off the gin." Jack laughed.

"Come on, you can tell your Uncle Jim," his friend said.

Jack rolled the bottle between his hands and then raised it to his mouth and took a drink. Edie watched fascinated as his throat bobbed as he swallowed. She licked her suddenly dry lips.

"OK so there is this one woman..." Jack said.

"I knew it! What's wrong then? She's married? Got a boyfriend?"

"Oh she's single."

Then she's a complete dog and won't leave you alone? You've got a stalker? She's panting all over you?"

"I wouldn't call her a stalker..." Jack said. Edie could hear the laughter in his voice.

Edie didn't think she could hurt any more that evening. But Jack's mocking words were sharp and like a razor.

"So I'm a dog am I?" she said.

"Then she's a dog," Uncle Jim stated.

"No and not a dog either." Jack said.

Edie's hurt lightened just a little.

"So the problem is..." prompted Jim the friend.

"The problem is that she's a prize bitch," Jack said and swallowed some more beer.

The razor hacked off some more of Edie's heart.

"Oh stay clear mate!" his friend said as he recoiled holding his hands up.

"But the thing is there is something about her that makes me think that I've got her wrong. Just a flash here and there, you

126

know? That there might be something worth knowing underneath it all." Jack said.

She yearned for him at that moment. The burned places and the pink new places inside her that peeked through the crumbling wall tried to expand, to send out tendrils towards him. But the solid part of her, the main part of her that still hid behind her cracked defences held back. Half in and half out, she was stuck.

"You don't want to go down that road again, mate. Remember Tanya? Yeah there was something underneath all that cold bitchiness and that was frigid bitchiness. Sometimes they really are just bitches," his friend said solidly.

Jack shook himself and pushed himself away from the wall.

"You're probably right," he said.

And he stepped out of the shadows. Edie looked closely, now she could see his eyes and hoped the light gradually fading in them wasn't him giving up on her.

The tendrils retreated behind the crumbled stonework again.

"So that's the kisser then," the Spirit had appeared next to her without her realising. "Boy, between him and that Tom bloke you don't pick badly."

No, she didn't pick badly.

They did.

"It's a pity he thinks you're a bitch," the Spirit carried on.

"I can see you completely flunked the 'small talk' part of whatever training you had for this," Edie said.

"Oh we don't sit exams for this sort of thing, you're either born to it or you're not." The Spirit had a lascivious grin on her face as she drank in Jack. "And then there are days when I'd give anything to snog someone like that." She smiled wider.

"Can we go now?" Edie asked, clenching her fists.

She wanted to step between the Ghost and Jack and tell her to back off from her man. Her man. Yeah right, the man thought she was a cold bitch. She shivered.

"Just one more quick stop," the Ghost said and sighing, she

took one last look at Jack. The rugby boys winked out.

Edie was in another familiar house. A place she had seen the outside of only last week. With another Ghost.

"I am not listening to my mother slag me off."

That was it. She was officially on strike.

She went to bite her thumbnail on her left hand and noticed it was mostly gone. She started to gnaw on the right thumbnail instead. She turned her face to the wall and stared at a graduation photo. It was of her and her mum, her dad hadn't been there.

"Suit yourself," the Spirit replied.

Her mother's voice suddenly came through from the kitchen. "It's what I've always said, Maggie. Men are spineless, inconsiderate and useless. Can't trust them as far as you can throw them," she was holding forth on her favourite topic and it sounded like it was fuelled by a few glasses of wine. Or maybe it was gin and tonic. That always made her belligerent.

"Edie thinks this mediation thingy will make our divorce more amicable or even get us back together." Maggie replied.

Or help you keep your mitts off other men, Edie thought as she turned her head to hear them better.

"Of course all we've done so far in the meetings is drag up every nasty thing we can about each other."

Edie flinched.

"Mediation? Edie wanted you to try mediation? She always swore it was a waste of time. Only practiced by namby pamby lawyers," her mother said. "You want it over and done with. Ripped off fast like a plaster. Get a lawyer like Hilary Satis. She'll see you right."

"What happened when you... well when you and Charlie..." Maggie stumbled over the words.

"What when we divorced?" her mother said, before making another drink.

"Yes," said Maggie.

"Yes," echoed Edie.

"You never knew what happened?" the Spirit asked.

"No," Edie said pushing away from the wall and moving to the doorway so she could watch her mother at the kitchen table.

"One day I came home from school and they sat me down and said they were separating. I used to think it was because they'd had a massive row about me wearing make-up. Stupid really, the things you think when you're a kid. As if the world turns round you." She rubbed the spot over her heart; she still wondered if she'd been better behaved, would he have stayed? "After Dad left I got to see him on alternate weekends and then suddenly one day even that stopped."

Without a phone call or a letter, a huge hole opened up in her life.

"Charlie and I hadn't been getting on for a while," Edie's mum started to tell Maggie. "So I did agree, reluctantly I might add, that we should have a bit of time apart. Give us all a break from the arguing and crap like that. So he would come here and pick Edie up every other weekend. Sometime he would come over in the week if I made excuses about house stuff. I thought we would get it all back together," Edie watched as her mother took a drink and then lean forward at the table.

Edie felt herself move forward as well. What had actually happened?

"And what stopped that?" Maggie asked.

Yes what had stopped it? Edie started chewing the nail on her right index finger.

"I asked you to have Edie one school night, I don't know if you remember, and I decided that I would dress up nicely and go over to his rented place and persuade him to come home."

"I drove up to the little cottage, you remember the one, out towards Great Hanningfield? Well there was a car in the drive I didn't recognise. I didn't want to burst in on him if he had work people round. How embarrassing would that have been? And in the pit of my stomach I wondered if… well. So I decided to drive

129

the car a bit further down the lane, park it and walk back. When I got to the cottage I hid myself in that little clump of trees by the gate. And then I saw…" Her hand clenched the glass.

"What did you see?" said Edie.

"What?" asked Maggie.

"A woman. A very attractive woman. She was coming out of the house and he was behind her; they were laughing. It felt like the joke was on me. He hadn't looked so relaxed and happy in years. He hadn't looked at me like that in years."

"And then what?" Maggie asked.

"Well then she got in her car and drove away."

"He was having an affair?" Maggie asked.

Edie's mouth opened and closed soundlessly.

"He swore he wasn't. But I'd seen her in his house. I don't know if you remember but you had Edie again that weekend. That was when I told him that we didn't need him any more. That he could take himself and his fancy piece and leave us alone. Edie and I would be just fine on our own."

"But I still needed him," Edie didn't realise how much she had needed him until she spoke.

"And he went? Just like that?"

"He didn't go that quietly." Edie's mother looked furious. "He fought me in court for custody but in those days and with a lawyer like Hilary Satis, well… the mother always won big. Every year he sent cards and presents for Edie, trying to buy her love, I reckon. It stopped when she was twenty-one. Like she would ever need him. I keep them locked in the dresser," her mum gestured behind her. "I couldn't bear to give them to Edie, but then I can't throw them away."

"He sent presents?" Edie's hands clutched each other for strength and to stop her from trying to wrench open the dresser drawer. She knew it was futile; she couldn't touch anything here.

The room seemed to bend and lengthen to the side and then lurch once upwards. When it stopped Edie didn't feel the same.

Things had shifted. Nothing fitted in their place any more. She felt bigger but also emptier.

"How could she have done that? Cut him out of our lives?" Edie looked to the Ghost searching for answers.

"Some people want to score points when love turns to hate. If she couldn't have his love, then he couldn't have yours. That is called 'putting conditions on it,' and it sounds like you learned it early on."

"Please," Edie said. "No more."

And she tumbled out of her mother's kitchen and into her bed.

Chapter 13

She had one week to change things round. She would not become her mother or Ms Satis, she would turn herself into a fully functioning member of society or she would die trying.

Edie stared long and hard at herself in the mirror the next morning. Around her eyes she could see lines of stress. She rubbed the spot between her eyebrows where a groove was being carved from frowning. She smiled to pull her face into a different position. It felt odd. And she realised that she had no laughter lines, no creases from smiling.

This week would be a step up from last week. It had to be. She would show everyone.

"Cold bitch indeed," she said.

She turned away from the mirror and carried on dressing.

Edie sat at her breakfast bar with a pad of paper in front of her and a pen.

How was it that everyone pitied her? Her, of all people? She was successful, heading to partner with a bullet and yet... what else was there? Marriage? She shuddered, that was the death knell of any successful relationship she had ever seen. And you couldn't have everything, could you? A career and a relationship? Something or someone always compromised and then...

Compromise.

Her flesh crawled and she shivered.

Edie felt all turned around, as if she'd been flipped inside out and when she was put back the right way her stuffing had been lost and her corners were all puckered. It was not a feeling she liked. Order, precision and everything in its place was how she liked it.

But the Ghost? She supposed that was the only way she could describe the dream. It should've faded like all dreams do but it felt so real. No, it had to be a dream, but that didn't mean she couldn't act on it.

The blank pad stared up at her. The list. She would write a list of what she needed to do this week.

Number one:

She'd phone her mum and ask about her dad. Then she'd know if it was just her imagination. Just a left over yearning of her little girl dream where her dad hadn't really left her. It was amazing; no matter how old you got you could still be a slave to your childhood yearnings.

But what if it wasn't a dream? What if her Dad had really wanted her? She rubbed her sternum to get rid of the pain. No, that was a fairy story; things didn't happen like that in real life.

No prince to wake you from your sleep. No fathers suddenly appearing to save you.

Actually, no, she wouldn't just call. She got out her phone and checked her calendar. If she left early from work on Monday she could make it to her mum's for the evening. This was the sort of conversation she wanted to have face to face. Or she could go this weekend... then she remembered the dress fitting. She wasn't sure which was worse - the dress fitting or facing her mother. Either way she needed to put her armour on for both of them. And if she saw her mum on a weeknight she had an honest reason to leave; that house made her feel claustrophobic.

Number two:

Maggie and Doug. Somehow she had to fast track the mediation. *If Jack Twist would let her,* the thought winged in straight away.

And following soon after was the kick to the stomach that he thought she was a bitch.

But she had been. Hadn't she?

She chewed the end of the pen and contemplated adding number three; persuade Jack Twist I'm not a bitch.

But how would she do that?

A scene flashed into her head of him crushing her up against the side of the lift where they'd first met. Her hands splayed on his chest. The cerise lining of his suit the last thing she sees before her eyes close and he kisses her. His body is hard, and as she presses against him she feels every single glorious inch. And the scent of him surrounds her, making her dizzy.

Then as his mouth finishes exploring hers and as he moves to nuzzle her neck, she hears his voice in her ear.

"I'm going to melt you," he whispers and the heat that spikes through her could melt a thousand ice queens.

She shook herself out of the daydream.

Where the hell did that come from? She opened her eyes, which had drifted closed. She touched her lips, to feel if they were swollen from the imaginary kisses. Her heart was racing and she was burning up.

No, she couldn't deal with Jack Twist this week as well. It would be too much. She hurriedly scratched through the 'J' she'd started to write, almost tearing the paper.

What else did she need to do this week?

Something for Rachel, perhaps? She could try and be nicer and maybe stop sending those emails to HR. Edie rubbed her head. These disturbed nights were getting to her. She'd think about it tomorrow.

Today she had a dress fitting. Her life was on hold until this whole wedding thing was all over.

Why did they need another bridesmaid dress fitting? She'd done her research and told Mel that two fittings would be more than enough but now they were on number five. And what more could be done just a week before the wedding?

It was as if Mel was squeezing every last drop out of her wedding experience. Which would be OK if Edie didn't have to join her for it.

She hadn't meant to keep tally of the time spent on the wedding preparations but when you charged your clients by the minute for your time, it got to be a habit. It was as if a stopwatch in her head constantly measured out the minutes and hours and days.

The wedding dress search had clocked in at four full Saturdays and one manic, desperate trip to a wedding fair. There were also the two hours she had spent talking Mel out of flying to New York to 'Say Yes to the Dress' at the shop featured on some reality TV show. Edie had then made the mistake of relaxing and had been horribly sideswiped when Mel had quickly moved on to the bridesmaid dresses.

Really, how hard could it be to find a dress for three women to wear for a few hours on a Saturday?

Well she'd found out. The bridesmaid dress-a-thon was currently at five Saturdays for actually deciding on the dress style and colour. And on each of those Saturdays there had been at least two tantrums and a sulk, mostly from Sophie.

Edie had personally clocked up twelve hours and forty-two minutes in fittings. She'd even tried turning up late for a few and running off early. Maybe she could charge Maggie and Doug for those hours when she sent them the bill for the mediation.

And now she had this last one to suffer through, which brought with it the joy of facing the other bridesmaids or as she thought in her head, bridemonsters. To be fair, Jo was fine, well except that she seemed to have bought into all the wedding nonsense. And Edie hadn't had to see the flower girl yet but Mel had promised she didn't have a permanently runny nose.

No, the real bridemonster was Sophie. There was no love lost between them before the hen weekend. And after… Edie cringed. It seemed Sophie was a rugby groupie and thought Jack should've been her property as she'd known him longer. And she was making it known that she wasn't taking Jack preferring Edie very well.

"I brought bubbles!" Sophie said and the squeals that greeted this went through Edie's head like an ice pick. Or maybe that was just wishful thinking. She was sure an ice-pick lobotomy might be marginally more enjoyable than this fitting.

She sat on the edge of her seat and hoped for it all to be over quickly. Or for death to take her. Whichever came first, she really wasn't fussy.

This is what was wrong with the whole wedding thing. It wasn't about the marriage itself, but it was about the production surrounding it. And the amount of money that people made out of them. At least her way of making money was a little more honest.

She looked around the dress shop they were in, whilst sat on a white painted wooden chair with satin white seats. Billowing swathes of satin and gauze hung from the rose in the ceiling and gathered up at the walls with big rosettes. Edie eyed the oversized chandelier that hung down in a cascade of crystals and wondered if she could get it to fall onto her.

She wished it even more when she caught sight of the poufy meringue of a dress in the window. It was white but had layer on layer of tulle ruffles that looked like they had been left in a smoker's room for too long and had been stained a brown yellow.

Nicotine chic.

But maybe it wasn't the dress designer's fault. The fact was that people were willing to spend obscene amounts of money on one day, and someone had to provide the goods.

"Oh my God! I've put on weight! I'm so fat." It was Sophie, the bridemonster. She'd been the one who had extended the dress search for at least three more weekends than necessary. She was the one who'd made a fuss about the colour of the dresses. So much so that by the end, the dress worked for her but not for the rest of them.

Edie looked over at her and sighed. Sophie looked amazing,

136

and she knew it. Toned from spin classes and Pilates plus a rather unhealthy addiction to kale, the dress fitted her like a glove. But of course the other bridesmaids and Mel fluttered round her reassuring her. Edie exchanged looks with the fitting lady, the only other sensible person in the room. Which, considering she worked in a bridal shop, was worrying.

"And now you, Edie" Mel was flushed with excitement. "I can't wait to see what it looks like on."

Edie wanted to ask her why this was so important? Didn't she know this was all window dressing? These were trimmings that disguised the real thing, a marriage.

But as she looked over at her friend, she saw that Mel glowed, and her smile was wide. And superimposed on it Edie saw the younger Mel who had been a bridesmaid with her as a teenager, the girl she'd seen a few nights ago. This was her friend who'd been planning this wedding since that day; she'd picked out her wedding music before she'd found the groom. Ghosts of the girls they'd been swirled round the dressing room and Edie felt like Macbeth at the feast.

She rolled her shoulders and dredged a smile up from somewhere.

"Of course," she said and grabbing her dress, she headed for the changing room.

Edie stripped off her clothes and without looking in the mirror she stepped into the heavy dress and pulled it up and over her shoulders.

It was very green, eye poppingly so. Edie's eyes hurt.

And, of course, green looked great with red hair, as Sophie hoped. But it was going to be hell to wear if the day was hot and it would show every sweat mark.

Attractive.

Edie longed for the forest green dress last night's Ghost had worn.

The bodice wrapped into ruching under her breasts and then

the dress fell, from a pleat at the front, to the ground. From certain angles she looked pregnant. She could be known as 'the knocked up bridesmaid'. She imagined the gossip from that.

They probably thought she'd be giving birth to the anti-Christ.

She tried to pull the ruching down a bit, to minimise any billowing.

No, it just sprang back up.

She would never wear this again, no matter how many times Mel kept telling her how 'wearable' it was. Even knowing how much money Mel had paid for it, or rather Mel's parents. Who should really have been holding on to any money to pay for their divorce. She shivered. She needed to get them back together. Then maybe she could stop all of that.

It would be her present to Mel, the one she didn't know she needed and hadn't registered for at John Lewis.

She could hear the giggling outside and some whispers.

"Oi Edie, are you ready yet?" Mel called and there was a snigger, definitely from Sophie. They were talking about her.

What else was new?

She'd ignored their saccharine smiles when she'd arrived. None had reached their eyes. It had been the hen weekend; it seemed peeling people off people on the dance floor and saving relationships didn't help you make friends.

"I'm coming."

She squirmed trying to get the right angle so she could do the top bit of the zip up. God, she hated dresses like this, dresses that couldn't be put on by one person. You needed someone else to zip you all the way up. It just highlighted that the world expected you to be paired up.

She yanked the dress down and held her arm higher and somehow got the zip up.

Yes, the dress did show marks when you sweated.

She took a deep breath. Smile Edie, she told herself.

She pulled open the curtain, causing the rings to rattle on

the rail. Suddenly she was the centre of everyone's attention. She squirmed. She wished for the anonymity of her hauntings. Most of the faces staring at her were hostile. She could feel the heat of their stares.

The exceptions were Mel and the fitter.

Mel just looked tipsy from the whole experience and not on the bubbles.

The fitter's face was full of pity, until she spotted Edie watching and her expression went blank.

And with her head cocked to one side, Sophie had a malicious smile playing around her mouth.

"Well, I'm sure Jack will love seeing you in that." It was said in a sickly sweet voice.

Don't react, Edie thought. What she really wanted to do was tell Sophie to back off from her man.

Hold on, no, Jack wasn't hers. Sophie was welcome to him, Edie thought even as her hands curled into fists.

No, she wouldn't ruin this for Mel.

"Thank you, Sophie. Mel chose a great dress, didn't she?" Edie emphasised.

Sophie wasn't going to score points off Mel to get at Edie.

"What? What do you mean? I think Edie looks great. Did I get it wrong?" Mel's voice got higher and squeakier.

Damn it, Edie rushed as fast as the dress would allow and grabbed the bottle of champagne and topped up Mel's glass, at the same time straightening it from the alarming angle.

"It's wonderful. I feel like a princess." she lied.

A Day-Glo, pregnant sweat stained princess.

She grabbed a glass; she needed a drink too.

Looking to see how much was in the bottle, she saw the label. Cava.

Sophie was a bloody cheapskate. Couldn't even be bothered to go the extra mile but made sure that she was the centre of attention.

There would be a few bottles of Pol Roger at Mel's on the

morning of the wedding, Edie thought. She'd need it to get through having their hair and make-up done. And maybe being drunk through the wedding would help because it looked like she wasn't making any headway with Mel's parents.

"It is a beautiful dress, Mel. I don't know what Edie is saying. She always takes what I say the wrong way." Sophie was backtracking and stabbing her in the back at the same time.

And the drink would definitely help dilute Sophie.

But fundamentally the dress was hideous on her. And one more fitting wasn't going to change that. She knew that, the woman on her knees making infinitesimal changes to the hem knew it. The other bridesmaids knew it.

Sophie, of course, looked perfect in hers.

And it definitely looked as if it were more fitted.

That bitch had had some sneaky alterations done.

Edie wanted to rip the seams open, until Sophie was in a billowing tent like the rest of them.

"My turn," Mel clapped her hands, just missing spraying cava all over Edie.

It would either have put the dress out of its misery or been like launching a ship.

Edie knew that this was the real reason they were here. The last chance for Mel to try on her gown.

The changing room echoed with 'oooohs and 'ahhhs' and was that someone sniffing and blowing their nose? If they were like this at the fitting of a dress they'd all seen before she could imagine the floods of tears come next week.

Edie felt herself take a breath as if to sigh, as she looked at Mel standing on a raised dais with mirrors and bridesmaids surrounding her.

No.

She wasn't getting sucked into this. It was just a reflex reaction, something hard-wired into women. They were supposed to respond that way when confronted with a bride.

It didn't mean she liked it.

Edie took a slug of champagne.

The acidic burn of bubbles on the back of throat reminded her of last night and the jolly bridesmaid Spirit. Her stomach churned. And that brought back memories of the little precocious flower girl Ghost.

OK, she needed to be positive.

Upbeat.

She shuddered at the alternative. Stuck forever in this horrible dress wrapped in a chain studded with fairy wings and penis deely boppers.

Edie plastered a grin on her face.

Chapter 14

"We must stop meeting like this," Jack said as he got in the lift with her on Monday morning. The dark voice sent quivers through her; goose bumps up and down her arms.

Edie sighed.

Her weekend had been spent dodging a replay of the hen night and then working out what she was going to say to her mum. So far, 'where is my dad?' was winning for its brevity and pointedness.

Jack hadn't featured much in her thoughts.

Except for that steamy fantasy, inner Edie, who was getting increasingly chatty, said. *Or of course that dream she'd had this morning when she'd woken up whispering his name.*

Edie could feel the heat start travelling up her neck to her cheeks.

Bloody Jack Twist. He was worse than the Ghosts. He haunted her days. And the nights… even if the Ghosts weren't there.

"Twist," she nodded briefly and refused to make eye contact.

Because even though she had R-rated dreams about him she could still hear his voice from Friday night.

Cold bitch.

It threw ice on her blushes. Why was she lusting after a man who thought that about her?

She stalked out of the lift and sailed past him.

Or at least she tried to. A large hand came out and caught

her arm.

"I was hoping we had moved past the cold shouldering and we could talk about the Remingtons?"

Edie stared hard at the dark hair that sprinkled his knuckles and back of his hand. Looked at the scars and the oddly shaped knuckles, damaged from rugby.

What would his hand feel like on her skin rather than the sleeve of her jacket?

Hold on. No. She imagined it not being on the sleeve of her jacket. That was it. Nothing else.

She coughed pointedly.

The warmth of his hand was still on her arm after he'd lifted it away. She could feel each individual finger.

"I don't think there is much to talk about is there?" She glanced up, caught the frown in his eyes and quickly focused on a point behind his left shoulder. "You are the one doing the mediation now." She said.

"But you are still Mrs Remington's solicitor. That hasn't changed," he replied.

"Oh I am, am I?"

OK, so she was being petty but she couldn't help herself. He made her feel exposed.

"Look Edie, what exactly is your problem?" he had lowered his voice so that it didn't echo round the building.

"Problem? I didn't think cold bitches like me had problems," she said.

Damn. She couldn't believe she'd said it.

Jack's jaw dropped.

"What the... How did you...?" he asked.

She took his surprise as a chance to escape and walked quickly down the corridor to her office.

Once inside she leant her back against it and stared up at the ceiling.

Please don't let him find out how I know, she thought. My God, they would have her committed.

Seeing ghosts.

But obviously what she had seen or dreamed was technically true. His reaction pretty much confirmed that.

"Bloody hell! He did call me a cold bitch," she said

Which meant if he had said it, then everything else she had heard was true. All of those people thinking that she was cold or a bitch or a borg. Even Mel couldn't defend her.

She cringed.

The door rattled and tried to open. It banged into her heels and her head.

Rachel.

And of course if everything from Friday night was true then so were Rachel and her problems. Maybe this was something she could use to show people she wasn't the cold unfeeling bitch they thought.

Edie staggered out of the way and went further into the room.

"Edie?" Rachel's timid voice sounded round a crack in the door. "Are you OK?" she sounded terrified.

Edie suppressed the surge of irritation. The woman was a rabbit.

"Yes, I'm fine," Edie lied as she rubbed her bruised heels. "Come in. Come in."

She winced at the sound of her voice, she was back to sounding like a crazed Head Girl from a 1940s boarding school.

Rachel's head peered round the door and then her body followed. She scuttled to her desk.

"Good weekend?" Edie asked.

"Whaaa?" Rachel's strangled cry came along with a crash as she jumped at Edie's question and knocked over a stack of files.

"Your weekend? Was it good?" Edie repeated, her faux jolliness starting to strain.

"You're asking me about my weekend?" Rachel said.

"Yes," it was a simple enough question. It didn't take a law degree. "You sound like you've never been asked that question before."

144

"Well I haven't, by you." Rachel replied and then realising what she said covered her mouth quickly with both hands, locking the door after the horse had bolted.

"I'm asking now," Edie felt hot but she carried on through the increased tension.

"Good. Great. Fine." Rachel looked round wildly for escape.

Edie gave up. Obviously small talk with Rachel was not the way to redeem herself.

But she needed to do something.

Throughout the morning, Edie found herself staring at Rachel while she wracked her brains for some way to make amends, to balance the books.

She wears cheap suits because the money goes somewhere else. This thought flashed through Edie's head. The suit was less offensive suddenly. That probably explained the lack of hairstyle and general air of unkemptness.

All the money went on Timmy.

Money.

Timmy.

Redemption.

The three thoughts collided and there it was; what Edie could do to redeem herself in people's eyes. Not only was she going to get Mel's parents back together, she was going to raise a huge amount of money to help Timmy.

Perfect. It was a win-win situation.

Now she just needed to come up with a kick-ass fundraising idea.

But how do you raise a load of money in a week? Well less than a week.

Because let's be honest, she thought, she had to show a little bit of progress before the next Ghost. It was due the day before the wedding and she wanted to be able to stand in front of it and point out all the good, meaningful things she had done that week.

Saved a marriage.

Check.

Raised money for a boy with Cerebral Palsy and Cystic Fibrosis. Check. Check. Check.

Now she knew what she was doing, Edie hit the internet and started researching.

There, it only took a few minutes but she'd found it. There was absolutely no training required and a place was available if she promised to rake in a load of money.

Quickly she set up a fundraising page and drafted a number of different emails to send out with the link attached.

Edie glanced over at Rachel.

It wouldn't be good to have her around when the emails went out. The whole idea of being there when Rachel fawned over her for what she was doing made her skin crawl.

Edie set the emails to go out at different times, when she logged out that evening on the way to see her mum.

She smiled.

An open mouthed Rachel watched Edie as she packed up at five thirty.

"Close your mouth, Rachel. It isn't dignified for a solicitor to look like a goldfish."

Rachel closed her mouth with a snap. Edie smiled to herself. There were some things that she was still in charge of.

There was a flash of memory, the little house with toys strewn over the floor.

She was a horrible person.

Edie turned to say something to Rachel; she needed to sooth the slap she'd just delivered.

She tried to smile but Rachel was hiding behind her hair again. A wave of irritation rose in Edie and threatened to overwhelm her. It didn't matter how good a person Rachel was, she was still incredibly irritating and wet.

Edie slammed the locks on her briefcase, picked it up and

banged out of the room before she could do any more damage. This week was about making amends not making things worse, but she couldn't seem to stop messing things up.

"I've signed up for the fundraising," she said to herself. "I'm in credit. And I'm going to stay there."

She stalked down the corridor towards the lifts, glaring at anyone who looked her way. People cowered against walls, making sure they didn't touch her as she passed.

Good, she thought. Don't touch me. Don't come near me. I'm poison.

Battling through London to Liverpool Street tried her patience further. The tube was packed. It was a humid, sweaty mass of people who were all getting in her way.

Really, the bus was a much better option. She pushed her way onto an Eastbound Central line train. When you were on the bus you could get off at any point, rather than feel trapped. Out of control.

A portly man whose neck rolled over the collar of his shirt, was dressed in a loud pinstripe suit, refused to move further down the carriage. Edie, squished between him and the middle pole, elbowed him in the kidneys.

"I'm so sorry," she said as he humphed and shuffled his way down the centre aisle.

Ha, she thought as he nodded and scowled at her. She knew he knew that she'd done it on purpose. Commuting in London was a series of small petty wins.

Edie spent the rest of the journey staring at the ceiling so she didn't see any stray glitter happen to alight on commuter's shoulders.

Surely there should be some sort of dispensation for travelling on public transport?

At Liverpool Street train station she threaded her way through the crowds and bought herself a ticket at the self-service machine.

Scanning the boards, she rushed to platform thirteen and got on the train to Chelmsford.

It was another jam-packed commuter train, and it trundled out of the station and headed through east London, past the Olympic Park and out into the Essex countryside.

As they flashed past Gidea Park, Edie could feel herself becoming younger and younger. She didn't need Ghosts visiting her at night, not when she was on this train. This train carried her own ghosts for her.

She swayed with the carriage, shoulder to shoulder to the young woman one side of her and the middle-aged man the other. She could almost see her past play out in front of her.

There, in those seats where a harried mother gripped her toddler on her knee under the disapproval of the businessman across from her, were the ghosts of all the family Christmas visits to London when she was a child.

Coming home surrounded by huge bags of shopping, dozing on her dad's shoulder with his hand stroking her back as she came down from a sugar high from too many sweets and their annual Christmas show.

And near the pole where a woman stood reading her Kindle, was the ghost of little Edie the year they'd been to see the Nutcracker. She'd pirouetted up and down the aisles. And used the poles as ballet barres.

"Watch me, Daddy. Watch me!"

She could almost hear her voice in the silence of the carriage. And Dad's face had been wreathed in smiles. Mum had tutted saying that she was 'making an exhibition of herself' and she was 'getting her dress dirty.'

Edie looked over to a double seat where two girls were sharing headphones and staring at one phone screen. They could've been her and Mel.

Edie remembered their faces being caked in make-up an inch thick, going 'up town' on a Saturday. Their handbags would be

148

bulging with their illicit packets of cigarettes and stolen bottles of wine. They'd try to pretend that they were eighteen or even twenty-one, hoping that they would be able to get into bars and clubs. Sometimes they lucked out, but more often they'd be on a train home working out what made up story they would tell in school the next day.

Or there were the afternoons they would be trawling up and down Oxford Street, in and out of shops. Arms full of clothes to try on in packed changing rooms.

Edie wondered when she'd last had a day out like that with Mel. Trying on wedding and bridesmaid dresses didn't count.

And, with her heart aching, there were the ghosts of her and Tom. Right there by that couple in the double seat, holding hands.

She'd be leaning against Tom, bracing herself to spend a weekend with her mother. And then Tom would hold her on the way home as she breathed a sigh of relief for surviving. Her mum's bitter words still ring in her ears, gradually soaking into her skin.

Edie turned away from the couple, rubbing her chest. Tom had made her feel happy and loved; she remembered how she couldn't wait to be home with him.

No, she stared out of the window at the green fields that blurred and smeared as they rattled past them. She didn't need some precocious child Ghost to show her the past. She carried it with her. It was etched upon her soul and in her heart. It was like a veil that she carried behind her, that wrapped around her. One she'd tried to ignore.

The tannoy squealed and the announcer said the next stop was Chelmsford.

Edie stood and grabbed her briefcase from the shelf above the seats. The whole time she tried to keep her face hidden.

That was the other problem with this train. It wasn't just a magical time machine that showed her the past. It sometimes produced someone from that past; an old school mate, a teacher, one of Mum's friends.

149

Edie snorted because of course they never saw the successful lawyer, all the sacrifices she'd made. No, they still saw the ballerina, the teenager, the woman in love.

And that was why she had to make a run for it as fast as possible. Pushing her way off the train, she allowed the crowd of commuters to carry her down the stairs past the Essex Cricket Club notice and out to the barriers.

Now if she could just make it to the taxi rank.

"Edie? Edie!"

The shout was from near the ticket office. It was the bugle call of the blast from the past.

She was busted.

Edie stopped and turned her head. There, hurrying towards her was her Mum's neighbour, Beattie Jones.

Should she ignore her?

But Edie could see her mother's face if she heard about it, which she would. You didn't make a bad impression in front of the neighbours. It wasn't done. Edie didn't want any more of the silent disapproval that she knew would envelop her when she asked her mum the question she'd come to ask.

"Hello," Beattie air kissed her cheek noisily. "I didn't know you were coming home. Your mother never said when I saw her this morning."

"I'm surprising her," Edie started to move off and round the building as she spoke, heading towards the taxi rank and trying to shake off Beattie's determined friendliness.

"Well let me give you a lift. The car's just in the car park." Beattie pointed to the multi-storey car park behind the station.

Edie stopped dead and barely felt the person bumping into her from behind and the soft swear words under their breath. What could she do? It wasn't as if it was out of Beattie's way, she lived next door after all. And if she refused, her mother would never let here hear the end of it. And then there would be that awkward parade of the taxi and Beattie's car all going in the same direction,

150

stopping behind each other at traffic lights. Edie could almost see the hurt look in Beattie's eyes if she caught a cab and turned and looked back to see her.

There were some weeks when you just couldn't catch a break.

"That would be lovely, Beattie." she said.

"Thank you", she said twenty minutes later and through gritted teeth as she got out of the car.

The twenty minute journey had been filled with Beattie's tales of the minutiae of her life plus all the comings and goings of pretty much the whole population of Little Hanningfield. People Edie had forgotten about or had wanted to forget about or had never known in the first place.

She was getting soft.

She should've withered Beattie with a single comment. Taken her down with a well-placed barb. But at home, it wasn't just that people saw you differently. It peeled layers of you back to an earlier incarnation. A better Edie? She wasn't sure but she knew she couldn't hurt this woman.

"Have a lovely time," Beattie said eventually letting her go having chatted for another five minutes after they'd got out of the car.

So much for trying to surprise Mum.

Their voices had made her peer out the window; Edie had noticed her.

And now she looked over at the house, where her mum was standing on the doorstep with a fixed grin Edie knew well. It was the one that was used in front of neighbours when she didn't want them to know anything was wrong.

Edie watched as her mum waved to Beattie as she waited for Edie to walk through the little wooden gate.

"Edie, this is a surprise."

It was said loudly, so Beattie could hear. Edie knew the drill; her mum was making sure that Beattie knew she'd been surprised.

Edie leant down to kiss her cheek but her mum hardly reached up for it. Instead Edie ended up kissing the air by her ear.

Her skin crawled as she walked through the front door. Any happiness she had, which wasn't much, felt as if it was being leeched out of her. A mantle of misery seemed to fall on her shoulders.

What had happened to the happy family home that she'd seen with the Ghost? It was the same bricks and mortar. The same walls, admittedly the décor had changed, but this had once been a home. Now it was merely a house.

Edie looked at the photos on the walls, the ones she'd seen on Friday night.

None of them had her dad in them. He'd been airbrushed out of her life. He wasn't even in photos from when she was a child and this had been a home.

Their home; they'd lived here together as a family.

But he left us the house.

Slowly Edie's lawyer brain started to turn.

If he left the house to them, her Mum's story that he didn't care about them didn't add up. And how had her mum kept the house going all that time? Her part time job wouldn't have been enough. Had he cared?

Or did Mum have a better lawyer?

But of course she had. She'd had Hilary Satis as her lawyer. And Edie had been tutored on the way she worked. Take no prisoners, just take the money.

Damn it, why didn't she remember more? She'd been a teenager so she should have some memories but when she looked for them they weren't there. One minute Dad had been there and then he hadn't, but none of the financial issues that she knew should happen in a divorce had been obvious. Just the sudden entrance of Ms Satis in their lives.

Why didn't she remember?

Edie followed her mum to the kitchen.

"I hope you said thank you to Beattie for giving you a lift," her mum said as she tied an apron round her waist. "And I wished you told me you were coming. You'll just have to do with an omelette as that is what I was going to have."

Edie watched her mum pull the eggs from a very well stocked fridge.

She knew even if she had called they would be eating the same thing. Her mum believed in routine.

"You'll never believe who I saw in the village yesterday? That Justin Douglas. He's lost most of his hair and he's gone to fat. I'm glad you never got involved with him. Something not nice about that family."

Edie grabbed the onions and started chopping. The sound of the knife on the wooden board a comforting counterpoint to her mother's words.

Her mum rehashed all the gossip Edie had just heard from Beattie.

Edie watched her mum's hands dance as she talked. Why hadn't she moved away? Why had she stayed here in this house, a constant reminder of her failed marriage?

Why hadn't Edie asked any of these questions before? Why had she believed her mother's story without checking any of it?

Because she hadn't wanted to know the answers.

She watched as her mum put the dishes on the table and then Edie poured some wine. She found herself mirroring her mum as they both straightened the place mats so they were lined up with the cutlery and condiments.

Edie sat down quickly.

She moved the fork to the left so it wasn't completely aligned.

They sat in silence for a moment before they both picked up their cutlery. For a few minutes the only sound was scrape of knives on the plates.

It was loud in Edie's ears, and getting louder.

It was now or never. She had to do it.

"Mum..." Edie took a deep breath, suddenly scared. It felt as if this were the line between before and after. Nothing would be

153

the same once she asked this question.

But what would change, really? It wasn't as if they were close. And what did she have to be scared about? Her father had already abandoned her; it wasn't as if there could be anything worse.

"Yes?" her mum said without raising her eyes from her plate. Edie watched her put the exact proportions of omelette and vegetable on the fork so that it constituted a perfect mouthful.

"What exactly happened between you and Dad?" Edie rushed it out.

Her mother's fork halted in mid air between the plate and mouth. She looked up and met Edie's eyes briefly before dropping them again.

Edie held her breath, her knife and fork left forgotten on the plate.

"I don't want to talk about him. He left us. That is all you need to know." Her mum said it as if that was it. There was nothing else to be said. Edie could see her mum's hand shaking slightly as she put the fork down on her plate and reached for her glass of wine.

"No, I need to know. Why did he never want to see me?" Edie had inherited the same tone of voice from her mother. She asked her question in the same implacable tone.

Edie saw the wine shimmering in her mum's glass as she took a big slug of it and swallowed.

"Mum. Why?" Edie wasn't letting it go.

She needed to know.

The glass wobbled. The wine sloshed up the sides and over the top of the glass and her mum crumpled.

It was strange; one minute her mum had been the straight, no-nonsense woman Edie had always known. The next she was like a balloon with the air let out. Edie was shocked. It was as if she had no foundations. Nothing had been holding her up, but hot air.

"Please, Edie. I don't want to talk about it," she looked scared and shrunken.

Edie's stomach swooped. What was happening? She still needed to know.

"Mum, did Dad ever send me stuff after he left?" She tried not to look at the drawer in the dresser, where she knew the letters and parcels were locked.

But she could feel the anger flooding into her again. She needed to keep calm otherwise her mum wouldn't tell her. But this was her life, a part that had been hidden from her.

"How did you know?" Her mum's voice was quavering.

Edie saw her glance at the dresser drawer.

Chapter 15

Edie felt like she'd been slapped. She felt herself stiffen. It was true. What the ghost had shown her was true. Which meant she couldn't ignore any of it. It meant people really did think she was the Ice Queen... But it also meant that her dad hadn't left her.

The whole of her world shifted.

"Why?" She could feel the cracks that the Ghosts were making in her heart stretch wider. She wanted to know. "Why did you hide them?"

Her mother didn't say anything. She stared down at the table and then, with a big breath, pushed herself up out of her chair. She suddenly looked like an old woman, she staggered a bit as she went to a pot on the sideboard and got out a small key from inside it.

Her hands were shaking as she opened the drawer.

Edie could see that it was full, so packed with packages and envelopes that it stuck slightly and had to be wiggled to get it free.

Edie put her hand over her mouth.

"But..." she whispered. She stared at the proof that she hadn't been left. That she had never been forgotten.

"Take them and then go." Her mother was starting to get her solidity back, refilling with air and, much like Edie when she felt scared, she went on the offensive.

Edie looked up at her mum, struggling to stop staring at the treasure displayed to her.

"Why?" she asked again.

"Your father left us. We didn't need someone like that in our lives. We did OK." It sounded more like a question to Edie, than a statement. "Why do you need him now? You never needed him before."

"He's my dad." Edie said. Why couldn't her mum understand?

Her mum pursed her lips together, then spat out.

"Just take them."

Edie couldn't stay. She was struggling to at look her mum. She might love her, but she didn't like her very much at that moment.

She grabbed a spare canvas bag she had in her briefcase and started stuffing the envelopes and packages into it. The handwriting looked so familiar even though she hadn't seen it for years. She wanted to linger over them.

No, she wouldn't cry. Not yet.

The bag was full before the drawer was empty. Silently her mum got her another canvas bag. Edie took it without a word.

When the bags were full, Edie called a cab.

Her mum sat back down at the table and carried on drinking her wine but not touching her food. She refused to make eye contact. They sat in silence waiting for the taxi to arrive.

The canvas bags propped against Edie's chair were like an elephant in the room. Edie touched them with a finger to check they were still there.

There was a beep on a car horn; thank God the taxi had arrived. Edie stood up, grabbed the canvas bags and her briefcase and stalked to the front door. She didn't care if her mum followed or not.

She heard the scraping of the chair and she paused at the front door and looked back at her mum following her.

"Goodbye," Edie said.

She was about to turn around and walk out but there was something on her mum's cheek.

Her mum came closer and caught in the hall light was the glint of pink glitter.

How had it got there? Maybe it had fallen from one of the cards onto an envelope and blown up to settle on her face. It winked at her. She could feel the weight of its expectations.

Edie really didn't want to be the bigger person, but she had to be.

Reluctantly she bent forward and pressed her cheek to her mother's. It felt soft and fragile like tissue paper. She closed her eyes against the tears that brimmed up.

She would not cry. She wouldn't.

She walked out the door and got in the cab and stared straight ahead without looking back. The canvas bag handles were wrapped round her fingers.

The train ride back to London was as full of ghosts as the earlier one.

As she read the work files she'd brought with her, Edie could see from the corner of her eye a happy little girl pirouetting up the aisle. Reflected in the window was a scared teenager just starting to build her wall against the world.

Edie cuddle the canvas bags to her side.

Edie climbed the stairs to her flat, the canvas bags banging against her legs.

Maybe she would just open one, she thought as she opened her front door. But how could she stop at one? Because what if that wasn't the one that explained it all? She walked into the living room and leant the stuffed bags against the sofa. They were bulging with her past. Out of place in her ordered world.

"I won't look at them", she said. "Not yet."

They scared her, but also fascinated her.

She stared at them again and then turned her back and went to bed.

Edie didn't brush her teeth for quite as long as she usually did. Or brush her hair as many times.

In bed she lay on her back and stared at the ceiling.

Ten minutes later, she sat up with a huff and punched her pillow into shape, turned it over to find the cool spot and then lay back down again.

Five minutes more and she put her right foot out from under the duvet.

Maybe I'm too warm, she thought. That's why I can't sleep.

But five minutes after that, she was still wide awake but now with a cold foot.

Edie found herself wriggling on the sheet looking for a comfortable place.

This was playing havoc with her sleep pattern. She expected it on Ghost visiting nights but not now.

Except that there was a ghost in the living room. Her ghost. And she wasn't going to be able to sleep until she'd dealt with it.

She sat up and pushed back the duvet.

She pulled on her robe and slippers. It was eleven o'clock, and she had work tomorrow. This wouldn't be a quick job. But she could either lie there and mither or she could go and deal with it. Either way she wasn't getting any sleep.

Edie strode into the living room. Her steps faltered as she saw the canvas bags full of her past, bags which could open up her future.

She definitely needed some help before she started on it.

She boiled the kettle and made herself a herbal tea and found her emergency chocolate supply, hidden at the back of the cupboard. Sod the newly cleaned teeth.

Armed and ready, she sat on the sofa and carefully started taking out all the envelopes and packages from the bags.

There were so many that she began by organising them into piles; letters and cards in one and packages in the other. She picked one up at random, the handwriting looked so familiar.

"Miss Edie Dickens" it said in precise block capitals. Her dad's writing.

She traced the down stroke on the D with her finger. But then she noticed the postmark.

They would all be postmarked. And if that was the case she could open them chronologically.

Her mother hadn't even bothered to take the brown wrapping off the parcels or the presents out of the jiffy bags. Their postmarks were there for Edie to see how they spanned back over the years. Here was the proof that she'd been looking for, the evidence that she had always been loved. That she hadn't been forgotten.

Tears welled up in her eyes, blurring her vision. She blinked them away and found the envelope with the earliest mark. It was dated a few days before her fourteenth birthday. Just after he'd stopped seeing her.

Her hands shook as she made a tear in the paper, and as she uncovered the card inside she saw it was covered in pink glitter.

Her hand dropped the half opened envelope and she turned and buried her face in the pillow, howling. Her heart felt as if it was tearing too.

Edie sat, surrounded by torn envelopes and wrapping paper with a pile of glitter covered cards carefully stacked beside her as the sun rose the next morning. There was a pile of gifts at her feet.

She'd started out calmly after her crying fit but as it went on she wanted to unwrap everything as fast as possible.

Now everything was open and she was left clutching a small jewellery box. It was what he'd wrapped for her twenty-first birthday. It was the last gift he'd sent.

Edie stared at it. This was her last link to him.

Slowly, she opened the box to see a fine gold chain with a locket nestled there. It was simple and classic.

Twenty-one year old Edie would've hated it.

But now, this Edie… it was perfect.

Her hands shook as she lifted it out. She turned the locket over to find words engraved on the back.

Happy 21st, Edie. With all my love, Dad x

The locket had a hinge and a small lock. Edie's fingers brushed the mechanism.

What would she find inside? A photo? Somehow opening it didn't feel right.

I'll open it when I find him, she thought as she put it on. It fell so that it nestled in the hollow of her throat; she stroked it with a finger.

The sun was streaming through the windows and she could hear the birds singing. It was early and she'd done none of the work she needed to, nor had she slept but strangely she felt better rested than she had in years.

Now the question was; could she find him?

A few minutes later as she stood in the shower and she shampooed her hair, she realised she couldn't wait any longer.

I'll phone Mum she thought. If I'm going to be haunted by Ghosts, then she can be haunted by me.

Edie started to wonder what her mother would think if she knew that her daughter was being haunted. She'd say it wasn't appropriate behaviour and what would the neighbours think.

But then an icy thought trickled down her spine. Maybe her mum had been haunted. And if she had and hadn't believed... hadn't changed, because it was obvious she hadn't learnt anything. Edie shivered as if the shower was icy.

She'd find her dad. She had to.

"Edie, can I have a word?" Edie looked up from her computer screen into the frowning face of Liz from HR.

Damn, she'd meant to go and sort out all that stuff about Rachel. Take some of it back, and soften it. Even if Rachel hadn't turned up for work this morning.

"If it's about the complaints I've made about Rachel, well I..." she started.

"Actually it is about a complaint Rachel's made about you." Liz interrupted and then quickly took a step back as if she expected

Edie to come out swinging.

"A complaint?" Edie repeated. Why was Rachel talking to HR about her?

"About me?" She checked again. She'd never had anyone complain about her before.

"Yes, Rachel seems upset that you have been exposing her private life to the whole office via a series of emails."

Edie felt as if she'd been attacked by a stuffed teddy bear that she'd thought was inanimate and benign but had turned feral overnight.

"She's complained about me?" Edie thought she'd better just check that Liz was really saying what Edie thought she was saying.

"Yes. She says that the emails you've been sending asking for sponsorship for your fundraising abseil tomorrow are a violation of her privacy."

"But I'm raising money on behalf of her kid!" Edie blurted out.

Liz looked apologetic.

"What can I say? Evidently she doesn't want the world to know about Timmy and she says that your emails listing his issues are causing her concern."

"So what do I do then? Apologise to her?" Edie could feel her lip turn up in a sneer. It seemed it didn't matter how nice you were trying to be to people, you just got smacked for it.

"It is a bit more complicated than that. I've checked the policy and she also brought up some issues around 'abusive language' and 'bullying.'" Edie could see Liz cringing as she listed each complaint.

So the teddy bear had claws and teeth, did she?

The old Edie wanted to go on the attack. Annihilate Rachel until nothing would be left but a smoking hole with scattered burned paper raining down.

She opened her mouth to say something, put her hand to her chest to gather strength and felt the unfamiliar weight of the locket that now sat in the hollow of her throat.

She closed her mouth on the hot words. She felt them back up like a traffic jam in her throat.

No. She couldn't. She wanted to. Why the silly girl was getting her knickers in a twist about a few words in an email, Edie didn't know. But she would be the bigger person.

Such nonsense over nothing.

"Fine. I can see that Rachel could've misconstrued some of my training techniques as uncompromising. She is obviously quite sensitive as we can tell from her issue with my fundraising."

"Oh." Liz stood looking shocked. Edie realised she'd been expecting the scorched earth response that she'd almost given.

She wondered if Liz had lost a bet with the rest of the HR team and that was why she'd been sent to confront Edie.

"So what do we do now?" Edie asked through her teeth. The hot words were still backed up in her and she held on to the locket to keep them there. "I've already raised quite a bit of money and pledged to the charity."

"I think it will be fine as long as you keep Rachel's name out of it and..." Liz paused again and then rushed out. "And I'm afraid the complaint goes on your record."

Edie gripped the locket harder. She could feel the edges cutting into her palm.

Damn, but this was hard.

"Fine." She said. "Is that all?"

She drew all the iciness she had left in her and wrapped it around herself like a robe. Hoping it would numb the hurt.

"Sure, Edie. Rachel thought it was best to take the rest of the week off and maybe we can all meet on Monday to decide what to do next?"

Edie nodded and waited for Liz to leave.

Monday. Well, she'd know where she stood come then. If she survived the wedding and the haunting. She kept hold of the locket as she went back to staring at the computer screen.

"Do you know how to get hold of Dad?" Edie asked without a preamble.

She'd managed to swallow back most of the words she'd wanted to say to Rachel and about her but it had blown her concentration.

That never happened to her.

So she'd taken the bull by the horns, and called her mother.

Edie hadn't forgiven her. She wasn't sure she could. She still had one hand clasped round the locket. She wondered if she'd have the shape of it and the engraving permanently etched onto her palm, in a reverse image.

"Why would I know where that good-for-nothing snake is?"

Obviously the past day had given her mum time to build up her defences. Edie wanted to shout down the phone that she'd stolen him from her. How could her mum call him a snake when he'd left her letters? Sent her cards and presents? When he'd tried to see her? But she couldn't say that.

"Mum." Edie's voice was quiet but anyone who'd worked for her would recognise it. It was her 'don't mess with me' voice. Her 'give me the house, the car, the children and the dog' voice.

There was silence for a moment on the other end of the phone. Edie let it grow. This was much easier to do when she didn't have to look her mother in the face. When she felt this angry, it was as much as she could do to even speak to her. But she was doing something; she needed to feel like she was moving forwards because after the chat with HR she felt like she was moving backwards.

She wasn't looking forward to the haunting on Friday. She shivered.

There was a sigh from her mum.

"No, I don't know where he is. It isn't like we're pen pals. But I suppose his mother will know."

"I have a grandmother?" Edie knew she'd had grandparents but her mother's parents were dead and she'd presumed her dad's were too. Another person she'd had taken away from her. The marks against her mother were growing. Edie could feel her hand trembling as she struggled to not shout or cry.

"If she's still alive, she never liked me," her mum said. "Have

164

you a pen?" she said it as if she were speaking to a stranger.

Edie grabbed a pen in time as her mum rattled off an address and phone number. Edie jotted it down. The address was in London, in Kensington. Only a few miles away.

"Thank you," she said absently and put the phone down without waiting for a response. She knew she needed to make peace with her mum if only because it would make an already hellish wedding even worse if they weren't talking. But not yet. Pink glitter or no pink glitter. Ghosts or no Ghosts.

She sat at her desk, staring blankly at Rachel's untidy desk. What did she do now?

She could phone up and announce that she was her grand-daughter. And give the old woman a heart attack.

But that was the same issue if she just turned up on her door-step. Edie could imagine the talk if she ended up scaring a little old woman to death. It was the sort of thing the office would probably expect.

What she needed to do was some reconnaissance. Her hand brushed the paper where she'd written the address. She traced it with a finger. This was scarier than the fundraising and Ghosts combined.

Chapter 16

At precisely six o'clock she left the office and headed for the station to take the Central line to Notting Hill Gate. Edie focused her energy on dodging the slower walkers that littered the pavement.

Did they deliberately step out in front of her? By the time she got to the steps to the ticket hall she was itching with impatience.

Her dad could be visiting her grandmother right this moment and she would miss him by mere minutes because she was stuck behind a tourist who was gawping at buildings older than their country.

Bloody typical.

OK, so it wasn't likely that he was there. In fact she knew it was a silly dream that he would be visiting his mum at the same time she was going there. But, he could be. That was the point. There were now possibilities where before there had been none.

Her heart gave a tug as it stretched to cradle the first dream it had held in a long time.

Did they know that her mum had kept everything from her?

Would they speak to her? Would they like her?

Would they leave her again?

Crap. With dreams and possibilities came heartache.

"This isn't your usual route." A voice came from behind her, and whispered in her ear.

What? she thought as her foot slipped and she started to topple down the stairs.

"Hold on!" Jack said.

A large hand gripped her elbow and kept her upright.

"Sorry. Didn't know you'd fallen for me." He laughed as he held her arm all the way down the steps.

His hand suddenly felt like the only real thing in the world. It almost pushed out her dream from her heart and replaced it with another.

No.

She shivered with attraction and then shook with anger. How had he got so near? She caught his scent over the stuffy and redolent tube station.

He made her feel too much when he was so close. He made her want that second dream.

"Thanks," she said as she wrenched her arm away and all but ran to the ticket barriers.

But he didn't leave her side. Jack Twist had long rugby playing legs that kept him alongside her.

Maybe if she ignored him and didn't encourage him he'd lose interest. Because his words rang too close to the reality. She was falling for him.

He walked behind her down the escalator. Now she knew he was there she could keep track of him by the way her body reacted to his, she was attuned to his frequency.

Radio Twist.

But she was strong. She could fight it.

Like a small child she kept her head firmly turned away from him.

Concentrate Edie, she told herself. Think of the bigger picture.

"Dad. Mel's wedding. Tomorrow's fundraising," she whispered it like a mantra.

They stood shoulder to shoulder on the platform.

"Kissing Jack," slipped into her whisper.

Bugger.

Had he heard?

Edie found herself picking at her thumbnail, worrying it with her mouth.

"I've noticed you do that when you're nervous," he said.

She quickly took her thumb from her mouth.

"Now I'm wondering what could possibly make you scared about a tube journey. Or is just me that makes you like that?"

She glanced over to find him smiling down at her.

"Nervous? As if," she couldn't help herself replying.

How old was she, using a comeback like that? Ten?

Thankfully the tube arrived in a rush of warm air.

I'll get away from him, Edie thought. She'd weave her way through the carriage while he was still trying to fit those perfect hulking shoulders through the door.

She had it bad.

She waited for the usual surge of people behind her, the push that would lift her into the carriage and away.

Where were they? Looking over her shoulder she found she had her own personal bodyguard.

Jack stood behind her holding a large swathe of people back by those self same shoulders, so that she wasn't crushed. He was acting as her breakwater.

He winked.

She turned back to the front, her face feeling hot.

Tube stations in the summer got horribly warm.

Forgetting her plan, she found herself corralled into the small doorway at the end of the carriage. There was no weaving, just Jack pressed up against her.

Damn him and his winks.

"So where were we?" he said looming over her.

Was there any air in here?

"We," she emphasised the word, "weren't anywhere."

At the same time she tried to hold herself as far away from him

168

as was possible in the crush.

Why was there no air coming through the window? She didn't care if it made her hair messy. She needed air.

The train took off from the station and the air arrived, warm and muggy. She felt hotter.

Damn it.

"That's a pity." He leaned closer as she leant back against the momentum of the tube. "I wouldn't mind being somewhere with you."

Hot. She was very very hot. It was the air. That was the reason her skin was suddenly on fire.

She opened her mouth to reply. Then shut it with a snap.

Nothing.

She couldn't think of a single thing except how, with every shake of the train and every clatter that made it sway and bring them together, her body remembered how much it liked to be pressed up against him.

She'd lost control of her mind when she started seeing Ghosts. Then she'd lost control of her work, bloody Rachel. And now she was losing control of her body.

She should be thinking about her dad. That was why she was on this train, but all she could think was how much she wanted Jack to kiss her.

And more.

Edie felt Jack lean down and she had a flash of an X-rated image of the two of them on the tube breaking she didn't know how many laws.

He was going to kiss her, wasn't he?

If she'd thought she'd been hot before it was nothing compared to the scorching heat that engulfed her. She glanced up under her lashes.

Damn it, he was only going to speak to her.

No, that was good. Talk good. Kiss bad.

"So where do you think we should go?" he asked, earning tuts and dirty looks from everyone around them.

Didn't he know better than to break the rules of the underground?

But there were so many rules she wanted to break with him. A treacherous inner Edie let another vignette past her defences.

Jack pressing her up against the window, her legs wrapped round his waist…

"We aren't going anywhere." Her voice was hoarse with want but she raised her head and glared at him.

I hope he can't read minds, she thought.

He smiled down at her, and it had enough of a naughty spark in it for her to wonder if he could. It would be just her luck; Ghosts and mind reading men.

"Well, they might arrest us for what I want to do if we stayed here," he said.

What? He could read minds.

Her heart slammed up to her throat and then dropped to her stomach.

Her mouth flew open in shock. His finger pushed her chin up so her mouth closed and then pressed it briefly against her lips.

She could taste him.

He raised an eyebrow.

The rest of the journey passed in a tense, taut silence.

Images of their naked and naughty alter egos kept appearing in her head every time his legs brushed hers. The muscles underneath his suit flexed as he braced himself against the train's movement.

She almost moaned as she imagined him naked.

She could feel the heat from his body; she wanted to melt into him.

His chest was inches from her face. She stared at a button and her fingers itched to open it and take a taste.

This was out of control, she thought as she fanned herself with a hand.

And Jack's words were only making it worse.

The train rattled into Notting Hill Gate station.

She breathed a sigh of relief. Disappearing fathers, lost grand-mothers and that damn fundraising abseil she'd signed up for were easier to deal with than Jack Twist.

She began her commuter shuffle, the special penguin waddle everyone does to get in the optimum position to get off.

Jack was in the way. Again.

He was a solid wall and she couldn't get past him.

"Excuse me, please." She spat it out; she couldn't help it.

It was that or pin him against the carriage and have her wicked way.

"Relax, Slow. I'm getting off here too." He smiled down at her. "We are going somewhere together it seems."

He was doing his charming thing again.

The universe, she decided was definitely making her pay.

Turned on and seething, which was very uncomfortable, she waited for him to move.

It felt an eternity before the door opened, although she knew it was only seconds. Passengers started to get off.

Jack had turned so his back was to her but not before winking at her again.

I will not hit him, she told herself.

But will you kiss him?

No. She wouldn't be kissing him either.

Edie stared at his beautiful broad back and followed him off the train.

He was so close she could touch him.

Dangerous thoughts.

She held back, letting people get between them.

As he got further away she started to breathe better.

Started thinking clearer.

She was here to find her dad, not to flirt with Jack Twist or have X-rated commuting fantasies about him.

Jack turned his head and looked behind him.

Hide! She thought.

Ducking behind an overweight man in front of her, she bent her knees to ensure she was completely hidden.

The things she's been driven to.

Jack's smell was replaced in her nose. Her chosen shield had been on the tube a bit too long.

Breathing through her mouth to stop the body odour smell hitting her too hard, she realised she should've appreciated Jack's personal hygiene more.

Peeking round the man's shoulder, she spotted Jack shaking his head and turning round to carry on away from the platform.

Yes, she'd lost him.

She accidentally caught the eye of her human shield.

Raising an eyebrow in his direction and looking down her nose at him, she stepped out from the slipstream of his stench and walked away.

Jack was still in front of her; he was too tall to be swallowed by any crowd. So much bigger and broader than the people around him, she saw people do double takes as he took the escalator two steps at a time.

Now she was outside of his magnetic zone, she relaxed.

Nice arse, she couldn't help but think.

Watching the way Jack climbed the stairs would be a successful spectator sport.

She wanted to slap a honey blonde in a skimpy summer dress who turned to watch him from the down escalator.

In the ticket hall she lost sight of Jack as she fumbled for her Oyster card.

No, she didn't miss him. No. Not at all.

She was still telling herself that as she climbed the stairs out of the station.

She looked round and frowned.

Crap. She'd been so busy thinking about Jack she'd come out of completely the wrong entrance. Looking across the four-lane street clogged with cars, she rolled her shoulders.

Concentrate, Edie.

Taking a deep breath she walked back down into the station. Finding the right exit, she walked tiredly up the steps and popped up on the opposite side of the street she'd just been looking at.

She had to get it together.

"Dad. It is about Dad." she said as she strode down Kensington Church Street, past restaurants and various antique shops plus a pub that was covered in hanging baskets.

How come she didn't remember her grandmother?

How can you forget a grandmother? She'd been thirteen when Dad had left. So there was plenty of time for her to have made some memories of a grandmother.

There were so many gaps in her life; she was wondering why this one could hurt as well. Surely she should be used to living in a Swiss cheese world.

She reached the junction of her grandmother's street and looked around, searching for clues. Wracking her memories for something familiar.

No, she'd never been here before.

She wouldn't have forgotten this, surely?

The large white stucco houses were like something out of a high-end property magazine or a Richard Curtis movie. Imposing.

Granny must have some serious money, she thought.

Slowly she walked down the street counting off the numbers.

She was close. And as she ticked the house numbers her feet started to go slower.

And then there it was, faster than she expected but years too late.

Number one hundred and fifty six.

It had gateposts, a small front garden with carefully manicured hedges. Gravel was scattered and raked between them instead of grass. The path pointed like an arrow to a shiny black door with brass fittings.

Edie knew she would be able to see her face in the doorknob. The plate to the side of the door held two buttons.

Now she just had to walk up the path and press the correct one. It was really that easy in principle.

Nothing to it.

Edie stayed standing at the gate.

What was she going to say? She was usually better prepared than this. She would have practiced every possible variation. And some impossible ones, just to be ready.

She should have been rehearsing on the train but oh no, she'd let her inner hormonal teen lust after Jack Twist instead.

"Hi, I'm your granddaughter." She whispered it under her breath. Testing the words.

Well it had a punchy immediacy and truth to it. But it if she wasn't careful it could cause a little old lady to keel over.

"Hi, you don't know me but I'm looking for Charlie Dickens," she said and stared hard at the house.

Could he be there, in one of those rooms?

OK it was a bit generic. It might work or she could get the door slammed in her face for being a salesperson.

Or a gold-digger.

She started biting what remained of her left thumbnail.

She turned her back on the house. She needed to concentrate. This could be a one shot deal. She took her thumb from her mouth and rubbed the spot above her heart.

One chance. She felt sick.

"Hi, I'm Edie Dickens and I need to speak with you..." had possibilities. And if her grandmother knew about her then she'd know immediately and Edie wouldn't have to finish an unfinishable sentence. And if she didn't know about her, well someone with the same surname would give her pause, surely? This was so confusing.

She had to do it, and do it now.

She span round on her heel and straight into the chest she'd been ogling only minutes before.

"Are you taking me up on my offer?"

She had opened her mouth to say, are you stalking me, but

instead she found herself wanting to say 'yes' to the question asked in a deep, velvety and seductive voice.

Jack was standing with his hands on his hips, smiling at her.

What the hell?

"No, I'm not. I'm here to see someone. So I think you'd better go away. This is private property. And stop stalking me."

Edie wanted to stamp her foot. She couldn't think when he was around and somehow he'd found her. Maybe he'd followed her from the tube? But surely he couldn't be too good at hiding. He was so big.

"Stalking you? I'm standing outside my flat and I see you hanging around the gate. What am I supposed to think?"

The laughter faded from his face as he said it. The look that was left was similar to the one she'd witnessed at the rugby party.

Right after he'd called her a cold bitch.

She could feel her face scald with embarrassment.

She drew herself up as tall as possible but then what he'd said hit her and she deflated slightly.

"Your flat?" she asked, screwing up her face in confusion.

He nodded, frowning down at her.

Surely that couldn't be right.

She peered past him. Two doorbells. Of course, well that explained it. But what were the chances?

"I've come to see your neighbour." Edie said decisively. She needed to claw back control of this situation.

"Mrs Pirrip?" he asked.

Pirrip? That didn't sound right. Surely she'd be Dickens, like her?

That was the sort of thing Mum would've told her, surely?

But Edie had put the phone down, hadn't she?

Because she hadn't want to talk to her any more. Great move, Dickens.

Control. Take control, that's what was needed.

And if she didn't have it... Fake it until you make it.

She nodded at Jack as if Mrs Pirrip was exactly who she was supposed to be seeing.

Edie wouldn't ask any more questions than she needed to, at least until she'd figured it out.

Best not to let on to Jack how confused she was.

She didn't need to give him any more power over her; of course he didn't know that with one look she would end up at his feet like all the other women.

No, he didn't need to know that.

And maybe this Mrs Pirrip, whoever she was, would know where her grandmother or father was.

She stared at Jack, willing him out of the way.

He looked at her with increasing wariness but eventually he stepped aside.

Edie wonder what was the statistical probability of Jack Twist living in the very house that her grandmother was supposed to live in. She knew that it was low. Astronomically low. Lottery winning low.

She'd think about it all later. She needed to focus.

She marched up the path as purposefully as she could, but with her stomach clenched and her knees quivering.

At least, she thought, I'm not going to give an old lady a heart attack.

But Mrs Pirrip might know something, a forwarding address maybe. Edie had a burning need to know, to fill one of the holes in her life.

Of course, Jack came with her.

"Are you sure you want to do this?" he asked, waiting beside her as she rang the bell.

"I'm not casing the joint," she said pressing hard on the buzzer.

Focus, Edie. This was about finding Dad.

The door opened and a slim, grey haired, very well dressed older lady stood inside holding the door and staring at her quizzically.

"Yes?" she said and then her expression cleared and she beamed when she saw Jack behind Edie.

"Jack, my dear. I see you've brought me your friend for tea." The lady turned back to look at Edie from top to toe. "And she's just how you described her. Beautiful."

What?

Edie had her mouth open to interrupt her and say one of the statements that she'd been practising but with these words she turned to look at Jack.

What had he been saying? Surely he hadn't been talking about her?

He was almost as pink as the ridiculous lining of his suit.

At long last, he didn't look all cool and collected. So he'd been chatting with his neighbour about her, huh?

Edie could feel a little smile building up inside her; it began to pull at the side of her mouth.

Interesting.

But the distraction meant she lost any chance to tell Mrs Pirrip she had got it wrong. Edie had come under her own steam.

Edie wasn't sure how but she found herself ushered into the flat and then sitting next to Jack on a sofa.

The sofa had been well worn. The stuffing had settled so that although she tried to sit at the opposite end of the sofa, she and Jack leaned into each other.

The half smile was frozen on her mouth.

How had she lost control of this all over again? The reins were slipping through her fingers and she felt like things were galloping out of control.

"Well dear, I'm so glad that you're here." Mrs Pirrip came back in with a tea tray.

What was Edie supposed to do, now? This wasn't what she'd planned.

She watched the old lady as she sat opposite them. Did she look like her?

Jack nudged her.

He had a very sharp elbow when it dug her in the ribs. She rubbed the spot and jabbed him back.

Her elbow hit what felt like concrete.

"Thank you, Mrs Pirrip. But actually that isn't why I'm here. It was just a coincidence that Jack and I…" she trailed off when she realised she was going off topic. She took a big breath.

"I need to ask you a question," she said.

Jack snorted. She stopped herself from jabbing an elbow into his side again. She'd have a bruise on it as it was.

She'd show him; did he really think the world revolved round him?

She waited for Mrs Pirrip to start pouring the tea.

She took a deep breath.

Here goes nothing.

"I'm looking for Mrs Dickens, Charles Dickens' mother."

When said like that it sounded nonsensical. She could feel Jack go still beside her, she waited for another nudge in her ribs, but there wasn't one.

Mrs Pirrip's cup rattled as she put it down quickly.

"I haven't been called Mrs Dickens in a long time." The lady pursed her lips as she whispered it and then she frowned. "But why are you looking for me?"

Chapter 17

Edie stared at the woman. This was her. This was her grandmother. Everything went blurry, she blinked away the tears that were starting in her eyes. She had to keep it together.

"I'm Edie." she said it quietly, keeping her fingers crossed that this woman, her grandmother, knew who she was. She could feel all the new pink parts of her heart swell outwards in hope.

The older parts contracted, waiting for the next blow to fall.

"Edie?" Mrs Pirrip's voice shook and her eyes brightened with tears. "Edwina. Oh, my dear." Her hand reached out towards Edie.

Edie's hand automatically flew up to grasp it.

Her grandmother's nails were perfectly manicured.

Edie's were all bitten nails and flaking polish.

No. She snatched her hand back and sat on it. It should be perfect. She needed it to be perfect.

Mrs Pirrip's hand fell into her lap and the smile dropped from her face.

Edie could feel her face burning.

She'd ruined it. She poisoned everything. Why couldn't she be like other people?

All the questions she had bubbled up, clamouring for a chance to be asked. But where did she start? How could she start?

"Where's my dad?" It came out like the question of a little girl.

Her voice wobbled. Her vision blurred again.

But then there was a hand on her back. It rubbed in circular movements. Soothing her. Keeping her from completely breaking down. It kept her grounded.

"Charlie? He's in Dubai." Mrs Pirrip said. Or maybe Edie should call her Grandma?

Dubai?

Why wasn't he here?

Edie didn't realise how firmly that dream of seeing her dad now, today, had settled in her heart. She felt as if she'd lost him all over again.

Which was silly as she'd lost him years ago.

The pink parts shrank back behind the older dark parts of her heart.

"Maybe I should leave?" Jack said quietly.

Edie realised the hand on her back was his.

He carried on rubbing even as he said it.

She didn't want him to stop. He couldn't leave; that touch was the only thing grounding her, making her feel less alone.

Mrs Pirrip, her grandmother, looked startled when Jack spoke and then upset, her hands clutching compulsively. She turned to Jack, panicked.

Edie realised they both needed him to stay.

Jack would be the very solid no man's land across which they could meet each other safely. A rugby-playing chaperone.

"Stay. Please." Edie whispered.

She'd deny it tomorrow at work, of course. Threaten him with some serious damage if he told anyone. But tonight, here, right now, she needed him.

"Yes," Mrs Pirrip agreed.

They smiled tentatively at each other.

Then there was silence. It was drawn out, pulling the strings that connected them all tightly.

"What do you know?" Mrs Pirrip asked Edie, cutting into it.

180

Releasing the tension.

She was watching Edie closely, as she perched on the edge of her chair, staring at her. Drinking her in.

Edie shrugged and lifted her hands and then clasped them tightly to stop them fluttering helplessly.

"Nothing." Her voice broke as she said it. "Nothing." That sounded better, stronger.

Jack's hand on her back radiated strength to her.

Mrs Pirrip raised her hand again. It was tentative, as if she expected to be rejected again.

Edie released her hands and grasped it.

It was cool and dry and fragile.

When was the last time she'd held anyone's hand? It must have been Tom. But when was the last time she'd held Mum's hand? When was the last time she'd held the hand of someone related to her?

She clasped it eagerly.

Underneath the fragility she could feel strength as it squeezed hers.

"Oh, dear heart," her grandmother said on a breath.

Edie held her hand tighter, clutching at it like a lifeline.

I'm going to crack, Edie thought.

She could feel the turmoil and feelings welling up pushing against her barriers, wanting to break through. Her heart was swelling out through the cracks.

"I remember the last time I saw you," Mrs Pirrip said. "You were seven and Charlie had taken you to see the Nutcracker at the Royal Opera House. Your mother was off shopping so that's why I met you there." She smiled in memory. "You twirled round in a pale pink tulle dress. You told me you were going to grow up to be a ballerina."

Edie could almost see her younger self, twirling for a lady she'd never met before. She remembered that trip, but she hadn't remembered Mrs Pirrip.

"But why didn't we see you after that?" Edie asked.

What had gone so wrong? This was all way before her parent's divorce, so it couldn't be that. What had been wrong then?

Her grandmother squeezed her hand again and then looked at the floor for a moment.

"I don't think your mother liked to share Charlie and you…" she said, and her body tensed as if bracing herself for an argument from Edie.

Edie frowned.

The thing is, it didn't sound out of the realms of possibility.

Mum wasn't known for her openness or sharing attitude. Edie grasped the locket around her neck for stability.

"Tell me more."

"Are you sure?" Mrs Pirrip asked.

"I need to know," Edie nodded as she said it.

"Well, my dear, I only know bits and pieces from what Charlie has told me and knowing your mother…" She took a deep breath.

"Your mum and dad met at work and I know Charlie was attracted to her because she was outgoing and funny but fragile."

Outgoing and funny? That didn't seem like her mum at all. Fragile though, that sounded right.

"I was happy that Charlie had met someone who made him so happy, but, I have to say I was a bit worried that she didn't speak to her mother."

"But her mum died. When she was a teenager." Edie said.

"No, dear. Her father died then but her mother didn't die until you were a little baby. Something happened between them and your mum wouldn't tell Charlie what it was, just that she'd made her choice."

"Charlie pieced it together later. Your other grandmother married very quickly after your grandfather died and I don't think your mum got on with her stepfather. I think your grandmother was made to choose, and she didn't choose your mum."

Mrs Pirrip's lips thinned at the thought.

"Anyway, with that kind of example, your mum wasn't very good at sharing her loved ones. She wanted to be the only person they needed."

She looked at Edie, pleadingly.

Edie nodded. It was exactly what her mum was like.

"So gradually, she started to see competition in everyone. She stopped Charlie from seeing friends in case they took him away from her and then when you came along, she didn't want me around either."

"Charlie would try and sneak you out to see me. But as you got older it got harder and harder. Charlie still loved her but she wasn't the carefree woman he'd married."

"He never cheated on her. No matter what that Satis woman said. But your mother was convinced that he had found someone else. And in her eyes that meant he couldn't have you. He fought all the way through your teens, he fought damn hard. But that lawyer," she shook her and shuddered. "That woman was horrible. Evil. The way she had your mum completely convinced that your dad should pay for what he did. Oh, Charlie didn't care about the money. That didn't matter. It was losing you that tore him apart. That woman made sure that you and he both paid the price."

Tears dripped from Edie's jaw and onto her lap.

The water darkened and puckered the pale linen skirt.

Classic Satis divorce strategy, Edie thought.

Hit 'em where it hurts. And she should know because she'd been doing it herself. Find their Achilles heel and grind a legal thumb into it until they bled.

Was she crying for young Edie and her dad? Or was she crying for all those little Edies and their fathers who she had left littered behind her.

No wonder she was haunted. Her chain probably wrapped itself round London.

"I'm sorry, darling Edie. I'm sorry for everything." her grandmother's hand tightened on hers.

"No, I am too." Edie replied. She took her hand from her locket to wrap it round their joined clasp.

The locket swung free and caught the light.

"Oh my," Mrs Pirrip gasped. "You got it."

Edie gave a watery smile.

"I got it on Monday. Just a bit late. Mum has only admitted she had all the cards and presents then."

"What a..." Mrs Pirrip stopped. "No, she is your mother and I'm sure she thought she was doing the right thing."

She looked like a ruffled sparrow as she said it.

"It is a beautiful locket." Edie said.

"Charlie and I chose it together. Have you opened it yet?"

"I'm waiting until I meet him." Edie felt shy calling him *Dad*.

"It will be soon. I can promise you that."

"Thank you, Mrs Pirrip." Edie said.

"I think you can call me something else." She smiled. "You used to call me Mimi."

Edie felt suddenly enveloped in love. Her hands held by her Mimi. And she had Jack guarding her back.

Pieces of her life she hadn't known she'd lost were slotting back into place.

She staggered out of the house, after refusing dinner but having had another cup of tea.

That was her grandmother, her Mimi.

Her head was stuffed to overflowing with thoughts and her chest burst with feelings she didn't know what to do with.

Her entire life had been thrown up in the air and when it hit the floor it had completely realigned.

She felt sick. Like vertigo.

No, she wouldn't think of vertigo, she'd be dealing with that tomorrow on the abseil.

Her father had fought for her. He'd fought.

He hadn't left because he wanted to.

The locket was warm against her throat.

What was inside it?

Soon, she thought. Soon she'd see her dad again.

Edie blindly made her way down the path to the gate.

It's not going to be as simple as believing one over the other. There would be shades of grey.

Could she handle the fact there were no absolutes? She worked in right or wrong.

She was going to have to compromise.

She pulled a face, but at least after years of only knowing one side of it she could explore the other side of things.

She had options.

"Can I drive you home?" Jack said.

"What?" She was in such a daze, she hadn't notice him.

How late was it? she thought. It was just getting dark.

It was almost the longest day, she realised.

She was so tired; her bones ached. She felt wrung out, as if she had been through a mangle and every bit of energy had been squeezed out of her.

Cab. It was safer.

She couldn't be in debt to him any more.

The weight of his hand was like a ghost on her back.

But she could still feel the solid comfort of it, grounding her in the moment and relaxing her enough to listen to what she was being told.

It felt like magic.

He had seen behind the curtain and her life.

It scared her.

She had to say no.

She opened her mouth to speak when Jack said,

"Come on, I'm cheaper than a cab."

But he wasn't, he was an expensive mistake that could cost her everything with the way he crept under her barriers and the ease with which he could read her.

But still she found herself in a familiar battered Golf.

How did he do that? She didn't have the energy to fight him. She would start again tomorrow, put the all walls between them back up.

Edie leaned back against the headrest and closed her eyes.

She just needed a moment, just a moment to regain her equilibrium.

"You need to let me know where you live before you fall asleep on me."

His voice was quiet and intimate in the car. It rolled over her and wrapped her in comfort. She muttered her address, and then she heard the beeps as he programmed the sat nav.

Chapter 18

"Wakey wakey."

Naked Edie wasn't sure why naked Jack was telling her to wake up.

They were in the middle of some very interesting experiments about what was possible in an underground carriage.

She brought his head closer and tried to kiss him but he wasn't there any more.

"Edie. Wake up."

He sounded like he was calling to her down a tunnel.

Then naked Edie whisked away and she woke up fully clothed, blinking at the now dark London night.

They were parked outside her flat.

She'd slept. It couldn't have been for more than twenty minutes but it was the best sleep she'd had since the hauntings began. And the best dream.

She squirmed in the seat, her body still hot from the fantasy.

How did he do it? Turn her on but also make her comfortable enough to fall asleep next to him?

Oh God, she hoped she hadn't drooled.

Or moaned his name.

She could feel herself blush.

"Edie," he started to say.

Oh, she wished he were saying it the way he had in her dream.

But this sounded serious. And she went from sleepy to alert.

His voice said he was going to ask more of her than she could give. She didn't know how she knew but she did.

Edie needed to get out of the car, before all the tender parts of her heart started making promises she didn't think she could keep.

"Thanks for the lift," she said and reached for the door handle.

"Edie, I'm not going to tell anyone about this." He said, his hand on her arm to stop her from leaving. It burnt her.

She frowned. That wasn't what she'd been worried about. She trusted him enough to keep her secrets. Which was more than she'd trusted anyone with since Tom.

But had she ever let Tom have that much trust?

No, she had kept everything tied up inside.

She was running away from Jack because she felt like her ice queen persona was melting as fast as an ice sculpture on a hot grill.

"But if you ever need anyone to talk to." He let go of her arm.

She opened the door.

No. She didn't need anyone, least of all him. She was fine. Really fine.

Edie needed to get away and refreeze. Even just for a little while.

"Thanks." She owed him that.

She turned to him and smiled. He looked amazing in the half-light from the street. Maybe she could defrost a little longer, she thought, kiss him just briefly?

She almost reached out a hand to touch his cheek.

But she'd done that before. And he'd rejected her.

She clenched her fist to stop from reaching for him.

No, not now. He'd thought she was a cold bitch. Now he was feeling sorry for her.

She had to save herself, he wasn't going to be able to save her and she couldn't afford to be distracted. She had things to do.

Quickly, she opened the door before she changed her mind and grabbed him.

She ran up the steps to the flat. Glancing at the pane above the door, she shuddered at the memory of Jessica being there.

She took the stairs up to the flat two at a time, finding energy she didn't know she had. She bolted the door but whether that was to keep people out or herself in, she wasn't sure.

Edie wanted to hide. She wished she'd kept herself locked in her flat. And never come out.

What could go wrong? she'd thought, when she'd signed up for this abseil.

Ha! Well now she knew. What kind of fool had she been, thinking you could raise money for charity in a week? Well it was possible, but you needed to do something pretty dramatic.

She'd looked into all of it. Marathons – you had to train for them. A fancy ball took months of organisation. So she had decided on an easy one to set up.

She'd do a sponsored abseil.

The fact that there was one being done from the top of a near tower block that week and happened to be sponsoring a charity for Timmy had been a godsend.

Were the powers that be doing a bit of interfering? She chose to believe not. Not with the serious amount of money she'd had to promise to raise to get a spot this late

The sponsorship page had been great and those emails she'd sent out before the bollocking from HR had the money rolling in. It was amazing what people would give to see her do something so out of her comfort zone and see her make a fool of herself.

But she had forgotten two vital things.

One. Well, she'd had the formal warning from HR abut Rachel. Who still hadn't been in the office, Edie ground her teeth. A verbal warning wasn't something she particularly wanted on her record but if it was for the good of mankind and saving of her soul, then she would grin and bear it. Rachel would come round when she saw the amount of money Edie would raise. Who wouldn't?

And Edie would apologise and maybe lay off sending complaints to HR for a while, if ever. That would settle that.

But the second vital thing she'd forgotten, was a more pressing matter at this moment.

She was scared of heights. Petrified of them. Known to have had vertigo on a stepladder level of fear.

"Alright, love?" the marshal asked her.

Edie tried to peel her fingers off the handrail. She could do this.

"Fine," she said, her voice almost failing.

It wasn't too far down. Honest. And it wasn't as if anyone she knew was watching, she tried to convince herself. She could get up there, get down, grab the official photo and boom, done. Pop it on the sponsorship page and it was another thing she'd completed off her checklist to stop the haunting.

Easy.

"Hey there! Thought we'd come along and give you some moral support," said a cheery voice from behind her.

"Yes, we're Team Dickens," a voice whispered in her ear with a twist of laughter and seriousness. "We couldn't let you do this alone. Someone had to check you were actually doing it. So when are you going up?"

Edie, currently frozen on the small set of steps in the lobby of the building heading towards the lifts, realised that life had just taken a turn for the worse. Her hands were gripping the handrail and refusing to let go.

She looked up into the face of Jack Twist, her mind screaming with fright but nothing came out. She was locked behind a pale mask. Behind him was a handful of people from the office but no Rachel.

Thank goodness she didn't have to face her yet.

Her eyes flew back to Jack's. She couldn't let him see her fail, she thought. He's already seen me too vulnerable. How can I do this?

His smile faded and he stroked her hand gently. It reminded her of him rubbing her back last night.

190

"Edie, are you OK?"

"That's just what I asked her," the marshal piped up in his fluorescent orange jacket. "She's been stuck there for ten minutes. The rate this is going she should be sponsored for how long it takes her to climb a stair."

"Are you sure you want to do this?" Jack asked.

Sure? Of course she wasn't sure. Somewhere in the cold dread knotted at the pit of her stomach a small flame ignited. She would not be made to look foolish again in front of this man. He would see she wasn't a frigid ice queen or a foolish girl with a screwed up family life or even a lawyer who couldn't get the idea of mediation. No, he would see her as someone strong, who could do things for others.

"No, no. I can do this," she whispered.

"Can someone go up with her?" Jack asked the marshal.

"No skin off my nose if you go," the man said.

Edie's stiff fingers were warmed in a pair of battered and scarred hands that then lifted them off the rail.

"Come on, I've got you." Jack said.

So much for looking strong and independent. Blindly she allowed him to lead her to the lifts.

Her stomach was a tight hard knot and her knees were liquid. She could do this.

She stood hand in hand with Jack in front of the bank of lifts in silence. Maybe all the lifts would breakdown? Then she couldn't get to the roof and this wouldn't happen.

Bing, a lift arrived.

"Any more for the abseil?" a voice cried out.

"One here!" Jack waved her into the mirrored lift.

OK, maybe they would get stuck in the lift. That would be OK. She'd rather be stuck in the lift with Jack than walk off a building on a piece of string. In fact, that would be fine, she wasn't claustrophobic. At least she didn't think she was. And Jack well... He was still a safer bet than falling off a building. Just.

She watched the floors tick off on the digital display. One, two, three…

"I wonder why Rachel isn't here to support you?" Jack said in the silence.

She flinched. At least the whole Rachel complaining to HR about her hadn't got round the office yet. Mind you, it was only a matter of time. Something like that always found a way out, no matter how 'confidential' the chat had been.

"I think it's a bit off when it's her kid you're doing this for," Jack continued.

Yeah, the kid that Rachel wanted to keep out of the office gossip, the kid that Edie had unceremoniously outed. That kid.

"Prior engagement," she said.

Eighteen, nineteen, twenty…

Surely she could get out now?

Bing.

The lift came to a stop on the last floor.

"Now you have to take the stairs on your right to the roof," the kind lift operator pointed out to them.

Edie found herself propelled out of the lift by a familiar hand that had only been stroking her back in support last night. Then Jack, using that same treacherous hand, pulled her gently towards the stairs leading up to the roof.

What was she doing?

Surely being haunted by a Ghost wasn't worth all this? She couldn't do this. She'd write a promise to donate a massive sum every month for the rest of her life if only they'd let her back in the lift.

But there, fluttering from an air vent in the ceiling came a shiny pink piece of glitter. Like a mote of dust it spun around and danced in front of her, reminding her it was this or an eternity alone with the penis deely boppers slotted through the links of a chain hanging from her waist.

"Right," she said and marched up the stairs. Wind whistled

down them, making her fight into the headwind.

"Never let the bastards see you cry." she whispered into the wind.

At the top, a fire door was propped open and a young woman in yet another high visibility jacket stood with a clipboard.

"Another victim for the jump then?" she said, beaming. "You must be Edie, the last one of the day," she made a tick against the sheet.

"Of course I'm sure you have read and signed the release forms and insurance doohickey. After all you are a lawyer," she laughed. "And have you come to make sure she jumps?" the girl said and glanced at Jack.

"Oh. My. God! Jack Twist!" the girl gasped and stared wide eyed past Edie's shoulder. She was getting used to feeling a spare part when she was with Jack.

"Are you abseiling too?" she said, or rather simpered.

Great waves of nausea crashed on top of Edie's already knotted stomach. She might just jump to get away from the love fest.

"No. Just here giving support," he said absently as he hustled Edie through the door.

She was on the roof.

Bloody hell, she was on the roof.

Wind battered her, pulled at her clothes. Surely it was pushing her closer to the edge.

Her knees gave way.

Jack caught her.

"You really don't have to do this," he said as he took her weight.

But she did have to do this. She had to do this more than anything she had done before.

And it wasn't for the money.

"I can do it," she said.

At the end of the roof was a group of people wearing harnesses and hard hats. That was where she had to jump.

She moved slowly towards them, her hand gripping Jack's and hoping he wouldn't let go. Even though she couldn't see the ground, she could feel it. It pulled at her, drew her to it. It wanted to embrace her. It wanted her to take the leap. It wanted her to fall.

"Edie! You made it!" a man said bustling up to her, carrying a harness and helmet.

"I'm Gary, the instructor. I'll be talking you down. And I see you've brought some moral support… excellent!"

Then it was all talk of harness and karabiners, rope and angles and notes. Edie's head buzzed with the information.

"So which one is the brake?" she asked confused.

"It'll be easier once we've got you hooked up," he said.

He rattled a harness at her.

"Now just step into the two leg bits, here and here." Edie stepped in gingerly. "And then this bit, here and here for your arms."

Reluctantly, Edie let go of Jack's hand and put her arms through the required loops. Her hand groped for Jack's again and catching it, she clung on.

"And now we do this doohickey up here," Gary slotted some metal pieces together closing the harness, "and then we tighten it."

"Arghhh!" Edie cried.

"Sorry, but it has to be snug," Gary said as he tightened the harness causing Edie's nether regions to lose circulation.

"OK, and now for the helmet," Gary plonked it on Edie's head and tightened the chin strap.

"All right?"

All right? Skin was now trapped in the buckle but the sharp pain focused her mind. She nodded, her eyes smarting as skin pulled out of the buckle.

And then Gary was going through the whole rope thing again.

"So if I do that I slow down?" Edie asked after a while.

She pulled a rope apart and fumbled with the other. She was going to plummet to her death. There was no way she would remember any of this.

"It's like this," Jack said.

He guided her hands to the correct ropes and took her through the procedure. The heat of his hands flowing through hers; her fingers chilly from the wind and fear twitched at the contact. They itched to turn and hold on to him tight.

"Ready then?" Gary asked.

Was she? This was her chance to step away from the edge and walk back across the roof and away from her fear. But hadn't she been walking away from fear for most of her life?

"Ready," she whispered.

Jack squeezed her hand tightly and then released it.

She shuffled in the tight harness to the edge of the roof.

"Now stand with your back to the edge," Gary said as he manoeuvred her into place.

Edie turned and faced Jack. He stood there, his arms crossed on his chest, his eyes staring intently at her, a small encouraging smile on his mouth.

"If you just stand on the very edge, just like that and lean back,"

Lean back? Were they completely mad?

She might not be able to see the drop but she could feel it. It tugged at her hair, at her jacket. It called to her to come and play. To see what it would feel like to free-fall. To feel the wind rushing past her stealing her breath. To give into gravity until Newton's law of motion brought her to an abrupt and painful halt.

"Lean back, come on. You need to be perpendicular to the building as you walk down," Gary coaxed her.

Theoretically she knew what this was all about and in theory she could do it. In theory she was leaning back and her heart was beating slowly. In theory she was breathing regularly and she wasn't feeling light-headed like she'd faint.

In theory she was already at the bottom of the building.

However, in practice she was still staring at a now concerned Jack. In practice her legs were braced hard against the jelly-wobble that ran through them every few seconds. In practice, the rope she held whipped back and forth like an agitated cat's tail.

"Edie?" Jack said. "You can still back out."

She could couldn't she? No one would blame her, would they?

"She's the Ice Queen"

"A cold bitch"

"An automaton"

"The borg"

All the words from her trip with the Ghost of Weddings Present began to echo in her head.

But she wasn't that person. She had promised to do this. People were sponsoring her. The Ice Queen would walk away. The cold bitch that Jack talked of would slink off with a cutting remark.

But he wasn't looking at her like she was a cold bitch now.

And little Timmy...

His laughing knowing eyes had looked too deeply, seen too much and had ultimately found her wanting.

"I'll do it," the words couldn't come out of her dry mouth.

She wet her lips, swallowed and tried again.

"I'll do it," the wind almost carried it away but it reached Gary, Jack and everyone on the roof.

"Then I'm doing it with you!" Jack said.

He was what?

Chapter 19

Within five minutes, Jack was harnessed up. He'd signed all the insurance forms and he was beside her. A pinstripe suited, helmeted force of nature. The charity photographer who had been slouched in a heap near the parapet had leapt to life when he realised the charity was about to get a hell of a scoop and some great publicity.

"Ready?" asked Gary.

"Ready?" Jack whispered to her.

"Ready," she replied.

And then in unison they leant back. Edie watched Jack's hands as they held their rope firmly, watched his feet in the borrowed trainers that gave more grip than the leather soled shoes he had been wearing.

"I hope you are going to follow directions for once in your life, Slow." Jack said as they hung out over the pavement far below them.

She would follow him anywhere if he got her back on the ground.

"I'll follow," she said.

"OK, I'll count and on three we slip down to the next level," he said.

"OK," she nodded.

"One, two, three,"

On three Edie screwed her eyes shut and loosened the rope as she shoved her feet off the wall.

She was falling.

"Brake!"

At his call, she braked and her feet were once again against the wall and they were off the top.

"That wasn't so bad, was it?" Jack said.

Grinning Edie turned to look at him.

He smiled back at her and then she made a big mistake.

She looked down.

"No." Jack shouted.

It was such a long way down. The fierce pull she had ignored briefly was back.

"No," he said and suddenly there was the warmth of his hand under her chin.

Her head came up, the pull of his magnetism overpowering gravity.

"The three places you can look at are the sky, the wall and," he released her chin and pointed two fingers at his face "my eyes."

It was an order. Jack was in charge and Edie was glad someone was. She nodded.

She took a deep breath, pursed her lips together and blew it out in a long stream.

"One, two, three," Jack said again.

And they were off again.

One, two, three. Brake.

Gradually they made their way down. Edie ignored the shouts from the roof; the waving workers in the building gathering to watch them. All she saw were Jack's eyes. Their watchers grew exponentially along with the camera flashes as the word spread that Jack Twist was hanging outside the building.

And as they got closer and closer to the pavement, the siren song it had been singing to Edie was drowned out by the cheers and encouragement from the crowd below.

"One, two, three," she chanted under her breath with Jack.

And then suddenly there was land. Her feet were no longer walking down a wall they were on solid ground. The moment they hit the pavement the tiny part of the siren song that still wove a tendril around her stopped.

"You did it!" Jack said.

She turned and she caught a glimpse of his huge grin before she was enveloped in a hug.

She'd done it. And at that her knees wobbled once and fell apart as did her emotions.

"Hey Edie, you did it," Jack held her up and pressed her head into his chest.

"Mwwwmahamam," she was incoherent but muffled by his suit jacket.

"You're not crying are you?" he asked.

Cry? Edie Dickens?

No it must have been some grit or the wind as they came down that made her eyes water. But she stayed with her head against his chest for a few more minutes until she was able to breathe properly. Or at least as properly as she was able when standing so close to Jack.

"Jack! Jack! Over here mate!"

As Edie's knees returned to firmness she began to hear the calls of the crowd around them.

"Jack! Amit Pindora from BBC London. Can we have a few words to camera?"

"Jack! Who's your lady friend?"

"Damn press," Jack whispered.

Edie now knew why the charity people had been so eager to get Jack to join her on the abseil. The story went from a nice human-interest filler piece to a story that might just make it on to the early evening news.

And here she was, bedraggled and shaking. Not the professional image she needed.

"Are you OK if I go and talk to them? Try and divert them

199

from you?" Jack asked.

She nodded into his jacket.

And then he was gone and she felt bereft.

And that was it; her great charity moment overshadowed by Jack. All the supporters from the office were either already in the pub or watching Jack avidly from behind the cameras. Edie limped her way to the waiting marshals, keeping her face down and hoping someone would get this bloody harness off her quickly before she lost any more circulation.

And then Edie lost herself in the crowd. Her bags recovered from the marshal clutched in white knuckles as she watched Jack turn on the charm.

He smiled for the camera and spoke at length gesturing upwards and then became serious for a moment.

Then he said goodbye to the TV reporter, slapping him on the back in camaraderie. She saw the moment he looked back to find her gone, but before he could do anything a group of fan girls grabbed his attention for autographs.

Was that what it would always be like with him? Having to share him with the rest of the world? And what would happen when the world wanted more and more? Would she get less and less until there was a Jack-shaped hole in her life? She had enough of those. She'd had enough people leave. She didn't want to turn into Mum and make him choose.

She shook her head. Why was she even thinking that? A few kisses and some steamy dreams did not make a relationship. *But you'd like them to*, her treacherous inner voice said. Liking and doing were two different things, and she knew the difference very well.

Without a backward glance, Edie turned moved out of the crowd. She'd thank him tomorrow.

"Well done, Edie."

"I upped my sponsorship. You were so brave."

"Got a hug from Jack Twist, you dark horse."

Edie kept her chin up and nodded as she passed her colleagues down the corridor the next morning.

She felt as if she was in a spotlight and it was burning all her layers away. She wanted to take a swipe at them all.

And that comment about Jack Twist. She should snap a comment out right now. Show them how the Shark still had a lethal bite.

Think of the money, she chanted inside while outside she glared and swept past.

She shut the door of her office.

Maybe she could hide in here all day? Rachel wouldn't be in till Monday. No one would bother her.

Edie sat at her desk.

Just get through the rest of the day, she thought. She was almost looking forward to the wedding. Then at least it would be over.

Ghosts.

One more left, she sighed. There was still one more chance to head it off.

She opened her calendar. Maggie and Doug were due in for their last meeting at ten o'clock.

Edie wondered if she could leave it to Jack.

No, that was a coward's way out.

Jack had done the hard work. Now it was for her to make sure Maggie and Doug put on a united front tomorrow. Preferably wearing their wedding rings and taking their wedding vows seriously.

Edie shuddered as she remembered the close up view of Maggie playing tonsil hockey at the hen weekend.

This was for Mel. Her wedding present to her.

And before she could back out, she ran the gauntlet of the office corridor again and went to find Jack.

"Jack," she stood by his desk, ignoring the curious looks from the people sitting nearest him.

"Hey Edie," he started to unfold from his seat.

No, she couldn't have him looming over her.

She put her hand on his shoulder.

"Don't get up," she said quickly.

"Are you OK? I missed you after the interview yesterday," he said as he sat back down. "I was going to buy you a drink. Or dinner."

He winked and just like that, she wanted to sit on his lap. Curl up there and let whatever would happen, happen.

No, be strong Edie.

She looked down into his eyes. The same eyes that had held her attention the whole way down the building yesterday.

She could feel the wind in her hair, and the ground pulling her downwards.

She grabbed the desk to stop from falling.

"I'm fine. I wanted to say that I'd deal with Maggie and Doug today. You don't need to come." She pushed off the desk with a hand, trying to give herself the momentum she needed to spin out of his orbit.

"But Edie, is that wise?" he grasped her hand.

Warmth crept up her arm, trying to melt her.

"It will be fine," she tried to smile as she tugged her hand out of his.

It would be fine.

If she had to lock them in a room and not let them out till they solved it.

She walked away and didn't look back.

"Maggie, Doug" she ushered them into the meeting room.

"Edie," they both said and, subdued, took their places at the table.

Edie itched as if someone's eyes were on her. She looked over her shoulder expecting to see Jack storm in and try to take over as if he'd worked out what she was up to.

Instead, she met the oil painted, brush stroked, accusing eyes of the Hilary Satis portrait.

Did they just blink?

First ghosts, now portraits. She rubbed her eyes.

No, they were just paint on canvas.

Tiredness and stress were getting to her. Just tomorrow to get through and then she could worry about going mad.

I'm probably there already, she thought. But this wasn't about her mental state, this was about getting these two sorted out. This was about Mel.

"Where's Jack?" Maggie asked.

She and Doug both peered round Edie, looking for him.

"Jack can't make it today, so I'm here."

Edie stretched out her fingers to loosen the stress and then she clenched them into fists.

"First we need to come to an agreement about how you two are going to behave tomorrow. I'm not having you upsetting Mel on her day."

Edie stared at first one and then the other, holding them until they looked away uncomfortably.

"Well, I say, really." Doug started to bluster.

"What, Doug? You have to walk your daughter down the aisle. Do you really want her knowing what you've been up to?" Edie said. She'd had enough of pussy footing round them.

She watched in surprise as Maggie reached over and squeezed Doug's hand, as he turned red and purple in the face from embarrassment.

"Really, Edie…" Maggie started.

Edie cut her off.

"We need to make sure that you two behave tomorrow. And maybe if you can do that, maybe you can carry on and patch things up?" Edie didn't realise she was still hopeful that these two could make it.

That they could show her that marriage was something worth

fighting for.

"OK, Edie. We get it." She watched them hold hands at the table.

See? I can do this, she thought and wished that Jack Twist was here to see it.

Instead she sat under the watchful gaze of Ms Satis.

Chapter 20

"You've got some nerve!"

The door to the office slammed open and banged off the wall.

Edie jumped, she'd been looking at her files and smiling to herself that she had the whole mediation/reconciliation thing sorted.

Standing in the doorway was a very dishevelled Rachel. Her hair was greasy and looked like birds could nest in it. She was wearing slouchy yoga pants and a cardigan pulled on over a button down shirt. All the buttons were done up wrongly.

Edie thought there was a very suspicious stain on the sleeve.

"Rachel? I didn't think you were due in until Monday."

Damn, thought Edie. I haven't come up with a good apology yet.

She frowned at Rachel; she could do without these histrionics. OK, so Rachel had made her feelings quite plain in terms of broadcasting her family issues around the firm but this was taking things too far.

"Rachel, I just wanted to say…" Edie started.

"*You* want? It's always about you and I'll say it again. You've got some nerve, lady!" Rachel's normally sallow face was flushed and she was glaring at Edie. She slammed the office door shut.

"What is it now? I was just about to say I'm sorry."

Really Rachel needed to get things in perspective.

"Sorry? *Sorry?* I'll make you sorry when I've finished with you. Do you know what you've done? Do you?"

Edie shook her head; speaking was probably not the best thing to do just now, she thought.

"Not only did you have to splash the whole of my personal life round the office but now it's all over London and probably the rest of the world!"

Ah, the press.

"And don't give me all that shit about it being charitable and the like. You just did it to get into Jack Twist's bed." Rachel flung the newspaper at Edie's face.

Edie grabbed it before it could hit her.

She unfolded the paper and there, on the front page of the Metro was Jack and herself.

Edie could see why Rachel might have got the wrong idea. She was plastered against him as if trying to merge with him. And in a small inset was the moment at the top of the building where he had held her hand.

HEARTTHROB TWISTS FOR LOVE?

Blared out the headline.

"Retired England International, Jack Twist took an impromptu abseil down a building in London yesterday. Twist, 35, claims he was helping a work colleague raise cash for Timmy Cratchit, stepson of fellow worker, Rachel Micawber. Looks like he was helping himself to some more extracurricular activity. Our sources have identified the mystery brunette as Edwina Dickens, a high-flying lawyer at Bailey Lang Satis and Partners, where Twist started working after retiring at the end of last year."

Edie groaned. This was not good.

"There is nothing going on like that. I really was trying to help…"

"Help? Help? You fucking cold-hearted bitch, you used my Timmy as a way to get what you wanted. What, were you trying to persuade Jack that you aren't the cold bitch we know you are?

206

And it didn't matter to you who you hurt? I'm going to kill you."

At that, Rachel pushed Edie's desk out of the way, tipping over her monitor. It crashed to the floor as she threw herself across the desk.

What the... Rachel's bulging eyes were suddenly right there in front of Edie, her hands were claws aiming for Edie's eyes. In the nick of time Edie leaned back and the wind whistled past as the hands mostly missed her but one of the ragged bitten nails caught the end of her nose.

"Ouch! Bloody hell, Rachel!" Edie said, her chair sliding back and stopping against the wall.

"I'll 'bloody hell' you. Come here!" Rachel screamed and she got a little further over the desk and her hands closed around Edie's throat.

Edie had never believed anyone saw stars but she was definitely seeing black splodges and her lungs hurt.

"Rachel," she rasped.

She was going to die, here. Now.

And ruin Mel's big day. Crap.

And she hadn't made amends yet.

As her sight started to go, as she grabbed at Rachel's hands trying to get them off, trying to breathe, she thought she heard the clanking of chain links over the sound of her heart beating frantically in her ears.

The door to the office burst open and people piled in.

And suddenly the pressure round her neck was gone.

Coughing, Edie collapsed over her desk gasping for breath and blinking the black spots away.

"I'm going to kill her! Let me at her!" Rachel shouted over the pounding in Edie's ears as blood started to flow back.

"No one is doing any killing here."

Jack. Yet again he had come to her rescue. Worming his way into a space in her life. Her body relaxed knowing he was there. It was so traitorous.

"Can someone call security?" he spoke to someone just outside in the corridor.

"Now Rachel, what is it that Edie's done? Embezzled the charity funds?" he said as he held her, arms pinned, against his chest.

"Charity? That bitch wouldn't know charity if it bit her on the bum! She's using my poor little Timmy for her own ends. And I won't have it!"

"Her own ends? Are you sure? It didn't look like that twenty storeys up yesterday," he tried to joke.

"Ha! She's already got you fooled hasn't she? Haven't you Edie? You've got him snared, so it's just a case of hauling him in," Rachel said.

Edie's head throbbed; all the emotion in the room was suffocating her.

"Rachel, I meant to help, I really did," she whispered.

"Help? The only thing you've ever done for me is get me put on report and officially disciplined. Why should I believe you want to help? Timmy is the one pure, unsullied part of my life. And you know what you have done with your stunt? Well you've only got Rob's ex-wife deciding she wants access and thinking maybe she'll sue for custody for him. That is the same woman who left him when he was a few days old. That's what your 'help' has done. So excuse me if I don't do cartwheels round the office."

Tears were streaming down Rachel's face.

Edie watched helplessly, all the hurt and the fear that someone she loved would be taken away from her were etched on Rachel's face. Edie knew that fear.

"I'm… I'm sorry. I didn't think," she said. Her stomach twisted and the pain in her chest competed with the pain on her neck.

"No you didn't think did you, you stupid cow!" Rachel yelled at her as Jack manoeuvred her out of the room and into the arms of the security guards.

What had she done? Everything she touched turned rotten. Even with the best intentions she was still mucking it up. Destroying everything and everyone around her.

"I'd be better off dead," she whispered.

"No one is doing any dying," Jack said.

Edie looked up to find him in the doorway of the office. His tie was askew, his hair was ruffled and his shirttails were coming un-tucked from his trousers.

He looked alive and sexy and safe. Safe? That wasn't the normal word she thought about with him but he did. Nothing would happen to her if he was standing between her and the world.

She shivered.

But what could she do to him? Ruin him? Destroy him? Probably. For his own sake, she needed to stay away.

"No, of course not," she backtracked. "It was the shock."

"Look Edie, it isn't your fault that Rachel has gone off on one. I've already heard from HR that she was crumbling under the pressure."

Had she been crumbling or had Edie pushed her? HR only knew as much as Edie had told them.

"It was only a matter of time before she would have been asked to leave," he carried on.

"They aren't going to fire her are they?" she asked. She didn't want that. No, she had to make this right.

Jack looked at her strangely.

"You don't really think they are going to keep her on after she attacked you in your own office?"

This was a disaster.

"But they can't…"

Jack came up and took her hand. It trembled and then lay still, absorbing the heat and safety that he exuded.

"Edie," he said gently, "I know that you have been hiding a heart of gold underneath that ice queen persona but even you can see that she needs to go. She's mentally unstable."

Heart of gold? Her?

Mentally unstable? Rachel?

Jack had it all the wrong way round.

Edie fought the tears that threatened to spill.

Edie had a heart of stone more like. And that had been no persona he had seen, plus she was seeing Ghosts. But Rachel did have a great heart. How had it got so tangled up?

She snatched her hand away. She needed Jack to get away, far away.

"I was thinking of the potential lawsuit," she let the ice and hauteur infuse her voice.

"Lawsuit?"

"Yes, I wouldn't want to see the firm dragged through the courts by some emotionally unstable woman like Rachel." Edie realised that she still found it too easy to allow the lies to slip off her tongue.

Jack recoiled; a look of distaste crossed his face before he could stop it.

Inside, Edie cringed and shrivelled, wanting to tell him she was lying. She wanted him to know that she was protecting herself, protecting him. Instead she lifted one eyebrow as she stared at him and then began to straighten her desk with steady hands.

"Thank you, once again, for coming to my aid. But I have lots of work to do, so if you wouldn't mind?" she gestured to the door.

"You're going to sit there and carry on working like nothing happened?" he asked.

"Yes, and your point is?"

"You've been attacked. Surely you could take the day off and go home. Relax."

Go home? Have a day off? And do what? Look at the four walls of her flat and realise that she had no one. No one who cared for her enough to attack someone on her behalf.

"I don't know what gave you the idea that I was a delicate flower that needed protecting. I am perfectly capable of looking after myself." She forced herself to look down at the file in front of her. She couldn't look up again to see the distaste she knew was on Jack's face.

"Maybe that ice queen act isn't so much a persona then?" he said. "Last night I thought you were like this because of your mum and that Satis woman, but this really is you."

Edie ignored him. The words on the page were blurring and tumbling as she stared hard at them.

Go. Go. Go. She thought hard at him.

She could see his legs out of the corner of her eye. The silence stretched between them. The tension screamed through Edie, her fingers twitched and her knee bounced under the desk.

And then he left.

Edie slumped in her chair, bought her hands to her mouth and bit her nails.

She was a horrible person. She knew it, the Ghosts knew it and now Jack knew it.

Edie needed to get out. She walked blindly through the office, not caring about the whispers she could hear in her wake.

Don't let the bastards see you cry. She repeated it until it turned into the rhythm of her steps. She'd do anything to stop the tears.

She waited for the lift and repeatedly pressed the button. She needed to get out, now. She clutched the locket with her hand, tugging at it to see if it could help her breathe better.

Edie could feel phantom hands around her neck.

She gasped as she felt her throat close in memory.

Maybe Jack should've let Rachel kill her. It would be easier for everyone.

The lift arrived and Edie hardly waited for the doors to open before she rushed into it and collapsed in the corner.

Edie had driven Rachel to breaking point.

She'd pushed Jack away.

She was holding Maggie and Doug together through sheer force of will but she knew it wouldn't last.

She was being haunted tonight.

She was damned. How could she ever get it right?

Leaving the building, she headed for the café, needing a coffee and maybe a pastry. Screw the diet and healthy eating. She craved sweetness, the melting sugar hit and caffeine kick.

Needing comfort that she couldn't ask from someone else.

As she pushed open the door, the bell above it rang and the guy behind the counter looked up. The smile on his face froze and then fractured and fell when he saw her.

Crap. She wanted to turn and walk away.

She wasn't even welcome here.

She hovered in the doorway.

Maybe she should go? She thought.

But then she thought of the office she'd just left. The whispers. Jack's disgusted face.

No, she needed this. Pastry didn't judge you, only the people who served it to you did.

She straightened her shoulders and carried on and joined the queue.

The woman in front of her seemed familiar as she dug in her change purse, frantically looking for money. A key chain with a cube of photos of grinning children swung from it.

This woman had a family, thought Edie jealously. People who cared whether she lived or died. No one would call her an ice queen or a borg.

"I know I have it, sorry," the woman said and looked over her shoulder and smiled at Edie.

Edie smiled back.

But the woman went white when she saw Edie. Edie tried to make her smile bigger and encouraging in return.

Tears started to form in the woman's eyes. Edie could see them welling and starting to dissolve the woman's mascara.

Edie frowned. What was wrong? She was pretty sure she'd seen her before.

Edie couldn't stand it any longer. The tension, the impending tears. It made her even shakier than she'd been before.

She took her purse out.

"I'll get this for her," she said.

There is sometimes a quality to silence that has weight, and this one packed a hell of a punch. Edie felt as if the world had frozen. The man behind the counter stopped chopping, his knife held in mid air and his mouth ajar. The woman stood stock still, a tear balanced on her bottom eyelashes. Even the espresso machine stopped hissing.

Edie offered the money to the man, pushing through the silence and breaking it.

"Are you sure?" the woman whispered.

Edie could feel herself heat up.

"It's fine."

"I can pay you back." The woman went back to digging in her purse.

Edie put a hand over hers.

"Use it to buy something for the kids." She turned again to shop owner who was looking at the money like it was going to spontaneously combust.

"Latte and a pain au chocolate," she said it quickly. She wanted to get out fast. Everyone was staring at her like she'd grown a second head. Or as if she was going to turn and bite them.

"Please." she added. That spurred him into action. As he made her the coffee, he kept turning around as if to check she was real.

The woman collected her tea and sandwich leaving the café in a flurry of thanks and more tears.

Edie eventually managed to leave the shop clutching the coffee and the pastry.

She went and sat in a small park near the office. It was a carved out place of quietness in the city. It used to be a graveyard, Edie realised. She'd never bothered to come in before, had often walked past it. A cemetery, it made sense for her life at the moment.

She took the pain au chocolat from the bag. She stared at the icing sugar dusting, the flaking pastry. Inhaling the smell, she had a half remembered memory flash through her head.

There was laughter and her mother with a sugar coated nose and a man she supposed was her father trying to lick it off. And her stomach ached from the remembered laughter.

Edie shook her head and the memory fractured. Had it been real?

She bit into the sweet stickiness.

Tonight she'd see the last Ghost and she didn't know how to stop it.

She'd failed. She licked her lips, trying to get every last crumb of comfort she could.

And then tomorrow would be the wedding.

She had a flash of her worlds colliding and exploding.

Maggie and Doug, her mum, Tom, Jack. If she didn't love Mel so much, she would be tempted to run away. All those people who saw different versions of her. The girl she'd been and then the woman she'd become.

Could she learn to change again?

She took a drink of the coffee. She wasn't sure she had a heart big enough or brave enough to try.

She stared at the ground and watched a small glimmer of pink in the dust.

Using her finger she dug into the corner of the paper bag the pain au chocolat had come in, each crumb as small as the piece of glitter that was in the dust. And each one a tiny explosion of memories.

Had her mum really been that laughing woman in her mind?

Her phone rang.

Work, she thought, but glanced at the screen anyway.

And as if she had conjured her up from those tiny flakes of pastry, it said it was her mother.

Edie's finger hovered over the screen.

Did she accept? Could she handle having to listen to her mum's side of the story when she was still trying to deal with what her

Mimi had told her?

But the memories were on her tongue.

And the glitter flashed a warning at her.

Maybe there was something she could do today...

One small step in the right direction.

She pressed the button.

"Hi Mum," she said, her voice still husky from Rachel's assault on her throat.

"Oh Edie, are you OK? Beattie says she saw your name in the paper this morning. And that one of those celebrity Internet site wotsits are saying you threw yourself off a roof with a rugby player? It wasn't because of what I said is it, about your dad? I didn't mean it."

Edie's mum was talking at high speed, upset.

"Mum." Edie said cutting through the words. "Mum, I'm OK. I was abseiling for charity. I'm absolutely fine," she said.

"Oh," she could feel her mum taking big gulping breaths.

"Mum, thank you." Edie said, gripping the phone tighter.

"What for?" her mum sounded suspicious.

Edie had to do this.

"For giving me my grandmother's address. I know this is hard for you, I know you were only doing your best. But I have to do this. I need to speak to Dad, make my own relationship with him." Edie wasn't sure where the words were coming from, but they felt as if they needed to be said.

Would she listen? Edie waited chewing her thumbnail, the last few tastes of her pastry melting in her mouth.

"Oh Edie..." it was a voice she didn't usually hear from her mum. Softer and less aggressive.

Warmer.

"OK Mum?" Edie asked.

"OK," her mum said.

Edie sat with the phone pressed to her ear for a moment. The picture she had of her mum in her head with a sugar coated nose made her smile slightly.

"See you tomorrow," she said.

"Bye," her mum replied, and hung up.

Edie leaned back on the bench and she crumpled up the paper bag.

Chapter 21

Edie stared at the TV screen.

There was sound and light coming out of it. And she was sitting in front of it, bathed in the bright light and she knew the sound was in her ears but she couldn't make any sense of what she saw or heard.

It could've been in Korean for all she understood. Her mind wouldn't process it. Or couldn't.

"I'm glad you've come and stayed." Mel had said when Edie had arrived on her doorstep two hours earlier.

"Where else would the maid of honour stay the night before the wedding?" Edie had replied through gritted teeth. All she really wanted to do was curl up in a ball on her own bed and wait for the end of time.

She might have made up with her mum but every other part of life was going to hell in a hand basket. And she didn't know how to fix it.

In less than twenty-four hours the wedding would be over and so would Edie's haunting. But would she be chain-less?

Of course the last Ghost did still have to find her at Mel's.

Edie had felt a smaller flicker of excitement at that thought.

She'd never get that lucky. They probably had her micro chipped like a pet or at least psychic equivalent of it. She wasn't getting away with anything, she realised that now.

She had to pay.

Music burst from the screen, jolting her out of her thoughts.

What were they doing? She watched as the two figures on the screen prance round in a pond or something.

The film was Mel's choice. Some romcom to get them into the right mood for the wedding.

"I want to wallow in my final night of freedom," Mel said as she'd put on the DVD.

Edie was just glad that the other bridesmaids weren't invited. This was the last time she'd have Mel to herself and she'd happily watch any kind of film she wanted to. Or so she'd thought.

But the mood in the house probably wasn't the one Mel had expected when she'd made her plans. There should've been giggling and reminiscing. Looking at photos of them as bridesmaids as kids, although Edie had seen quite enough of that in real life recently.

"I told you we should have hired a professional DJ! But no, you wanted your mate Dave to do it and look what has happened!" Mel was screaming down her phone whilst pacing back and forth in the kitchen.

Edie flinched. Nope, no giggling at all.

"Don't you dare tell me I am overreacting. You have done nothing. Not one tiny little thing towards this wedding. I've done everything."

There was a crash as if Mel had thrown something and then there was quiet, which made Edie feel queasy.

Back down, Barry, Edie pleaded in her head. He could do it if he just tried...

"No, I will not calm down, you patronising shit. If this is what you are going to be like when we are married then maybe we shouldn't be getting married at all."

No. No. No. Edie chanted as she stared at the screen. *Barry, please*, she begged silently.

"Yeah, really? Well if that's the way you feel then this wedding is off!"

Edie put her head in her hands.

The only thing worse than an actual wedding was an eleventh hour cancellation. This couldn't be happening.

I'm cursed, she thought. I've brought this on Mel. I've poisoned it.

"The wedding is off!" Mel stormed back into the living room, kicking Barry's mountain bike as she passed it. The spokes in the wheel bent.

"Isn't that a little hasty?" Edie ventured.

"Ha! Hasty! I think not, over the last couple of weeks Barry's shown his true nature and the DJ was just the icing on the cake. I'm not marrying a man like that. I want a marriage like my parents. A marriage of equals."

Like her parents? The same parents who had spent the last two weeks discussing their divorce. Bloody hell.

"Marriage isn't perfect," Edie started.

Was it really going to be left to her to be the advocate for marriage?

"But what you and Barry have is special. This is just wedding craziness." Edie quickly topped up Mel's glass. "Have some wine, watch the movie and then call Barry back."

Mel sighed… "Maybe I'll just let him stew for a while." She took a massive swig of wine.

"And another thing…" Mel slurred and gestured with her wine glass. It was half an hour since Mel had called off the wedding.

Surely that was plenty of stewing? Also, Mel seemed to be getting sloshed.

Edie quickly moved the wine bottle, which was in the trajectory of Mel's glass.

She needed reinforcements and she needed them fast.

"Need the loo, will be right back," with that she ran out of the room clutching her phone.

"Come on. Answer goddammit!" Edie muttered as she waited for Mel's mother to pick up.

"Yes?"

"Maggie? It's Edie, you've got to get to Mel's right away. Why? She's called off the wedding, something about wanting what you and Doug have! Yes I'd swear too."

Edie clicked off the handset and prayed she had done the right thing.

"Right! Where is she?" Maggie said as she arrived through the front door, a few minutes later. She'd obviously run from the hotel she and Doug were staying in round the corner. In separate rooms.

"Mum?" Mel called through tears and wine from the living room.

"Baby!" and Maggie ran in.

Edie slumped against the wall; she was off the hook and someone else was in charge.

She took herself off to the kitchen, poured herself a massive glass of wine and waited.

"You WHAT!"

Edie flinched. Mel had obviously been told about her parents less than stellar marriage.

"EDIE!"

Sighing, she walked back to the living room.

"Yes?"

Mel was huddled in the corner of the sofa. It was going to be a long night.

"You knew they were splitting up and you didn't tell me?" Mel sounded so hurt.

"But…" Edie tried to say but she was losing what was left of her voice after this afternoon's kerfuffle.

She should've called HR before she left for the day but she'd been too tired after the emotional roller-coaster, she thought, as she coughed and started again.

"But how could I tell you? I've been trying…"

Mel's phone rang, cutting off Edie's explanation that she'd been trying to get them back together.

"It's Barry," Mel said staring down at the screen where a photo of a wildly gurning Barry flashed up.

"Talk to him," Edie said.

Mel rejected the call.

What the hell?

"I'm never talking to that bastard again! Men are all the same; you've always said it, Edie. We're better off on our own. I mean, if Dad can't keep it in his pants what hope do Barry and I have."

"Surely that's a little drastic…" Edie started.

Mel glared at her.

"If you are going to stay here, Edie you'd better bloody well be on my side." Mel said, glaring at Edie.

Edie wondered whether she could get haunted right about now. It seemed to be a better option than the evening or what lay ahead of them tomorrow, in cancelling this wedding.

"I've text him to tell him not to bother calling." Mel said and threw her phone across the room.

Even being attacked by Rachel was looking favourable.

Exhausted, Edie slumped into the bed in Mel's spare room.

Nothing she had said helped. Mel had divided her time between shouting at her mum and Edie. Apparently hiding the truth wasn't what a friend should do.

And how was Edie to know that Mel had been listening to all those things she'd said against getting married and what a bad idea it was?

She was definitely reaping what she'd sown.

The problem was that Mel was doing the reaping too.

Honestly, Edie didn't think she would wake up for any amount of Ghosts that decided to haunt her.

Why did love have to be so painful?

She rubbed her heart. Surely it was better to lock your heart away and barricade it from harm. As she drifted off to sleep, she thought she heard the clanking of chain across a wooden floor.

She shivered and pulled the duvet higher over her shoulders.

The alarm on her phone went off. Groggily, Edie groped for it in the dark. She knocked it to the floor but the alarm stopped so she flopped back onto the pillows.

Had she even set the alarm last night? She couldn't remember… and it was damn dark for seven o'clock on a summer morning.

Now she had to pick her phone up and check.

The last Ghost, the thought swam into her consciousness, as she tried to get the energy up to lean over the edge of the bed.

She sat up quickly and looked around the room.

Nothing.

The phone started beeping again. She scrambled to edge of the mattress and grabbed it. She switched off the alarm and saw it was one am. She definitely hadn't set that alarm.

Someone or something else had.

Damn Jessica and her bloody predictions; Edie thought. She looked up from her phone and saw her last incorporeal visitor.

Chapter 22

She shuddered.

Gliding towards her wreathed in mist and cobwebs was a wizened old woman encased in tatty yellowing lace and chiffon. Her cheekbones were sunken and her face lined and creased. Her white hair, also yellowed, blended into the dress and cobwebs. Her eyes were dark and all pupils.

Edie was reminded of Monet's painting of his wife on her deathbed, grey unfinished charcoal lines fading away to nothing. There was also something familiar in her face, someone Edie knew. There was a whisper of recognition.

The Ghost approached slowly, gravely with great sadness. Depression and gloom flowed before her and pooled behind her like a train.

Edie's heart gave a thump. She remembered her thoughts as she had fallen asleep. Was this what came from hardening your heart? The closer the Ghost came the more depressed and grey Edie felt, as if it was sucking the life from her. That she was being drained of all hope.

They stood staring at each other. Unlike her other visitors this one seemed like the silent kind.

"Are you the Ghost of Weddings Yet To Come?" There was something about her that made Edie's language formal.

From the darkness of the Ghost's eyes came a spark with a disquieting glow, but instead of answering Edie's question it pointed forward with a gnarled and arthritic hand.

"So you're going to show me the future?" Edie found herself talking slowly and distinctly as if the Ghost might be deaf. The withering look it gave her before nodding its head made her feel about an inch big and very stupid. It was a familiar look, if only she could place it.

Along with the familiarity and the stupid feeling, came the symptoms of knees like jelly and she wasn't sure she could move even if the ghost demanded it.

Miss Havisham had figured in some very horrible teenage nightmares.

Was this what Edie had to look forward to?

She had to pull herself together. This was for her own good. Maybe if she got through this she could start making things right. She had to.

"OK Miss Hav…" she stuttered to a stop when the Ghost gave her another look. "Erm… shall we get on with it? Happy to follow you, you know, anywhere?" She let her voice go up at the end, inviting an answer.

The shrivelled, lace-cocooned old besom merely lifted her hand, twisted and swollen, and covered in crocheted fingerless gloves. She pointed out past Edie and towards what should've been the wall of the room. It had been there a moment ago, but now it was grey mist that billowed and retreated as if breathing.

Edie's whole body joined her knees in the jelly symptoms.

"Right you are then, after you." Edie decided to brazen it out, but she was beginning to feel she was speaking as if she were in an Ealing Comedy; albeit a depressing and not very successful one. She felt the urge to giggle hysterically.

The Ghost of the Disappointed Bride, or Miss Havisham, as Edie secretly thought of it, shuffled passed her. As Edie went to follow, her feet tangled in the train from the yellow and dusty gown.

224

She threw her hands out to stop herself from falling, but instead of tripping, it had wrapped itself around her legs, starting at her ankles and then up and round her body, pulled tighter, swaddling her. It seemed to grow and then it carried Edie up and out in the ghost's wake.

At first all Edie could see were the grey clouds billowing round her, almost as if the wedding dress had multiplied and swollen so that it covered the world, until it was wrapped in sadness.

And then through the mist came the City. A building here and a building there, sprouting up until she was surrounded by skyscrapers that reached through the lacy clouds until they melted away.

They alighted at the bottom of the Bailey Lang Satis' office building. The veil that had carried her gently dissolved until it was normal length again and Edie stood uncovered. Edie found herself brushing her pyjama bottoms, trying to rid herself of the feeling of sadness that still clung to her.

The Ghost nudged her and she looked to see a clutch of the firm's trainees coming through the revolving door from the office. Both men and women looked like their suits had been sprayed on as they creased and pulled badly. Edie wished she could pull down a jacket or a skirt to sit better.

And she cringed at one of the boy's over styled hair.

Edie caught Miss Havisham watching her in disgust.

OK, she was being shallow, but it hurt that they didn't make the best of what they could be.

No one should stop them from being the best they could be. Not even themselves.

Edie felt her shoulders slump. That is what she'd been doing.

The trainees all started off down the road and the Spectre slipped alongside them with Edie following in its wake. They turned in at a local wine bar. The place was dark and dim but there was enough space for the Spirit and Edie to slip in next to them.

If Edie could bottle the space making abilities she had during the hauntings she could've made a fortune.

She had to concentrate. She needed to know what she had to do.

"No, I don't know much more than the office email that came round earlier, but she definitely is dead," said one of the male trainees whose hair sculpted into spikes.

"Are you sure? She's the sort that would come back and haunt you." Edie looked at the girl, remembering her. The trainee was earnest and usually frowned in concentration. And never said boo to a goose. Now she still looked nervous but also secretly delighted.

"How did she die?" Another girl, who Edie grudgingly had to admit was a good lawyer, looked both horrified and gleeful.

"I heard that she walked in front of a bus. She was too busy shouting on her phone, obviously taking someone for everything they had and she didn't see it. Squish."

Edie could've done without the hand gesture. The spikes in the guy's hair bobbed excitedly as his hand slammed into the table. Drinks sloshed over the sides and they all giggled and nudged him as they tried to clear it up.

"Are you sure she wasn't pushed by some angry husband?" one of them said.

There was a brief pause before they all fell about laughing. Once they'd calmed down, they raised their glasses.

"Ding, dong the witch is dead." The spiky haired boy said and they all chorused it as they touched glasses.

"They'll probably have to give rent-a-crowd a call to make up the numbers at the funeral," the earnest girl said.

"Hey, if they put on free booze then I'll go. I want to make sure that she is definitely dead and buried. You know she reported me once for going to the loo too many times in one day? I swear she was keeping a tally." The second girl smirked.

Edie was confused. Who were they talking about? And what did it have to do with her? She looked over at the Ghost who was wearing a mocking smile.

"Who...?" she started to ask but the Spectre glided off out of the bar and into the street. It head back to the door of Edie's office building.

Through the doors came two of the partners. They wore their pinstripe suits over paunches hard won through client lunches. Edie watched them, partially envious from having achieved the pinnacle but also in confusion.

What could they tell her?

"Well I can't say that it won't be nice to have her off our backs. Office meetings were so unpleasant," the more senior one said, shifting his belt up on his trousers.

"I know what you mean. HR will be having a party, now they no longer have to deal with constant emails from her. With both her and Hilary gone, I'll bet they feel like they are rolling in clover."

"But you know we'll lose some clients. She was a shark; she learnt from the best. She could've been like Hilary. And no one could take a chunk out of people like she could," the younger man replied and then they paused for a moment.

"It's a pity that she got her last trainee fired, I think that was something like the third one she'd canned," the first man continued. "That trainee, at least, would know some of the cases. But as she's trying to sue us for constructive dismissal and work place bullying, I don't see her coming back to help."

They looked at each other and grimaced.

"We're just going to have to bite the bullet and get someone to look through Edie's files," the senior one said.

The Miss Havisham Spirit with her yellow lace billowing in an invisible spiritual wind stood quietly beside Edie.

Waiting.

"But... surely." Edie scrunched her face up in confusion. She didn't know what to think. What were they talking about? She was dead?

"But I'm going to get Rachel her job back." It was the only thing she could think to say. But then a voice in her head asked why she hadn't done it before she left work on Friday.

The scene dissolved like the most perfect movie cut, Spielberg would've wept but Edie hardly noticed. She was trying to work out whether they were saying she was dead or not...

"Our daughter is in there, crying her heart out over Edie and all you care about is that the funeral will make you miss your golf game." Maggie Remington's voice brought Edie out of her reverie.

Looking round, she recognised it as the Remingtons' house. One that she had spent many years in as a child and teenager.

But that house had been warm. It had felt like a home. A place that had reached out and held her as a girl. But there was none of that in this version of it.

It felt spiky and angry. Edie could feel it prickling on her skin. Or that could've been the waves of antagonism coming off Maggie and Doug.

"Oh, they stayed together," Edie smiled realising the significance of them being in the house together.

She'd got something right.

But then her smile fell.

"Oh shut up, Maggie. Stop guilt tripping me. I'm here now aren't I?" Doug snapped back.

This wasn't a happy marriage.

Maggie sighed.

"Look we agreed that we would stick together for Mel. She never recovered from breaking up with Barry. Thank God they never actually married." Maggie's mouth screwed up in distaste. "And now this with Edie. We all know that Edie is a big reason that Mel and Barry broke up. She always had too much influence over Mel. But Mel still stood by her. So we stand by our daughter. Yes?"

Doug nodded, even though he was shooting Maggie a look that said he'd shut up on this but they weren't done.

Edie wanted to collapse into one of the chairs that were scattered round the room. Her legs were jelly but the chairs looked as uncomfortable and spiky as the atmosphere.

"Oh God, they really hate each other." Edie said. "Am I the

reason they are this unhappy? Are they actually supposed to split up?" She almost wailed.

She was confused. So Maggie and Doug would become a bitter and unhappy couple if they stayed together. She rubbed her head to try and rid herself of the headache that was stabbing behind her eyes.

The door to the living room opened and Mel walked in.

"Oh Mel," she whispered.

Her best friend appeared to have aged twenty years. Where was the blonde bubbly petite pixie? She looked short and stick thin, like a scraped matchstick. Her hair was more grey than gold. Edie wanted to cry when she saw her now, to see her wearing a shapeless black dress that looked like it had been made for someone twice her age and size.

"Can we go?" Mel's voice was monotone. Her eyes were hard.

And as she turned to leave the room without waiting for an answer from her parents, Edie was sure she heard the faint clang of a chain scraping across the floor as Mel walked out of the room.

Edie looked closely. She saw a pink glitter trail following Mel like an obscene wedding train.

She'd doomed Mel.

"What can I do?" she said.

Edie wanted to pull Mel back. Claw off the chain and send her back to Barry. Save her from the fate that Edie faced.

She rushed towards the door.

The Ghost grabbed her arm. The elderly hands were as cold as ice and as strong as steel. Edie couldn't move. The Spectre shook its head as Edie tried to break free.

"Please let me go. I need to tell Mel. I've got to..." she shouted into the face of the Spectre.

They flashed to another scene. Another house; a kitchen that could've been straight out of an interior design magazine.

"He says he has a business meeting but I know he's gone to see her." The voice was harsh and cut through Edie's shouting.

Edie looked round from Miss Havisham to find the voice. It wasn't one she recognised.

But then she saw a face she knew. Admittedly she had only seen it once before, in another haunting.

The face was older, harder and sadder but perfectly made up. The hair was the requisite gold of a yummy mummy. The yoga pants clung to a perfectly sculpted body.

Kitty, Tom's fiancée.

Edie glanced at Kitty's left hand.

She corrected herself. Wife. Edie hadn't buggered that up as yet.

"Well, I don't care that he has his 'little friends,' he'll never leave me and the children. And if he did I'll just make sure I take him for everything he has." Kitty was talking on the phone while her manicured nails tapping on the kitchen work surface in a fast and angry tattoo.

"It's a pity about his ex, Edie. You heard about her? Dead. Just think I could've hired her to take him to the cleaners. Now that would've been perfect. His first love carving him up for his soon to be ex-wife." Kitty's laugh was brittle and hard.

"But how did I do this?" Edie was confused about how this related to her. They were married weren't they?

She hadn't actually seen Tom in real life in years and she'd never met Kitty.

The Ghost laid its hand on Edie's chest, just by her heart. It echoed the actions of that first wedding ghost. Edie's heart stuttered and knowledge unfolded in her head.

"He never truly let himself love again, did he?" she said in wonder and pain. "He settled for what was easy, a life that ticked the boxes."

She looked around the perfect London house. Everything was in its place, designed to cover up the cracks in their life. And he'd caught himself a wife that had turned into the clone of a yoga yummy mummy.

Edie could feel the guilt crushing down on her, drowning her.

"Please, no more. I didn't know. Please." She begged.

The Spectre ignored her, turned and with a twist and flick of its wrist, the veil started to wind round her ankles, and Edie was somewhere else.

The Ghost was beside her, a silent witness.

They were at a place that Edie knew well; the same church that she had visited with that very first ghost two weeks and a life time ago. But this time it was cloaked in gloom; no summer flowers, no bunting, no wedding.

It was empty, she thought, but then she noticed people. Mel stood, looking pale in the awful black dress by the front door. She stood between her parents who were refusing to look at each other.

And standing beside them like a praying mantis wearing a small black veiled pillbox hat, was Hilary Satis.

Edie recoiled when she saw her.

The shoulders of her power suit stretched widely and emphasised her emaciated frame. And her face. It was grotesque. Taut yet puffed and glossy in the dull light. The fillers and plastic surgery made a mockery of her original features. Hilary had tried to stop the clock and keep her youth. She had ended up looking like a monster. The pendent of hammered rings swung from her neck, they looked like links of a chain.

"Is this all there are?"

It was the vicar. A different vicar from the one who'd preformed the ceremony for her teacher and Tom's brother all those years ago. He was young and bookish and was looking at his watch impatiently.

"We need to get going, I have a christening at one."

"Her mum passed away last year and I don't know how to get hold of her father," Maggie offered.

"I think this is it." Mel said, and they went into the church.

This was her funeral? She felt her heart spasm. Her mum had died... Edie was glad she'd spoken to her. No matter what happened after this, she knew they'd had a brief moment of closure.

Edie followed behind the small group of mourners.

But where was her grandmother? Surely she would come. Edie thought.

And someone would say something good about her? Mel would say something nice about her; she had to. And Hilary, well she had been her employee, surely she would.

Eddie began to tremble.

And then she saw it. It stood right in front of the altar.

It was a white monstrosity.

"Who the hell chose this? What kind of fool has a white coffin?" Edie asked, distracting herself from the ache in her heart.

Edie hadn't thought it was possible for Miss Havisham to look any sourer until now.

"OK, OK. Maybe a little off the plot." Edie conceded. "But white…" she whispered.

On top of the white coffin was a small round of flowers, white roses and baby's breath. It was a parody of the circlet of flowers that the jolly bridesmaid ghost, The Ghost of Weddings Present, had worn.

Edie peered closely and saw that it was from the office. They were the only flowers. No one else had bothered.

Edie's four mourners settled themselves, with the Remingtons in a huddle on the front pew and Ms Satis sitting behind them in solitary splendour. Edie wished there was such a thing as a rent-a-crowd; then this wouldn't happen.

The vicar coughed and rustled his papers, preparing to start.

The main door creaked and caused him to glance up.

Edie turned saying, "See there will be more people. They're just late that's all." ●

Thank goodness.

And coming through the door was Jack Twist. Her heart skipped a beat. He'd come.

He held the door for the slight figure of Mrs Pirrip. Edie looked for another figure to arrive behind her but the door closed on her grandmother's heels.

Where was her dad?

They made their way down the aisle slowly. Jack was helping her grandmother who seemed to have shrunk and bowed since Edie saw her last.

Was it really only earlier this week?

As Jack brushed past Miss Havisham, the ghost rustled its gowns in an almost flirtatious way. No one was safe from him, thought Edie.

They took seats next to Mel. Ms Satis looked at him hungrily from the pew behind.

"You came." Mel said.

Mrs Pirrip looked crumpled and grey. Edie wanted to take her hand again and feel the strength she'd felt the other night.

"Yes," her Mimi whispered.

"But where's her dad?" Mel asked the question Edie most wanted answering.

"Why isn't he here? I'm dead for heaven's sake." Edie said.

Mrs Pirrip's face dissolved into tears.

"Jack?" Mel peered passed Mrs Pirrip to ask him instead.

Jack's face was stony as he put an arm round his landlady.

"He didn't think she'd want him here. She made it very clear that she wanted nothing to do with him. He said he could only take so much heartbreak."

Mrs Pirrip sobbed.

"But..." Edie wanted to say that Jack was wrong, that she wouldn't do that.

She stopped herself.

She could do that. Had done that. Had been doing it for years. She always drew back; refuse to forgive; would cut someone out of her life to save herself from hurt. She was an expert at wielding that power.

"I can't believe she's gone for good." Jack sighed and rubbed his face. "Such a bloody loss."

Edie glowed.

"See, he did care."

Her heart lifted, all those pink parts of her heart, newly exposed and now bloody and bruised.

Maybe she had made a difference.

"What do you mean?" Mel asked.

"If just once she could've let someone in, instead of hiding behind a wall while she shrivelled until there was nothing left behind it. She could have been… ah hell." He grabbed the prayer book and waited for the vicar to begin.

"I could've been what?" Edie tried to grab his lapels. "I could've been what?"

Her hands went straight through him; she was as insubstantial as air. She could feel tears trickling down her face.

"I thought she was once of the best trainees I ever had." Ms Satis said, or rather declared.

"That isn't any recommendation," Jack fired back.

Ms Satis looked at him as if he were a moron. Something about her face rang a bell. Edie looked to the Ghost. Miss Havisham was Hilary Satis without the plastic surgery.

Edie shivered.

She looked back at Ms Satis. Is this what she could become?

Turning to the Phantom she shouted.

"Stop it! Stop it! I don't want to hear more." She thought her heart would break. She couldn't sit through listening to the emptiness that her life would become. How empty her life was now. How empty it had been.

What had she achieved? Six mourners at her funeral who were only there out of pity?

Five mourners who all had reasons to hate her.

And one mourner who had a hand in her downfall.

"Take me home!" she sobbed.

The Spirit frowned at Edie; its lips pursed as if sucking lemons and shook its head.

The dusty wedding dress wrapped itself around Edie again; greyness enveloped her. She felt suffocated in grief. She could hardly catch her breath.

The dress fell away and Edie found herself in front of a familiar Lego identi-kit house.

Compared to its neighbours, it was unkempt, the grass grew high and weeds tangled up through the broken stones in the path. The wooden soffits were grey and flaking. The windowsills looked as if an animal had chewed them.

The Ghost and Edie melted through the front wall of the house as if it were a hologram.

"This is Rachel's house" said Edie redundantly but it was different from before.

She frowned as she looked around.

The cosy, toy strewn room was gone.

There were no toys anywhere. Dust and cobwebs covered surfaces and corners. It smelt mouldy and fusty.

It was as if the heart of the house had gone.

Edie's stomach churned. The hairs on her arms rose.

"What happened? Where's Timmy?" Her breath started coming fast; she could feel her heart pounding.

The Ghost pointed a gnarled arthritic hand towards the kitchen. Edie hurried to it with her heart in her throat. She knew these weren't dreams any more. This wasn't her imagination. This was what was to become. What would come true. And it didn't look good at all.

Sitting at the table was a man with straggling greyish hair. Edie barely recognised him as Rachael's fiancé, Rob Cratchit. His face was drawn, lines etched and carved into his cheeks and forehead. His eyes were blank.

Edie saw Rachel.

She was by the stove, stooped and bloated. Like an automaton, she was stirring a saucepan of soup. Edie might have always thought she was wet and annoying, but now there was no life in her.

No spark.

And still no Timmy.

"Where is he?" Edie turned to the ghost. "What happened?"

The Miss Havisham Spirit stared at her with those dark fathomless eyes.

Edie could feel the tears welling up behind her eyes, a sob forcing its way up past a blockage in her throat. She ran past the ghost and thundered up the stairs and fell into the bedroom she'd visited before. The bed was empty and stripped of sheets. The colourful bubble tube was silent and still.

"His mother got custody? That's it isn't it? He's at his mum's. Take me to him." Miss Havisham who had appeared beside her looked at her with sad, knowing eyes. Edie went to grab her dress. She needed to shake the truth from it. Or get it to tell her a lie so she could pretend it had ended well.

But before she could grab the lace, the veil reached up and snagged her wrist. Mist swirled round them, blanking out the bed.

She prayed she'd find Timmy in another bed, laughing at her and lit by a different bubble tube.

The mist cleared and Edie found herself in a cemetery. She stood in front of a small white marble headstone.

"No," she whispered and fell to her knees. With a finger she traced the letters T I M that were carved coldly in the stone.

"No," she said with tears falling from her top lip into her mouth where the salt stung and filled her mouth with bitterness. "I never meant to get her fired."

The Ghost raised an eyebrow.

"OK, I'll admit at the beginning I did. But I'd stopped that; I was trying to help. I was raising money for Timmy. Would he still be here if she had a job?"

Miss Havisham looked at her pityingly, as if she'd left it too late to ask the question.

Too late.

This is what she had done.

Too late.

"Take me home," she sobbed

And with a hot blast of wind and a whisper of lace around her ankles, she was back in Mel's spare bedroom. She collapsed on the bed; Miss Havisham gave her one long last look. It bored deep down into Edie's soul, as if checking what it saw there. The Ghost nodded once, as if satisfied and then faded away like an old Polaroid until nothing was left.

Edie burrowed her head into her pillow. She felt eviscerated, turned inside out. Her whole mind was in turmoil. All the barriers that she had set up to protect herself from the world lay in dusty piles around her. She'd never felt so exposed.

Could she do this?

She took a deep breath. The vision of the white coffin flashed in her mind. The hard look on Jack's face. The cold marble of Timmy's gravestone tingled on her fingers.

She had to.

A shaft of sunlight smacked her awake by shinning straight in her face. Her eyes burned and her eyelids were stuck together from crying herself to sleep. Waking up, she didn't even try to pretend last night was a terrible dream. She had to make things right. It was her last chance.

It was everybody's last chance.

Chapter 23

Edie grabbed her phone from the side table; six thirty. She did some quick calculations. If she got herself together she had time to get to Rachel's and be back in time for the wedding.

This wedding was going to happen; it had to. She wasn't taking no for an answer. Those two were saying 'I do' if she had to be a ventriloquist and throw her voice to say their vows.

She threw on yesterday's clothes and rushed out into the sitting room where Maggie was sitting on the sofa clasping a cup of tea and staring into it as if looking for answers.

"Maggie, you are in charge. Make sure Mel starts getting ready to go to the church." Edie said as she ran past her and headed for the front door.

"What?" Maggie said.

"I'm not marrying him if he's the last man on earth." Mel said.

Edie stopped with her hand on the door and turned to find Mel standing in the doorway from the kitchen, looking pale and shaky. There were dark rings under her eyes.

"Mel, trust me. You want to marry Barry." Edie thought about what she'd witnessed last night and shivered. "You really, really do. Now let me worry about the groom. I'll be back in time for hair and make-up. I promise."

And now she had to keep that promise, no matter what. She

was glad that Mel had gone for a three o'clock wedding. She had time. She hoped.

She didn't wait for an answer, but ran from the house in a desperate rush. Edie hadn't fixed anything yet, but she felt lighter than she had in years. As if she'd shed a massive weight.

She shimmied her shoulders as she unlocked the car. They definitely felt lighter.

But she didn't have time for this, she told herself. She had a mission and she was going to do it or die trying.

She had to be the best version of herself she could be, because she had been failing at it for far too long. Today was the day she shed all the masks she'd created, so the real Edie could emerge.

In the car she turned on the engine and, slamming it into gear, she screeched out and up the road whilst simultaneously dialling a number on her phone.

"Barry?" She shouted at her hands free as the call was answered.

"Edie? He's not talking to you and he's not talking to Mel. I don't know how you managed to infect her with your sickness but you did."

Damn, Tom was screening Barry's calls. Edie had forgotten he was the best man.

"Tom, you're going to have to do this for me then." Her stomach knotted. She was going to have to convince a man whose heart she'd broken and knew what she felt about marriage to believe in what she was saying. So he could convince Barry. Another Edie, even yesterday's Edie would have slumped in defeat. She would've walked away shrugging it off as a bad deal. Cut her losses.

But that was yesterday.

Today's Edie stiffened her shoulders and with every ounce of her will started her sell.

"Listen, I know what I've said before, I know what I've done. I admit to being the cynical Ice Queen bitch that everyone calls me and talks about but I've changed. I can't explain it to you but I have."

She took a hard right then slammed on the brakes to avoid a pigeon in the road.

"Mel and Barry are meant to be. All Mel has ever wanted since she was a little girl was to get married." She got going again, only to be stopped by a red light.

There was silence on the other end of the phone. She bit her lip as she sat at the traffic lights, tapping the wheel with ragged nails.

"Hold on I'm putting you on speaker." Tom said.

Edie waited. She was to have an audience. She couldn't blame Tom. If he tried to tell anyone what she'd just said to him, they'd die laughing, but not before slapping him on the back and telling him what a good joke it was.

"OK, go."

"I know I'm the last person you want to hear this from, Barry, but I believe this. I really do." Edie took a big breath. This was it. She had to make it good.

Edie launched into her speech, as the lights turned green and the streets of London whooshed past.

"Mel was brought up to believe in true love. She believes in the happily ever after. For her whole life, she has had her parents as examples. You marry your soul mate and live happily ever after. Mel, when she loves she loves unconditionally, I mean she's stuck by me for years."

"Too right," she heard Barry say. He was listening. This was good. "But last night, everything she believed was shaken. How couldn't it be? Her mum and dad are on the verge of divorce. Maybe everything and everyone are different? Maybe love isn't everything. And what if after all the time she's believed in a happily ever after, she gets left and ends up all alone?"

"Last night, she was going to call you back but when she heard what had happened with her parents she lashed out at the one person who can hurt her the most. You, Barry. If she didn't love you she wouldn't have attacked you. It was her way of defending herself. She wanted to protect herself. Hell, I've been swiping out at people and things that scare me for years."

She screeched to a stop at a junction. The traffic lights were blurry but when she tried to clean the windscreen she realised that she was crying.

"Barry, she loves you. You need to make her feel secure again. You need to rebuild her foundation. If you don't..."

She choked. She remembered Mel's face from last night's haunting. Heard the scraping clank of the chain, which even now was beginning to forge links and wrap itself around Mel.

And she knew then when her own foundation had been shaken, when her own chain had begun to be forged. Her dad leaving. And that was when her mum's foundation had gone too. And the pair of them had crumbled into the sea of despair. There had been no one to save her. So they'd built the chains that anchored them there.

And Hilary Satis had helped them.

She gulped in air and carried on.

"If you don't help her, you'll regret it till the end of your life and beyond. True love, Barry, it is unconditional. It's in the Ts and Cs."

There was silence at the other end of the phone.

Edie pulled away from the lights and took the dual carriageway.

"Edie?" It wasn't Tom now, it was Barry and he'd taken her off speaker phone.

"Yes?" Her hand shook as she changed gear.

"I'll be at the church." And he hung up.

Edie thumped the steering wheel. Now she needed Maggie to make sure Mel got there. She dialled the number and when it was answered, without waiting for Maggie to speak, she shouted.

"He'll be at the church. Make sure Mel is getting ready. I'll be back in time to talk her through it."

She cut the call. It wasn't ideal but Mel's wedding wasn't the only thing she had to fix that day.

Twenty minutes later, Edie pulled up in front of a familiar town-house. It still looked as if it were built of Lego and she breathed

241

a sigh of relief that it was still neatly kept.

The windowsills were whole and smartly painted, and the grass a regulation few millimetres long. She stared at it, the cold empty feeling from last night, which still clung to her like the trailing ends of the veil started to melt away.

She checked the time.

Eight am.

Early for a Saturday but she didn't have much time. It wasn't as if she was going to get a warm welcome, whatever time of the day she showed up. She could do this.

She opened the car door and got out, a lot more reluctantly than when she'd got in. Edie walked up the path and as she came to the door, she briefly touched the wall she had melted through the night before.

It was solid.

Shaking out her arms, which were stiff from holding onto the steering wheel for dear life, she raised a finger and rang the doorbell.

She could do this. She waited for someone to answer the door.

"You!"

Edie supposed it was too much to ask for Rachel's partner to open the door. Quickly she stuck her foot in the door before Rachel could slam it shut in her face.

Ouch.

Edie smothered the involuntary scream as Rachel slammed the door on her foot. If the wedding did go ahead she would be limping down the aisle. And dancing would be somewhat difficult.

"Please, let me talk," she said.

"Talk? Why should I talk to you? You've ruined everything." Rachel leant on the door. Edie's shoe creaked in protest.

Why couldn't it be winter so she could've been wearing boots?

"Please, I want to explain." She wasn't sure how she could explain but she was going to give it a damn good try.

Lives depended on it.

"What's wrong?" Rob Cratchit appeared behind Rachel.

"The Queen Bitch here is trying to explain how she's ruined our lives."

Edie had never guessed that under Rachel's meek exterior lay this lioness. Maybe there was hope for Rachel as a lawyer yet. But maybe more general family law, not divorce.

"Let her in, love." Rob reached out and stroked Rachel's arm.

Edie could see Rachel relax and lean into him at his touch.

She felt a stab at her heart.

Damn, she was jealous of Rachel. She would've laughed from the sheer obviousness of it if she didn't think it wouldn't have set Rachel into a rage.

Of course she was jealous. Rachel had people and connections. Edie had none. Edie owed it to her to fix what she'd tried to sabotage.

Rachel held on to the door a moment longer while Rob held her arm. She glared at Edie whilst putting a bit more pressure on her squashed foot. Edie's eyes started to water.

Then the pressure eased and Edie fell in through the door.

The room was exactly how she remembered it from her first visit; light and messy, clean and full of toys. It wasn't too late.

Babbling came from the kitchen and Edie found her attention drawn there.

Timmy.

She needed to see him, to make sure he was OK. She started towards the kitchen.

"No. You can't." Rachel said.

She darted in front of Edie to try and cut her off but Edie faked a pass and slipped past her.

Timmy was sat at the kitchen table smiling at her as if asking 'What took you so long?' With everything else that had been going on, Edie wouldn't have been surprised if he tapped a clock and told her off.

"Hi Timmy," she said.

He made a gesture and smiled at her.

It soothed all the jagged edges that were still inside her, including the shame of having been jealous of Rachel.

"That means hello." Rob said from behind her.

"He's amazing," Edie said in wonder as she smiled back at him.

"Stop it." Rachel grabbed her arm and started trying to pull at her away. She was trying to drag her out of the kitchen.

She had to make this right for all of them. Edie shook off Rachel's arm and turned to face them both.

"Rachel, I'm sorry. More than you can ever know. For everything. I'm sorry for being a bitch to you. I'm sorry for sending those emails to HR, all of which I will be taking back on Monday morning. I'll also be looking to ensure that you are rewarded for the work you do and see how we can work around your family here." Edie gestured to Rob and Timmy.

Rachel still looked sceptical and had an eyebrow raised but at least she'd stopped trying to drag Edie out of the kitchen. Her mouth was mulish.

"Most of all I'm sorry for invading your privacy and causing the issue with Timmy. I truly wanted to help. But I'm not good with people."

"Too right," said Rachel.

"It was supposed to be my way of making amends but I was too self-involved to actually talk to you. To work out what would actually help. And with the custody case... I'm going to make sure that you get the best representation and anything you need in terms of references or personal statements."

There was silence.

Rachel was still tense, watching her like a cat at a mouse hole. She looked as if she was waiting for the punch line. Or for Edie to kick her. Rob was watching her intently.

Edie waited. She didn't know what else she could do. There was no punch line. She didn't know how to be more sincere. All those years of being a bitch to people meant it was hard for them to overcome their doubts and for people to take her seriously. The silence stretched uncomfortably.

Then, just before Edie was about to fall on her knees, wrap her arms round Rachel's legs and howl to be saved, help came from an unexpected source.

There was a stream of sound from Timmy with more hand gestures.

"No." Rachel said sharply.

"What did he say?" Edie wanted to know; she looked at him. His eyes were gleaming and his smile was wide.

"He said 'she's sorry, be nice.'" Rob said.

She had Timmy on her side. How, she didn't know, but she did. She could still feel the letters of his name carved into marble on her fingertips. They were carved in her heart. It gave her goose bumps.

Not on her watch. No.

They all looked to Rachel for an answer. She was biting her lip. *Listen to Timmy*, Edie tried to will her to hear. For some reason he could see past her masks and walls and see the real Edie. The one she was just rediscovering.

"Do you mean it?" Rachel asked at long last.

Edie almost collapsed sobbing on the floor. Maybe she could do this after all.

She left half an hour later having signed a statement swearing that she would do what she'd promised under pain of some really uncomfortable professional embarrassments. She'd also drafted the email to send to HR and sent it while Rachel watched over her shoulder.

Yes, Rachel had a good future as a lawyer.

Edie jumped back into the car. Time check; eight forty five am. Plenty of time to make it back to Mel's for hair and make-up and to persuade Mel that she needed to show up for her own wedding. She turned on the engine, put the car in gear and raced back the way she'd come.

Chapter 24

"Where the hell have you been?" Mel was wide-eyed and pale, wringing her hands as she sat on a straight-backed chair in the front room.

The mountain bike seemed to have been moved elsewhere and all the available space was taken up with people.

Mel was surrounded.

The make-up artist, the hairdresser, the bridesmaids and Maggie standing in the hallway, hair wild.

And Sophie was smugly holding Mel's hand.

"Really, how can you be so selfish running off like that, Edie? Poor Mel has been sitting here, panicking. Personally, I think we should be cancelling everything. I couldn't even get Barry to listen to reason last night, and I'm his sister." Sophie said.

Edie saw Mel quiver as if she'd been shot. She wondered whether slapping Sophie would undo all the good she'd just done?

"I had to sort a few things out but I'm here now." Edie said as she rushed to Mel's side.

She bumped Sophie out of the way with a careful elbow and hip. She didn't think she left bruises but wished she had.

"Mum says that Barry will be there." Mel had a death grip on Edie's hand. "But he isn't taking Sophie's calls, so we can't check."

Sophie had even managed to annoy her brother.

"Yes, he'll be there. He promised." Edie patted Mel's hand, which was now crushing hers.

She needed a glass of champagne, stat. She looked round; there was none.

"Maggie, can you get the bottles I put in the fridge? We need them."

"I don't think we should be celebrating." Sophie said.

She was really getting on Edie's wick.

"Shut up, Sophie." Edie said.

"No, I won't. It isn't like you 'do weddings' is it? How can we be sure you aren't setting Mel up just to prove your point?"

The room went silent and everyone paused. Edie could feel herself blush, her cheeks hot.

"Yes, Edie. What do you care? You hate weddings. You don't believe in true love. How can you be sure?" Mel said, her grip loosening on Edie's hand.

Edie's raw, exposed heart flinched. Here was the proof of how far she'd fallen. Even Mel didn't believe her.

But she had to make her believe.

"I do care. I care a lot. I've spent years pushing people away to protect myself. Years telling myself that it didn't matter. That true love was just a ruse. That none of it mattered. But I was wrong. Mel, I was wrong." Edie said trying to sound convincing, putting her all into it.

She could hear Sophie tutting.

Edie needed more. She was feeling desperate. She could tell that the successful feeling was slipping away from her. She could feel the chain around her waist getting heavier.

Looking round she saw it; Mel's wedding dress, hanging swathed in plastic in the doorway. Edie couldn't help but smile. Mel had looked amazing in it at the last fitting. She'd glowed with happiness. She had been a vision.

She had been the embodiment of true love.

Edie gestured to it.

"See, Mel. Your dress. Remember how you looked in it? You glowed in that dress because you were wearing the gown that you will be marrying your true love in. It is more than today, the wedding. It is about a marriage. It is about forever.

Edie paused, then said "You love him. You really love him. What does it matter if your parents have lost their way? That is their life, not yours. You and Barry can handle anything and everything. You always could." Edie's voice broke and she realised she was clutching Mel's hand just as tightly as she was clutching hers.

Sophie sighed and tutted some more.

"Shut up, Sophie." Jo, Maggie plus the hairdresser and make-up artist all said at the same time.

Edie looked up. Everyone but Sophie was in tears.

"Oh no! But it's too late, Edie. I told him I wasn't marrying him." Mel slumped back in her chair, her shoulders shaking. "He isn't going to come is he? I've blown it."

"Of course he's coming." Edie said. "I spoke to him this morning. He'll be there. He promised. I promise." Edie finished, realising that saying Barry had promised might remind Mel that he'd promised to sort out the DJ but hadn't.

"You do? You promise?" Mel sat up a little straighter. Hope on her face.

"I promise and I'll be there every step of the way." Edie reiterated. This was part of her present to Mel. She couldn't let her be damned like Edie had been.

There was a snort from Sophie.

Jo elbowed her.

Edie smiled. The day was getting better.

"Now let's get that champagne out. We've got a wedding to get to."

She let go of Mel's hand and went to help Maggie pour out the bubbles.

"Sophie! You're stepping all over my dress," Jo complained as they loaded up the cars, which were clogging up the small street in front of Mel's house.

Edie watched from the corner. She, luckily, was in a car with the flower girl and Maggie.

She helped Mel get into the white Bentley, smoothing out the long skirt of the dress to minimise creases. Doug got in the car next to Mel.

"Dad!" Mel wailed as Doug sat on the dress.

"Sorry!" he shifted off it.

"It will be fine, see? All gone," said Edie as she patted it flat.

"See you at the church." Edie said as the chauffeur shut the door, got behind the wheel and drove off.

Behind her small posy of flowers that echoed Mel's larger bouquet, Edie had her fingers crossed, while she waved with the other hand.

This was going to work out. It had to.

"Edie!" Maggie called her over.

Edie stopped waving and picked up the handbag with her essentials in it. She got into the waiting black car and put the bag in the footwell.

Mel was off to the church safely. Jo and Sophie were in the car in front. Edie could see Sophie waving her hands around.

Poor Jo, she thought. But they had their posies and they were on their way. She could relax now until they got to the church.

They headed slowly down the residential streets of south London. The church was only a few miles away but Edie knew with Saturday traffic it would take them about half an hour.

She relaxed into the seat; there was nothing more she could do until they got there.

Please, Barry, she thought. Please be there. But what if he wasn't? Well then, she'd make sure that Mel didn't turn into a bitter person like she'd been. They'd work it out together. They'd move on together.

Edie smiled at Maggie who was looking regal as only the

mother of the bride could.

Everything was going to go right, Edie decided. Positive thinking.

Edie felt the vibration of her phone against her foot from where her handbag sat. She leant down, her heart thumping.

Please don't be Barry backing out, she prayed.

It was an unknown number.

She pressed the button to answer.

If this is a sales call, she thought, she wouldn't be responsible for her actions. No one would blame her, least of all the Ghosts.

She braced herself to hear about how she could claim for a car accident she'd never had.

"Edie Dickens" she answered.

"Edie?" it was a vaguely familiar male voice.

"Yes?" Please don't let it be the vicar, she thought. She chewed the skin at the corner of her thumbnail, there wasn't enough nail left to chew on.

She was going to have to hide her hands for the photos, she thought, while she tried to place the voice.

"Edie, this is your dad." The voice was husky and hesitant.

Her dad? Her father was talking to her.

Chapter 25

All the blood rushed out of her head, she felt dizzy. Her heart halted, then started hammering hard in her chest. It felt like it wanted to jump out of her.

She couldn't breathe. Her lungs felt paralysed.

She gulped down some air but she couldn't say anything.

She was mute.

Say something, Edie, she shouted in her mind.

"I hope you don't mind. Mum gave me your phone number," the voice, her dad carried on.

All Edie could do was press the phone closer to her ear to be as near to him as she could.

The voice was warm; it felt like a hug.

"Edie?" he asked.

She realised she still hadn't said anything.

"I don't mind," she croaked.

"Look, I know it's short notice but I'm in London today. I fly out again later tonight and won't be back for a fortnight so I was hoping we could meet?"

He was in London

Did she want to meet him? Of course she did.

She wanted to grab the driver and tell him to take her to the airport or wherever he was. To leave now, do not pass go, do not collect two hundred pounds or stop for a wedding.

The wedding.

She had to go to the wedding.

Edie started to work out how quickly she could get away from the church and go meet him.

But you promised, Mel, the voice in her head told her.

And that was the problem.

Edie didn't need to see the sparkle of glitter flashing in her eye from the flower girl's ballet shoes, to remind her that she had other commitments to keep.

"I'm sorry, I'm at a wedding today." She cringed as she said it. Would he think she was deliberately standing him up? "I'm the maid of honour. It's Mel Remington's wedding. I can't. I want..." she stuttered to a stop.

Please let him understand. Edie's heart thundered. Don't let him think I'm pushing him away. She shivered as she remembered his no show at her funeral.

Was this the beginning?

"No, I understand. I was just so desperate to see you and didn't want to wait another two weeks," he was smiling; she could hear it in his voice. She remembered that he was a smiley person. How his grins had reached out to her as if he were hugging her.

She missed his hugs too; she hadn't realised before.

She could feel his phantom arms around her, holding her close and making her feel safe.

"But maybe we can talk?" He said. "While I'm away. We could Skype?"

Then she'd see his smiles as well as hear them.

"Yes," she said. "I'd like that."

There was an awkward silence but she knew he was smiling down the phone at her, because she was grinning down the phone to him.

"Bye then," he said.

"Bye," she whispered. Pressing the phone to her ear even harder she heard the line disconnect.

"Daddy," she finished.

Edie could feel her face pulling into a smile she hadn't worn in years. Maybe he would teach her to be a smiley person too.

She clutched the locket around her neck.

"Edie? Are you OK?" Maggie interrupted her thoughts.

Edie jumped. She'd forgotten she wasn't alone.

"That was my dad." Edie said in wonder.

"Oh Edie," Maggie reached across and patted her knee.

"He's in town for a few hours but..." Edie gestured at the dress and the posy.

"Well maybe afterwards?" But even Maggie sounded doubtful.

Edie clutched her phone in one hand and the locket in the other.

Maybe she could sneak out? She could tell Mel. She'd understand. Edie could call her dad back and then she could see him, even for a moment.

She could, couldn't she?

"Edie?" Maggie asked.

"We'll work something out." Edie said.

And then she knew it was the right time to see what was in the locket. She'd avoided opening it until she met her dad. Well that call almost counted as meeting him.

If it had been a photo of her dad inside and she never got to see him, she hadn't wanted to open it. But now she would be seeing him so the photo wouldn't matter.

It was time.

Gently she clicked the lock that held the two pieces together and it swung open.

There was no photo.

But there was more engraved writing.

Remember - never let anyone stop you being the best you can be

It was there, engraved in a locket by her heart.

And then she knew why her father's voice had sounded so familiar. It was the voice she heard when that saying went through her head.

But for so long she'd been the one stopping herself being the best.

She closed the locket again and smoothed it down to rest on her heart.

"So what are you going to do?" Maggie asked.

"I'm going to do my best." Edie replied. It was all she could do.

The car turned the last corner and they arrived at the church, a Victorian red brick building in a south London suburb.

And somehow they'd arrived before Mel.

Please let it be the driver being fancy with his sat nav rather than Mel having a change of heart, she thought.

Please. Please. She sent the words upwards and hoped someone would hear.

Edie stepped out of the car smoothing her dress down, trying to get rid of the wrinkles. Not that there was really anything she could do about the rest of the dress.

Edie shifted from foot to foot, waiting for Mel to arrive.

Maybe she could be at the service and the photos then race back up to Heathrow and meet her dad. Surely that would be fine? It just took a bit of planning.

Then turning the corner came the white Bentley, sweeping up to the steps of the church. Edie got to the door before the chauffeur to help Mel out.

"Do you think he's here? Edie, can you check?" Mel was pale under her makeup, the blusher standing out on her cheeks.

Edie had to concentrate; this wasn't about her meeting her dad. This was about Mel.

"Of course." Edie said.

Anything to make Mel feel better, Edie had put her faith in Barry. He would turn up. He had to.

She could only deal with her side of things.

The feeling of being out of control threatened to swamp her.

She could feel herself tightening up, shutting down her emotions to deal with it.

She was freezing over.

No. She needed to learn a new way to cope.

Losing her barriers, her need to trust in love and other people would mean that she felt out of control.

She'd get used to it.

She smiled, cracking the thin layer of ice that had started to form, and she squeezed Mel's hand.

Edie left Jo and Sophie to fuss over Mel and walked up the steps and crept into the church; the long skirts of the Day-Glo green silk bridesmaid's dress swishing on the cold stone.

"Whoever sent me those Ghosts, you have to make this right. I'm doing everything you asked. I believe. Goddammit, I believe." She said.

She wondered if she had to clap to show she believed in love or would that only work for fairies?

And from above came a small flash of glitter, it fell from the rafters and settled on the back of her hand.

She stared at it. Let it be a sign, she thought.

She hid behind one of the towering flower arrangements. Spiky petals thrust to the ceiling.

She parted the foliage and peered through. There were three figures at the front of the church, waiting at the altar.

Barry was tugging at his tie and fidgeting.

Tom was standing beside him and was chewing on his lip.

And towering over them all was Jack Twist. He had his hand on Barry's arm, talking to him and he seemed to be reassuring him.

She looked at the glitter again. It flashed in the light from the stained glass window. She now had to hope Barry would go through with it...

But she had to leave it in the lap of the gods and, by the looks of things, Jack Twist.

Edie let the foliage sprung back and smoothed a crumpled bloom, until she realised how it could look and quickly snatched her hand away. She hoped no one saw.

She crept back out and into the vestibule where the bridal party were now huddled, waiting for an update.

"So? Is he here?" Mel asked as soon as she saw Edie.

"He's here." Edie smiled encouragingly.

"Thank you," Mel said clutching her bouquet, tears beginning to appear in her eyes.

Mel's father, Doug, was also misty eyed and his face was red with emotion. He was patting Mel's hand.

"Baby, see Edie fixed it. You'll be fine. And I'm sorry that your mother and I almost ruined this for you. We love you. We'll work something out, but that is for us to do. Not you. And we're so happy for you and Barry." He slid a look at Edie, his face went reddish purple and he looked away quickly.

Edie looked away, her face also red. There were things she now knew about Maggie and Doug that no one should know.

Maybe she'd be able to face them without blushing sometime in the next decade.

"I love you, Daddy." Mel said.

"Love you too, baby." Doug replied, threading her arm through his.

Edie wished she could say that, she desperately wanted to hear it too. Maybe today. Mel would understand. But as she thought that, she touched her locket and she remembered.

She had to be the best she could be. And that meant that for today she would do what Mel needed, and if that meant missing seeing her dad...

Her heart squeezed.

There was a wheezing sound from the church, then some whistling, which suddenly erupted into the start of the processional music. The organ was elderly, probably as old as the church

This was it.

For better or for worse.

Edie prayed that Barry didn't do a *Four Weddings* moment and declare it was all off right at the altar. If he did she was going to show Jack Twist what a rugby tackle really looked like.

"Ready?" Edie asked Mel who nodded back, her face now flushed beneath the make-up.

The small flower girl, who in no way resembled the Ghost of Weddings Past, for which Edie had been thankful for, started down the aisle. She flung fistfuls of pink and white petals instead of scattering them and as a result ran out halfway down the nave. She stood for a moment, staring into her basket before she ran up the aisle to find her mother, where she buried her face in her lap.

Edie smiled. There was no point worrying.

Then came Jo, who bounced down the aisle on the balls of her feet. Followed by Sophie, who was too slim, red-headed and bitter to be Ghost of Weddings Present.

And, before she was quite ready, it was Edie's turn.

She hoped she'd shed any of the despair and sadness that had wrapped itself round Miss Havisham, the Ghost of Weddings Past.

She wanted to channel the jolly bridesmaid of the present, or at least her own version of it.

Edie could feel everyone staring at her. Their looks held weight and she felt she was dragging them with her as she walked down the aisle. They were like the chain she wasn't sure she still carried. The further she walked, the more she saw; some were watching her with hatred and others with contempt.

She squared her shoulders and carried on. This was the beginning of a long journey. She couldn't change people's opinions overnight. There was a long way to go to make things right but... She thought of her locket. It was all about being the best you could be and no one said that was an easy way to live your life. But some things were worth the pain, she realised.

The organ crashed, wheezed and whistled its way to a crescendo before it paused and then the wedding march started.

Edie smiled as she reached the altar and saw Barry turned round and look past Edie. His face was pale, but it lit up from within, his hand dropped from his collar. He drew himself up and pulled his waistcoat down. His face broke into a wide, wondering grin.

He's seen Mel, thought Edie. Everything would be OK.

She let herself relax, and she felt the weight of the stares lessen as they all turned to watch the bride.

So far, so good.

Edie watched Mel walk down the aisle.

Gone was the scared flushed girl she'd left in the vestibule. It was as if with every step she took towards Barry, she gained the inner glow Edie remembered from the wedding dress fitting. And as she reached him, she was incandescent.

Edie crossed her fingers behind her posy. This could actually work.

She caught Jack staring at her.

He towered over Barry, but for once he wasn't the centre of attention. Only Edie was watching him.

His eyes were narrowed with suspicion as he looked at her.

Let him worry, she thought as she grinned back at him. This was going to be good. Mel and Barry would get married and everything would work out.

There was a brief collective holding of breath when the vicar asked whether anyone had any just cause or impediment to stop the marriage.

Edie ignored the weight of stares from the congregation. She wasn't stopping this.

And then finally there were the 'I dos' but Edie didn't stop crossing her fingers until Mel and Barry were locked in their first marital embrace.

Yes. She gave a mini fist pump with her posy.

As the congregation applauded and the organ wheezed back into life, Edie heard above it, the sound of a clink as if some links from a chain had fallen away.

The scrum in the vestry where they signed the register was joyful. There was room only for Mel, Barry, Edie, Tom and the photographer.

Through the door she could see Jack frowning at her.

"Edie," Tom whispered in her ear. She jumped.

How had he got so close?

It was weird to think that at one point she'd known where he was without thinking. Like she could now with Jack.

But before she could reply, they had to move round and sign their names.

And before she knew it, they were all walking behind Mel and Barry down the aisle.

Sophie had grasped Jack's arm and dragged him with her. So Edie walked ahead of Tom and Jo, on her own and out into the sunshine.

Edie felt the sun on her face and turned up to it like a sunflower. She almost skipped down the steps. But instead, she promptly tripped over the first step and a hand had to haul her back before she went down them face first. The hand wasn't calloused or big enough to be Jack's. And it didn't make her stomach break out into butterflies.

She looked up and saw it was Tom. He'd let go of Jo's arm and run to catch her.

Edie could feel the guests holding their breath as they realised that this could become a scene.

"Thanks," she said and moved out of his hold carefully.

She saw a small hand with a large glittering stone on their ring finger take Tom's from where it hung as if he was going to grab Edie again.

She stared at Tom.

This was the man she could've married. She remembered the way his curls had felt between her fingers. The kisses that had woken her up every morning. The feel of his hand curled round hers.

And she glanced down to see that hand clasping someone else's.

259

Chapter 26

She waited to feel a slam in her chest, that punch of regret. Instead all she felt was a wave of sadness breaking over her for what could've been. For what she'd thrown away. And then there was a brief tug of happiness that they'd once been in love, as she felt the tide on their relationship go out.

It seemed to have happened to another person. A different Edie.

"Edie." He sounded eager but wary behind a front of cheerfulness; it was odd that she could still read him that well.

"It's good to see you," he carried on and she could see he was searching for something in her face. Looking for the girl he'd known.

She could feel her mouth pull up into a smile. She never thought she would smile at him again. It felt nice, as if she was flexing a muscle she'd been too worried to move in case it hurt.

"Tom, it's good to see you too."

Edie then waited for the introduction to the woman at his side. The woman she'd already seen before in her hauntings. She didn't think it was socially polite to make out that she'd overheard them at dinner. Or, of course, what their future could hold.

Not socially polite and of course the quickest route to the mental hospital.

"Edie, this is Kitty." Tom introduced Kitty as if she was a prize.

Like he was laying a conquest at Edie's feet. And he wasn't looking at Kitty, but at Edie as he said it, waiting for her reaction, as if he wanted her to praise him.

Edie also realised the whole wedding congregation was watching her just as closely. As if she were a ticking time bomb about to go off.

They were all going to be very bored, very quickly.

"Kitty, it is great to meet you." Edie smiled.

She was happy for them; although she was also apprehensive.

What was she supposed to do with the knowledge of their future? Was she meant to fix it?

Edie wasn't going to do anything, in case she mucked it up. If she wished hard enough maybe they would have a happy marriage and Kitty wouldn't become the bitter woman she'd seen.

Edie looked back up at Tom who was eagerly waiting for something.

But maybe she was supposed to tell them?

Edie was confused. Why didn't this whole experience come with instructions?

Is this what he wanted? Marrying a woman who would be happy for him to cheat? Marrying someone he would cheat on? It seemed so sad. Or was Edie supposed to stop it?

Or maybe Edie had done this?

Part of her wanted to shake Tom and remind him of what it could be like, but what right did she have? She'd spent the past ten years hiding.

A whole decade spent frozen.

She'd always thought Tom was fine; he'd left because he hadn't loved her any more. But she'd seen him in that restaurant. She'd watch what she'd done to him.

No one came out unscathed. But she couldn't save everyone. Could she?

She looked back at Kitty whose eyes were cold behind the smile.

"I hear congratulations are in order?" Edie could do this.

Maybe she couldn't have done it yesterday and definitely not a week ago but things had changed. She needed to get through this wedding with grace and determination and make it the best day for Mel and Barry. That didn't include a scene that everyone seemed ready to settle down to watch with popcorn.

"Yes, we're very happy," Kitty purred. She wrapped her arm round her and Tom's linked hands and drew him closer.

Edie smiled. She had to leave them to sort it out. Look what had happened when she'd interfered with Doug and Maggie.

She moved past them and down the rest of the steps.

She'd done it.

"Edie." Jack was coldly polite as they stood for photos in front of the church. She was trying to keep as much distance as she could between herself and Tom. Plus she was avoiding Sophie. Which meant that she was stuck next to Jack.

Rocks, spikes and hard place came to mind.

"I don't know what you're playing at." Jack spoke out of the side of his mouth.

"What do you mean?" Edie's face hurt from the grin she couldn't lose, no matter what was happening. Admittedly it made everyone think she was on drugs or mentally unstable.

"I've been playing Cupid," she said.

"You. Cupid?" Jack spluttered and ruined the photo.

"Can we all concentrate?" the photographer shouted as she leapt round like a frog on a hot plate.

Edie posed again and said out of the corner of her mouth.

"Why not? Everyone can change you know. Maybe I've decided that this love lark is worth something."

She could feel Jack was looking at her and she guessed it was probably with an incredulous expression on his face.

He was going to ruin another photo.

"What happened to the Edie of yesterday? The one who didn't care that she'd ruined someone's career and life?" Edie flinched and she knew her smile slipped.

She felt as if he'd struck her.

"I went to see Rachel this morning and we've hatched a plan about getting her job back," she said.

"But that could ruin your career."

Edie nodded as she felt the smile coming back.

"There are more things in life than work, Jack. Haven't you learnt that yet?" she smiled and looked up through her eyelashes at him.

"Ha!" Jack smiled back bitterly and confused. "Who are you, and what have you done with the real Edie Dickens?"

"Maybe I am the real Edie Dickens and the other was just a bad dream?" Edie said.

He hummed and looked sceptical.

"How long does this version of Edie Dickens stick around for?" he asked.

Edie smiled sadly; here was someone else who wasn't buying her change. It wasn't going to be as easy as she thought. What she wouldn't give for Jack to be one of the people who believed in her. But she hadn't exactly given him any kind of idea that she would change. She'd been either kissing him or being a bitch for the past fortnight.

She turned her attention back to the photographer.

"She's here for keeps," she said and hoped he'd start believing her.

As the photographs drew to an end she looked at her phone.

Five pm.

Time had bled away and she realised with a sinking feeling that her plan to see her dad wasn't going to happen.

How had she ever thought it would?

Some of the fizz that she'd had went flat. She wasn't going to get her happy ever after just yet.

She stood slightly apart from the rest of the wedding party as they waited for the cars to take them to the venue.

She looked at them all.

Barry and Mel staring at each other with goofy smiles on their faces.

Maggie and Doug keeping a distance from each other.

Tom and Kitty clinging together but staring away in opposite direction, checking out who was watching them.

And Jack. Jack was watching her with a thoughtful but frowning look on his face.

She shrugged off the feeling of deflation. This wasn't about her. All she had to remember was to be the best version of Edie she could be.

And as she remembered that, the goofy grin bubbled up inside and spread to her face.

She moved towards the wedding cars that had finally turned up, carefully avoiding Jack. She didn't want to be stuck in an enclosed space with him. She didn't trust herself. She wanted to throw herself at him and it looked like he wanted to throw her out.

She watched as Sophie dragged Jack into the car next to her, telling anyone who would listen that they were old family friends.

"Edie."

It was her mum. She laid a hand on Edie's arm.

How had Edie forgotten she was here? Where had she been?

"I've been hiding out at the back of the church," her mum could read her mind. "I'm trying to be more positive but I didn't want to be the spectre at the feast."

Edie shivered at her mother's mention of ghosts.

"Edie, Maggie told me that your father called. Why haven't you gone to see him?" Her mum's voice was calm. The edge that was usually there when she mentioned Edie's father was absent.

"Because today is about Mel and I made her a promise. Also," Edie laughed as she covered her mum's hand. "I'm trying to be the best version of me I can be."

"That is what your father always said." Her mother sighed. "Maybe I should've remembered that."

They smiled at each other and Edie bent down and kissed her

mum on the cheek, drinking in the smell of her, the scent of her perfume taking her back to her childhood. The childhood she now wanted to remember.

Chapter 27

"Edie."

The speeches were over and the dancing was about to begin, so she'd slipped out of the reception for some time on her own but it seemed everyone wanted to speak to her tonight.

There was only so much she could take, when all she wanted was to throw herself at Jack, and tell him she wasn't the bad person he thought she was. But she knew that words were hollow, easy to say. Hell, she was a lawyer.

She had to prove it to him. She had to fix the things she'd broken.

And after everything that had happened she couldn't blame Jack for not trusting her word that she'd changed. Show, don't tell.

So a bit of peace and quiet was what she craved before she went back. And the night was clear and warm, so it wasn't a hardship.

But someone didn't want her to be on her own.

Maybe if she moved onto the fairways? She started to move further down off the terrace and out on to the grass.

If it looked like she hadn't heard them then maybe they'd leave her alone.

The music and the laughter and lights coming from behind Edie reminded her of that teenage wedding, so much nostalgia wove around her. She felt as if she was swimming in it.

"Edie," the voice called again.

He wasn't giving up; she was being haunted by more than Ghosts this weekend.

"Tom." She whispered his name, turning to look at him.

He hurried towards her onto the fairway. His morning suit looked so like the suit he'd worn all those years before. And in the darkness, the lines on his face melted away until he almost looked the same age he had when he'd rubbed her back as she threw up.

She looked around for Kitty. He was alone.

"Shug." He said his nickname for her and stood in front of her smiling the same old smile, the one that tugged up the corner of his mouth.

That smile stirred some residual warmth in her, like the embers of a coal fire flaring before dying down.

But what if he'd been wearing something else, looked less like the boy she'd loved. The flare wouldn't have been quite as bright.

"Doesn't it remind you," he began. She started to nod. "Of that first night we kissed at Justin Douglas' wedding," he finished.

Edie thought back to the night she'd only relived last week. And although that kiss had been amazing and had set her life on a different path, it was the other wedding that stuck with her. The one when they had been young and innocent, the wedding before her life had changed.

"I was thinking it reminds me of your brother's wedding," she said.

"The Hurling Incident." They said it together like it was the title of a film and laughed.

The echo of the laughter settled over them like a comfortable blanket and cocooned them as without speaking or agreeing, they started to walk together away from the wedding reception.

Tom was walking just a little too closely.

"Do you ever wonder what it would've been like if we'd stayed together?" he asked after a moment, as they headed towards a clump of trees that was silhouetted against the night sky.

This wasn't the man who'd been so bitter at the dinner party.

This man wouldn't have called her the Ice Queen.

What had changed? Or had he said those things because Kitty had been there?

Her head hurt from trying to untangle all the possibilities.

"Why do you want to know?"

She knew why she'd been feeling nostalgic, she'd been neck deep in her past only a few weeks ago, but why was he? He had Kitty.

"I've always wondered that if I'd only tried harder, maybe stayed and fought for you, whether you would've calmed down on the work front and we would have worked."

The 'what if's'.

They could curse you. Anchor you to the past.

What could she say to him?

That she hadn't loved him enough to put him first. Hadn't thought him worth fighting for. Had shut down when he left, rather than change. Had kept herself anchored to the past.

She could blame her parents or even Ms Satis but really it came down to the fact she hadn't been ready, she hadn't cared enough. But that wasn't what he needed to hear.

She needed to set him free.

Then maybe he and Kitty would stand a chance.

"Part of me wishes you had stayed. Maybe it would've been different but we can never know," she said as she turned to face him.

He was close, looking down at her, his face was twisted in pain.

"But never mind the 'what ifs' of you and me, you have Kitty now. And too much time has passed; we're not the same people." He looked like he wanted to argue.

He was living in the past, wanting a ghost or a version of Edie that had never existed.

"You deserve to be happy, Tom." She stretched up on tiptoe, put her hands on his shoulders and kissed his cheek.

He wrapped his arms around her and hugged her. She hugged him briefly back.

"Are you sure?" he whispered in her ear.

She felt sorry for him, and for Kitty; he was still chasing ghosts. She needed to put this one to rest.

"Positive."

She pulled away. He let her go reluctantly. His hands lingered on her hips until she took a step back and they fell away.

She took his arm and turned him round. Pushing him back towards the wedding reception.

"The future is that way," she said.

With one last look over his shoulder, he walked away.

She watched him go, and a part of her wondered what would have happened if he'd asked that same question a month ago.

But he wouldn't have, because the Edie of a month ago or even yesterday would've acted like a harridan and been appalling.

"He's engaged, you know." The dark voice came from a tree to her side.

And here was someone who did know what an awful person she could be. *Had been.*

"Are you stalking me?" she asked.

Suddenly, she was angry that the one person she wanted to believe in her transformation, to see that she really had changed, couldn't.

She could've had her first love back but he wasn't the one she wanted now.

She wanted her last love.

Maybe this was purgatory? She was no longer going to be in the hell that was floating round in chains and glittery fairy wings, but she'd be paying by spending the rest of her life wanting Jack.

And never having him.

Her heart clenched.

So be it. If this is what loving unconditionally is. She had to take the rough with the smooth.

And maybe inner Edie would stop with the sexy fantasies one day.

"I came out for a breath of air and when I was coming back

round those trees I find you wrapped around your ex." Jack said

He was as angry as she was.

He strode up to her and grabbed her arm. He was frowning down at her. Edie wished she could see better; had he completely lost faith in her?

And suddenly she could feel the anger drain out of her, as if a plug had been pulled and it poured out of her.

She felt so tired. Right down to her bones.

She'd been up since dawn trying to make things right. Getting the wedding back on track. Keeping the bride's parents from killing each other, and not making inappropriate passes at the wait staff or ushers. When she'd left the reception, all seemed well.

Making things right with Rachel.

Fending off Tom.

Missing her dad.

"Jack, I can't do this. Believe whatever you want. I've sent him back to his fiancée. What happens now is in their hands. I can't fix everything. I can't fix the fact I broke his heart all those years ago. I can't kiss it better and turn back time, even if I wanted to. If I'd loved him then maybe I wouldn't have got myself in the state I got myself in. But I've told him he's looking at a mirage. So think what you want but I'm done."

She turned to go. Inner Edie was silent for once.

"Damn it, Edie."

He grabbed her, twirled her round and pulled her into his arms. He kissed her.

It was an angry kiss, as if he was pouring all his frustration with her into it. And she opened up and let him. Took all that anger that he had, but returned it with soft kisses.

And then he cradled her head and his kisses soothed and gentled until the kisses they exchanged were full of yearning.

Eventually they pulled away from each other, breathing hard.

He leant his forehead against hers.

Edie was gasping for breath. Her heart was pounding in her

ears. Her stomach tied up in knots.

"Damn it," he whispered.

She could feel her lips shaking. And now that her barriers had been knocked down, the tears kept leaking out of her. She was a breached dam.

She could taste the salt on her lips, burning where they felt bruised and swollen.

She could fix everyone else's life but she not her own.

"Jack, please don't." She pleaded.

She pulled away from him. She couldn't stay and listen to him tell her why this was all wrong and how he hadn't meant to kiss her.

She walked back to the venue.

Each step away from him hurt and as she put one foot in front of the other, she felt the tears streaming down her cheeks.

Edie scrubbed her face.

She'd go in, grab her bag and escape to her room.

She couldn't let people see her like this. Make-up all cried off. She didn't care what anyone thought; but she knew it would upset Mel.

She'd done as much as she could, surely she could leave now?

Edie slipped back into the function room and threaded her way through the guests. The lights had dimmed and most people were drunk enough not to look at her in quite the same way they had earlier. Some even smiled fuzzily at her. And Edie smiled back even though inside her heart was torn. Her fragile pink heart that she'd only just found. But she wouldn't hide it behind a wall again.

She needed to live and if that meant having a torn heart, so be it.

"And before I throw the bouquet, I've got one more person to properly thank." Mel's voice boomed out over the PA.

Edie looked up from where she was trying to find her bag. It seemed to have got stuck under one of the chair legs.

Mel was on the stage in front of the emergency DJ that Barry had arranged. She had a death grip on the microphone. Barry stood beside her looking happy and proud and slightly embarrassed to

271

be up in front of everyone.

Mel was tipsy, Edie knew. She recognised the slight tilt, but she looked beautiful.

This was what it had been about. Getting these two who were meant to be together *together*. Everything else was just window dressing.

"Oi, Edie! Where are you?" Mel shouted and the crowd all turned to look at her.

Edie hoped no one would be able to see the mascara she was sure was streaking down her cheeks.

"That's Edie over there." Mel waved. "She's been my best friend forever and even though she hates weddings, she agreed to be my maid of honour. And she has done an amazing job. If it hadn't been for her, there wouldn't have been a wedding. She made Barry and I see that we could overcome everything." She winked at Edie. "And I know that you gave up something huge to be here today. And I am so touched." Mel blew her a kiss.

Edie realised that Maggie had obviously told Mel about the phone call from Dad. "So I want you to give it up for my own guardian angel who made this day possible. Edie Dickens."

The crowd cheered and started to chant her name.

Edie felt the tears starting to leak from her eyes again. They turned the lights into glitter and sparkle.

She heard a clatter, as if iron links were falling to the floor.

It eased the hurt that Jack didn't believe in her, even if he did want her. It eased many things. Whatever happened, she knew she'd done this. She could face the future and live it the way it was meant to be lived.

"And now the bouquet."

Edie watched, as the dance floor became a scrum. She smiled.

"Aren't you going to try?"

"Can't you leave me alone?" The words were torn from her, as her heart yearned to turn into his arms.

"I'm sorry," Jack said. "That is what I was building up to saying when I went out for a walk earlier. I was working out what to say, that I want to believe you've changed. I so want to believe, and I had a great speech worked out but when I saw you and Tom..." He shrugged and looked sheepish. "It seems I have a bit of a jealousy thing going on there. I didn't like the way he looked at you, as if he owned you.

Edie stared at him. Jack had been jealous.

Inner Edie started to do a happy dance.

Jack smiled and wiped under her eye with his thumb.

"Go, grab the bouquet and I promise I'll be here to listen when you get back. And then maybe a dance?" he asked tentatively.

Chapter 28

Single Ladies (Put a Ring on It) came blaring out over the sound system.

Edie jumped and then smiled.

Jack had been jealous.

"The bouquet is mine!" Sophie was in the middle of the scrum of screaming women.

At last she'd found something to distract her from chasing Jack for a few minutes.

"I think you can take her." Jack leant down and whispered in Edie's ear, giving her a push.

Edie shivered.

This had always been the point of the wedding that she and Jessica had stood at the back, watching with their arms folded and lips pulled up in a sneer.

And now?

Edie could feel her hands itching.

Mel's bouquet was beautiful. And Edie's tender heart, the one that had been stripped and exposed, fluttered with excitement.

She let Jack's hand propel her forward and smiling, she joined the throng of women standing in front of Mel.

It didn't matter if she didn't catch it, she thought. For once, her competitive nature was quiescent. This was about taking part.

"One, two…" the wedding party chanted.

"Three!"

Mel had her back to the crowd, she leant forward bending her knees and swung the bouquet like a kettle bell, then up over her head in a two handed swoop. At the apex of the swing she let go and the flowers spun out end over end.

A forest of hands went up, the bouquet flying through the air, tumbling and Edie realised it was coming straight at her. And following the flowers was a shower of pink glitter like a comet trail.

Ah, she thought, someone or something was intervening.

She cupped her hands ready to catch it but coming straight towards her, hair flying and face fierce was Sophie.

Edie knew she didn't have time to get out of the way.

With Sophie and the bouquet bearing down on her, Edie braced herself to catch the flowers and be ready for the impact of the inevitable tackle.

This wasn't going to be pretty.

But from nowhere, came a large jolly bridesmaid in the most beautiful forest green dress. She stuck out her foot.

Sophie tripped over it and fell full length in front of Edie, her fingertips just brushing Edie's toes.

The bouquet landed with a soft thump in Edie's hands.

She stared at the flowers, at the white rosebuds just opening to show a blushing centre. And here and there were a flutter of butterfly wings and a spark of a firefly on the greenery.

It seemed the bouquet had been transformed during its flight.

Edie looked up into the glowing face and the shining eyes of the Ghost of Weddings Present.

"Thanks," she said.

"My pleasure. Oh and congratulations."

The Spirit winked and moved into the centre of the gyrating women dancing to Beyoncé.

"Nice catch. Have you thought of playing rugby? Or is it a case of needing the right incentive?" Jack said from behind her. She buried her face in the bouquet, hiding her blushes.

"Got any man in mind for that bouquet?" he asked as he came round so he was in front of her.

She looked up and shook her head. She couldn't speak, in case she ruined the moment. They stood there, staring at each other.

"Let's dance." he said with a wink and held out his arms.

She melted into them.

As she span round the dance floor she saw the Ghost swigging from a champagne bottle while dancing wildly and waving her other hand. Edie couldn't help but smile.

"You look beautiful when you smile." Jack said.

Her heart stuttered. She looked up into his eyes.

"Not an ice queen?" she asked. She needed to know, even if it hurt her.

"I think the ice has melted," he whispered in her ear as he pulled her closer. She rested her cheek on his chest.

As he twirled her round the room, she saw a familiar small blonde flower girl spinning in circles and giggling. She waved to Edie.

Held in Jack's arms, she felt lighter than she had in years. It was as if shackles were unwinding themselves. Like she was shedding a chain.

"Hey, Slow"

She looked up into Jack's face. He was smiling down at her and in his dark hair was a sprinkle of pink glitter. She lifted a hand to brush it away but he caught her fingers and brought them to his lips, warm breath tickled them and then he kissed them.

Her stomach fluttered.

His head dipped and she reached her head upwards. Her eyes flickered closed, his mouth captured hers and there was a ringing in her ears, the clanking of chains fading away completely.

"Definitely not an ice queen," he said against her lips.

She giggled.

She hadn't giggled in years.

He lifted her up and span her around. She threw back her head and laughed. When she looked out again, over Jack's head, she saw yellow lace and grey hair sneaking out of the door. Edie nodded at the Spirit. Miss Havisham smiled.

Acknowledgements

If it takes a village to raise a child it took a small country to get this book to publication. First and foremost I'd like to thank my family; my mum, dad and sister, Annalise for their support. My parents taught me to read which opened up the world of words to me. I know sometimes they wished they hadn't, especially as they are currently storing a large part of my book collection. Annalise has been the best big sister a girl could ask for giving me love and support and kicks up the arse when needed. She is currently keeping me fed and watered and bullying me into getting some exercise.

I'd like to thank my writing family; the ties that bind us are as real and strong as blood. Julie Cohen for so much insight on writing craft, if only I'd listened better, and for all the years of crazy chats, late nights and obsessive fandoms. Anna Louise Lucia for the stone circles, warmth and love and laughter. Kate Walker for being the Virgin Mother and taking me in all those years ago.

My writing sister and critique partner, Liz Fenwick, without her wise words and judicious application of wine this book would not be where it is today. I also would be a poorer person. And to Liz's family for letting me 'borrow' her and I apologise for leading her astray.

For The Heroine Addicts, my blogging home, where Anna

Louise, Julie, Liz plus Christina Courtney and Susanna Kearsley who let me burble on even when publication was just a dot on the horizon. Thanks for the faith and fun.

When you decided to become a writer you need to have a touch of the obsessive and a whole lot of faith. You also need like-minded people to drag you along. I found my tribe at The Romantic Novelists' Association. If you have a problem, if no one else can help, and if you can find them, maybe you can hire the… Hold on that's the A-Team. The list of RNA members who have supported me could fill a book, but I appreciate every one of you. Special mention to Louise Allen (Melanie Hilton) for putting up with the last minute delivery of my NWS manuscripts every year with such good humour.

One extra special RNA person must be thanked, our glorious leader, Katie Fforde. Thank you. First for being so warm and friendly when I was first starting out and was star struck. Secondly, and most importantly, thank you for choosing me as the Katie Fforde Bursary winner in 2010. I don't know how you did it, it must be magic, but you chose me just when I was about to give it all up. Your bursary made me feel as if I really could do it. Even now when it all feels too much I remember you put your money where my words are. Oh and I apologise for calling the trophy, Le Dick Noir...

Thanks to Kimberly Young, the amazing HarperCollins publisher, who never minded me drunkenly chatting to her at RNA parties and never held it against me when it came to submitting. She took a chance on my short stories and led me to HarperImpulse. She also introduced me to Charlotte Ledger, my editor, my saviour, my tormentor and my friend. Charlotte bought this book when it was half the size and saw its potential. She also allows me to run riot on the HarperImpulse Twitter feed and happily takes photos of me as my alter ego in her office. Truly a woman with fantastic taste.

Thank you to those friends who don't look at me too funnily when I zone out and daydream. I'm looking at you, Matt Turner, for the coffee runs, white van man moments and DIY. And you, Caroline Turner, thanks for all the silly texts and our nights watching Harry Potter. And I will never tell you what I said to Sam West. And you, Molly Mikita, for the runs and letting me hang out at the store when I should've been writing this book. And Rachael Maryon for having my back for so many years, love you.

People say that social media distracts you from writing; all I know is that I've met the most amazing friends on there. They've kept me going through it all and made me laugh through the tears. Thank you Twitter buddies and Facebook friends. I salute you.

Chris McVeigh, the legend, thanks for all the support and Wham! Rap sing-alongs. Sam Missingham for being a superstar and Queen of Twitter. And Elizabeth Jenner for all round loveliness.

And thank you to #flame. You gave me the gift of time, without it I would never have finished this book. I can never thank you enough. Whatever road we end up on, you helped grow the first shoots for 'Brigid World'. I loved being your girl on fire.